MURDER AT THE BALL

A 1920s Cozy Mystery

A Lady Felicity Quick Mystery
Book 4

ROSIE HUNT

ISBN: 9789083290638

With thanks to early readers Sarah Alderman, Peggy Craddock, Federica De Dominicis, Kelly Hodgkins, Nancy R Willis, and others

Editing by Effie Wilson

Cover art by DLR Cover Designs

For my sister.

A legendary South Devon party girl.

A Note on Language

This book is written in British English. There are two reasons for this:

- the story is set in England, and
- I, the author, am British.

Part of my British writing style is the use of s where z is used in American English. For example: pulverise instead of pulverize, and fantasise instead of fantasize.

However, you may have noticed that in the blurbs and marketing for this book, it's called a cozy mystery and not a cosy mystery.

This is because the American spelling is standard for the genre. Spelling it this way helps people (and algorithms) recognise my book more easily.

But outside of book genres, it's cosy all the way.

Cast of Characters

Quick family

Lady Felicity Quick, journalist and occasional amateur detective

Pip, Felicity's Yorkshire Terrier

Miss Helen Quick, society girl and Felicity's cousin

Doctor Edwin Quick, eye surgeon and Felicity's cousin

Carrington family

Lord Archibald Carrington, first son of Earl Carrington and step-brother to Helen and Edwin

Lady Ariadne Carrington, step-sister to Helen and Edwin

Mina, Lord Archibald's Borzoi

Guests at Grimstow House

Mr Leonard McQueen, businessman and Helen's fiancé

Sir Vernon Adams, friend of Leonard

The Honourable Clemency Bourgoyne, society girl and friend of Helen

The Honourable Patience Bourgoyne, society girl and friend of Helen

The Honourable Rex Debenham, equestrian sportsman and Clemency's fiancé

Miss Ruth Fairchild, Edwin's guest

Lord Charles Lorrimer, friend of Edwin

Jambo, Leonard's Ridgeback

Staff

Mr Nigel Horrocks, butler for the Carringtons

Mr James Wilkinson, footman for the Carringtons

Mrs Laura Rudd, housekeeper for the Carringtons

Miss Maisie Ingles, maid for the Carringtons

Mr Ian Gibson, driver for the Carringtons

Mr Tom Jarvis, stable master

Mr Dennis Peabody, stablehand

Others

Mr Alexander Cooper, reporter for the Western Daily News

Chief Inspector Luscombe, police detective

Extract from the Western Daily News, 1922

The Mystery of the Not-Missing Jewels

If a thief escapes empty-handed, is he still a thief?

CHERITON ST MARY, 23 January — As the dust settles at Grimstow House on the macabre set of affairs about which much has already been written, another case emerges from the tragic remnants of that terrible night.

A certain London-based publication, which shall remain nameless to avoid generating undue publicity, has printed an exposé from a witness to the events at Grimstow. The witness claims a thief guilty of stealing from guests at the ill-fated stately home is still at large.

However, when pressed on the matter of the objects stolen, the witness cannot confirm any appurtenances to be missing.

While this esteemed publication will keep its readers abreast of any developments, our reporters will also take care to only publish the most accurate and useful information relevant to the case.

I know what you're doing. I'm not afraid to tell.

You'll get your comeuppance.

Anonymous letter received by Miss Helen Quick
19 January 1922

Chapter One

GRIMSTOW HOUSE, EAST DARTMOOR, DEVON, 20 JANUARY 1922

Lady Felicity Quick, reporter for the Western Daily News and — only if strictly needed and on an entirely unofficial basis — occasional private detective, glanced out the leaded windows of Grimstow House's library and considered for the briefest of moments the grand country seat's one obvious flaw.

Completed two years ago to Earl Carrington's exacting standards, Grimstow House boasted all manner of modern comforts. A seamless blend of medieval stone grandeur on the exterior and contemporary styling in dark wood and sumptuous fabrics internally gave the residence gravitas and timelessness. However, extremely vigorous revving of Felicity's newly restored two-seater Alvis had been required to climb Grimstow House's perilously steep tarmacadamed driveway. The extravagant residence clung to the sheer edges of the moors as if through force of will alone.

That said, the view across East Devon's undulating landscape was indisputably glorious.

The fuggy orange glow of the sun quickly setting in a milky sky confirmed the weather warning Felicity's brother had given her before she set out. The night would bring ice, especially on the moors. Departure from Grimstow House before dark was therefore essential, as Felicity had little experience of driving in freezing conditions, and there was the safety of more than just herself to consider. Her dear little motor had also only just been returned to her.

"You've read the letters, Cici."

Felicity switched her attention to the library's interior, doing her utmost to hide any trace of concern about the drive back to Bradley Court. She'd committed to assisting her cousin, and help her she would.

"What do you make of them?" Miss Helen Quick, daughter of the late Honourable Reginald Quick — brother to Felicity's own father, the late Lord Kingsley Quick — wore a riding jacket and a distractingly modern pair of cream-coloured jodhpurs, having arrived from riding practice at Grimstow House's generous equestrian facilities to meet Felicity at the front entrance. Helen's flat-brimmed riding hat and short crop lay next to the letters in question on a broad, oval table beside which Felicity was seated. "I don't take them at all seriously, of course." Helen paced in shining black boots across the library's waxed wooden floorboards. The partial escape of her reddish brown hair from the bun at her neck gave Helen an air of insouciance, while her straight posture and nose held high implied deliberately cultivated grace.

"I've nothing to hide," she continued. "So why should I be scared?" Helen's defiance struck a familiar tone, prompting Felicity to think fondly and sadly of her late father. Why didn't Felicity see more of her cousins? Family ought not to be taken for granted.

"That's an understandable conclusion to draw." Felicity looked again at the letters spread across the table. There were in total seven sheets of paper, the plain sort found at any general stationers, and each bore just two or three short lines of type-written text, expressing variations on the same, anonymous message. The writer claimed to know something about Helen of which the writer disapproved.

The writer also threatened to reveal what he or she knew and hinted that Helen would, in some unspecified way, be punished.

Helen had received the first six notes while at her residence in London, where she spent most of her time, and in various situations, from discovering a folded sheet pressed into the pocket of her mink coat to finding an envelope lying on her dressing table. When the most recent note had been found pushed under her bedroom door at Grimstow House, Helen had summoned Felicity.

Helen picked up her riding crop and tapped it against her palm. "So…?"

Felicity frowned slightly. "I'm afraid I shall need time to consider matters." While keen to assist her cousin, she wouldn't hurry into things. The expectations others had of her abilities as a sleuth often outstripped Felicity's own.

"Perhaps your assistant has some light to shed on the subject?"

Felicity twirled in time to see fellow reporter for the Western Daily News and — thanks to the meddling of Felicity's grandmother — her 'assistant' on this particular case, Alex Cooper, raise a normally unflappable dark blond eyebrow. Dressed in a subtly fashionable slate-grey woollen suit, he'd remained standing behind Felicity, positioned between her and the library door.

"Mr Cooper and I are equal in all matters pertaining to this enquiry," corrected Felicity with insuppressible emphasis, which she immediately regretted, for it drew attention to her own discomfort. Did Alex want to be involved in her sleuthing, or was he simply humouring her? Felicity had only known Alex since he'd become a colleague at her brother's newspaper the summer before, but unlike Felicity's brother, Alex could be incredibly stoic.

Felicity had left Bradley Court in a hurry. Her beloved

Yorkshire Terrier, Pip, had stolen a string of sausages from the kitchen and gone dashing through the garden. Although successfully caught after a dramatic pursuit, Pip was too dirty with mud and sausage grease to accompany Felicity to visit her cousin. Deeply flustered, Felicity miraculously collected Alex from Exeter's main railway station at the agreed hour. Their conversation on the run to Grimstow House had been rather stilted, but it was only after Alex alighted from the motor that Felicity noticed he'd been sitting on the scruffy tartan dog bed Pip usually occupied, and he'd said nothing about it. Felicity had wished for the ground to open and swallow her whole.

"Will you take up the case or not, Lady Felicity?" In a clipped South African accent and with an exhale of cigar smoke, Mr Leonard McQueen, renowned financier and Helen's fiancé, posed his question with neither an air of impatience nor of apology. Wearing a roomy brown suit to accommodate his large frame, and with black greased-back hair and a thin moustache, he solidly occupied a chair on the other side of the broad oval table. Beside him sat a powerful and alert Rhodesian Ridgeback with a red wheaten coat and a thick leather collar attached to a robust chain that sat firmly in Leonard's grip. The tag on the collar read 'JAMBO'.

"Leo, please," sighed Helen. "This isn't some business deal you can force through. Cici's family."

"Forgive me." The financier waved his cigar apologetically.

"If I may take the letters with me for further study," suggested Felicity, "I can then come back to you with an analysis?"

Helen ceased pacing. "But whatever for? I've the suspects already lined up."

Felicity threw a quick glance at Alex. He widened his eyes.

"You do?" asked Felicity of her cousin.

Helen tightened her grip on her riding crop. "It's either one of the Bourgoyne twins—"

Felicity drew back her chin but said nothing. Weren't Helen and the Bourgoynes close friends?

"—or my twisted little step-sister," continued Helen.

"Lady Ariadne?" Felicity remembered Ariadne's sullen, pretty face at the marriage of Helen's mother to Earl Carrington. She was barely more than a schoolgirl.

"Whoever it is, they've got to be stopped. I've got enough on my hands thinking about our wedding." Helen cast a kittenish look at Leonard, which was answered by a puff of cigar smoke that disguised his face for a moment. Jambo whined and pulled on his chain.

"You can question them right away," continued Helen. "The suspects are all here at Grimstow."

"They are?" Felicity couldn't hide the surprise in her voice. The investigation was romping away without her. How did Alex not show any shade of reaction in his face?

"But of course." Helen wrinkled her elegant nose. "Tonight's the ball, silly."

Felicity indeed felt silly. "What ball?" She didn't see her cousin as often as she ought, but Felicity couldn't possibly have forgotten an invitation to a ball, could she?

"You mean you didn't… Well." Helen's hands dropped to her sides with theatrical exasperation. "Perhaps your invitation got lost? You know better than me what provincial postal services are like."

Felicity swallowed. "They're usually quite reliable," she said quietly.

Alex remained unreadable as the sun sank ever closer towards the East Devon hills. The moment to leave was fast-approaching.

"In any case," Helen sighed. "You're here now, Cici. That's the important thing. And Mama and the Earl have given me carte blanche while they're on their second honeymoon. Or is it their third?" She turned a smile on Leonard.

"Helen." Felicity spoke firmly but also warmly. "I received your telegram requesting my help with the letters, but there was no mention of a party." Felicity glanced down at her ink-blue woollen skirt and jacket, which she had matched with a cream silk blouse, a string of simple pearls, and a favourite pair of blue T-strap shoes. "I came completely unprepared."

Helen laughed as though Felicity had just told a joke. "Cici, you tickle me. You absolutely do." Crossing to the library's somewhat redundant fireplace — for modern, unobtrusive radiators generated a comfortable heat — Helen pressed a black Bakelite button situated to the side of the mantelpiece. She approached Felicity, bringing with her the smell of kicked-up earth blended with a powdery floral perfume.

"A journalist and a sleuth," Helen said, looming above Felicity, her riding crop still in her hand. "Honestly, Cici, I don't know how you do it. One career is considered too many for most women, and my head feels quite full with just the preparations for my wedding. It's no surprise the invitation for my little get-together slipped your mind." Helen fingered the lapel of Felicity's ink-blue jacket.

Felicity smiled weakly. She and Helen were of a similar age, but their lives were indeed rather different. Was her cousin impressed with her achievements? There was something in Helen's tone Felicity didn't like.

"Shall we get you dressed for the occasion?" asked Helen.

Felicity looked again at Alex. He gave her a slight raise of his eyebrows. Was he darkly amused or increasingly irritated? Either way, Felicity was becoming desperate to depart from Grimstow House as quickly as possible. She looked out the library window. "That's awfully kind of you, Helen, but the weather's looking rather iffy, and I couldn't possibly—"

"Cici, darling. It wouldn't be any kind of imposition. That you can help clear up these ghastly letters at the same time as attending my little event is an absolute bonus."

"Please," added Leonard flatly. "We'd love for you to stay."

Felicity blinked. She was backed into a corner. It wasn't just Helen's plea for help with the threatening letters. Considering they saw so little of one another, to turn down Helen and Leonard's hospitality would have been damaging.

She glanced apologetically at Alex, then nodded. "Very well. But you understand I can't promise to solve anything today."

"Oh, you're a marvel, Cici." Helen tapped Felicity under the chin. "An absolute marvel. It's no wonder you haven't the time to find yourself a husband."

Any warmth that Felicity had been feeling towards her cousin suddenly cooled to the point of freezing. Time had rubbed the edge off the memories, but Felicity now clearly recalled why she didn't seek Helen's company.

There was a knock at the door. A tall man with wavy grey hair in a butler's uniform entered the room.

"Horrocks, my cousin Felicity will be with us for this evening's proceedings. Please ask Mrs Rudd to ensure Felicity is settled into one of our guest suites, and that she's suitably attired in alignment with the event's theme."

There was a theme? The ball was becoming less appealing by the moment.

Alex stepped forward and cleared his throat.

"Mr Cooper, you're welcome to depart in the Alvis," said Felicity. Alex's discomfort was at the forefront of her mind. Helen wasn't his family to tolerate. "I can only apologise that I didn't inform you well enough before bringing you to Grimstow House." The sky was darkening above the jagged lines of the pine forest visible from the library windows. "You should have enough time to get off the moors before the roads freeze."

Alex shrugged and gave a half smile. "If you've no need of me, Lady Felicity."

Felicity's stomach squeezed almost painfully. That wasn't what she meant.

Leonard stood up from his chair, cigar in one hand, dog chain in the other, the Ridgeback treading carefully in alignment with his master's heels. "Mr Cooper is useful to you in your investigations, if I'm not mistaken, Lady Felicity."

"In a manner of speaking, yes," replied Felicity. It was better than calling Alex her assistant, although not by much.

"I've worked with Lady Felicity in similar situations on a number of occasions," said Alex, ever the stoic.

"Then isn't it best Mr Cooper stay to aid you in your investigation?" continued Leonard.

Helen's eyes narrowed. She wasn't keen. The butler stood stiffly at the side of the room, his low-lidded eyes watchful but not intrusive.

"If Mr Cooper has no objection to attending the ball," said Felicity, eager for Alex to speak his mind.

Again, Alex shrugged. "I've no objection."

Helen snatched up her riding hat from the table and turned to face Leonard. "Forgive my lack of insight on the matter, but just how will Mr Cooper be introduced? When does a lady attend an event in the company of her male assistant?"

Felicity bristled. "My apologies for being a stickler, Helen, but Mr Cooper is not my assistant."

Somehow, Alex looked thoroughly amused.

Leonard drew on his cigar. "Mr Cooper will be with me. One of my guests. He can keep his eyes and ears open that way. The more manpower we have on this matter, the better. Wouldn't you say, Mr Cooper?"

While Felicity was grateful for Leonard's inclusion of Alex, it appeared to be accompanied by a dose of scepticism in a woman's ability to get the job done.

Alex gave a little bow and smiled winsomely. "I'm at Lady Felicity's disposal." His smile was always extremely charming.

Helen sighed loudly. "Horrocks, please also see that Mr Cooper is prepared for the ball. Find him a room."

"Understood, Miss Quick," replied the butler.

"And have you fetched the necklace I'll be wearing from the safe in the master suite?"

"Yes, Miss Quick. Everything is arranged."

"Jolly good. The gems Leonard bought me will look absolutely darling next to that classic piece." Helen turned to

Felicity. "And we'll get this whole ghastly matter of the letters solved tonight, shall we not?"

Felicity smiled at her cousin, but it was hollow. She couldn't promise to solve anything, and the chance of getting off the moors before nightfall was disappearing fast.

Chapter Two

The strains of a foxtrot echoed down the passageway as an austere yet amicable housekeeper in a prim black dress led Felicity along labyrinthine stone corridors towards Helen's gathering. Passing tall sets of mullioned windows beyond which the silhouettes of treetops were only barely visible against a dark sky, a cool draught whipped around Felicity's ankles, and the frock loaned to her rattled as she walked.

It was a sleeveless number adorned with countless tiny beads in forest-green glass flecked with gold that reached to just below mid-calf. The dress was matched with a headband featuring a dyed-green ostrich feather, a pair of dark green velvet gloves that reached past the elbows, and a generous organza sash in the dropped-waist position. A pair of green velvet slip-on shoes with a moderate heel finished the look and pinched Felicity's toes with every step.

Felicity's trusty notebook lay abandoned along with her ink-blue woollen suit in the guest suite, for the borrowed outfit had no pockets. Not that she would have been able to use it. Felicity's investigation of Helen's letter-writing suspects was not to be carried out in the open.

"Have you been at Grimstow House long, Mrs Rudd?" A hint

of nervousness was making Felicity chatter. She realised immediately how silly her question to the housekeeper was.

"I've worked here since it was completed, your ladyship—" which Felicity knew very well was only a couple of years ago "—but even before that, the Earl involved us staff in designing the place. He had his architects consult us on upgrades to make our work easier and more efficient."

Felicity was impressed. "The Earl sounds like a very thoughtful employer."

"Oh, that he is, your ladyship. That he is." Felicity detected something of the North of England in Mrs Rudd's accent.

The housekeeper smiled politely and withdrew as they reached a door outside which a young, bespectacled footman stood. He nodded solemnly, and Felicity's stomach tightened as he opened the door. There hadn't been a chance to speak to Alex before they were whisked away to change for the ball, but she hoped he'd at least been supplied with a well-fitting pair of shoes. If the matter of the anonymous letters could be cleared up quickly, everyone's discomfort would be minimised.

"Lady Felicity Quick," announced the butler as Felicity entered the room. She blinked and smiled graciously as she took in her surroundings. Modest chandeliers twinkled from relatively low ceilings. Panelled walls were painted pale green, with chintz furniture moved to the room's sides. The jaunty foxtrot Felicity had heard was playing on a gramophone in the corner. Most of the room's occupants — and for a ball, there weren't many — looked her way, including an older man with a monocle who raised a glass in her direction.

Felicity did her best to keep her chin high and her smile genial as she glided uncomfortably into the space. When a familiar dark blue gaze met hers, the battering of her heart settled.

Alex blended seamlessly into Leonard's entourage, looking every inch the gentleman in a dinner jacket that might have been made for his broad shoulders and narrow hips. He smiled at

Felicity conspiratorially and joined the monocled man in raising a glass to her.

"Felicity?"

With a wide, kind face covered in freckles, and standing not much taller than Felicity in an ill-fitting black tailcoat that was an act of resistance to contemporary fashions, Doctor Edwin Quick had never had much in common with his glamorous sister, Helen. The distance between them seems to have grown greater with the years.

"Edwin?" Felicity matched the tone of delighted surprise with which her cousin had greeted her. "My goodness. It's been too long, has it not?" she said between kisses on the cheek. He was several years older than Felicity, so they'd never been close, but Edwin always had a gentle, caring nature and had dedicated his life to the medical sciences. He still leaned on a cane because of shrapnel from artillery that hit the field hospital he'd overseen in Cambrai.

"I must congratulate you on your recent achievements," said Felicity. Via her grandmother, she'd heard Edwin had been engaged as a specialist eye surgeon at a prestigious London hospital and was at the forefront of developments in his field. She ought really to have sent a laudatory note to Edwin's London address, but it was too late for that now.

"Yes, well." Edwin blinked nervously. He wasn't the type to enjoy any kind of limelight. "I understand you've embarked on a career yourself." Was his nervousness brought on by the hubbub of the party, or by Felicity's career?

"Upon my soul. If it isn't Cici."

Felicity didn't immediately recognise the man in the dark blue dinner jacket with lightly tanned boyish features and wavy side-parted hair. Then she realised. "Charlie?"

Lord Charles Lorrimer, first son of the Viscount of Rothwell and Edwin's friend since childhood, beamed as he stepped forward to greet Felicity with a kiss on the cheek. The last time Felicity saw Charles had been on a balmy summer's afternoon in the grounds of Rothwell Manor, where she and her brother Jasper had been invited with their cousins Helen and Edwin for a picnic and treasure hunt as part of the celebrations for Charles' birthday.

"It's been an absolute age," he said, his warm brown eyes sparkling.

"Since before the war," concurred Felicity.

"Been rather busy since then. Diplomatic affairs and all that. Edwin assured me tonight would be special, worth the run down from London." Charles cocked an eyebrow at his friend.

Edwin looked grave. "It's not exactly the ball my sister hoped it would be. I believe the fireworks have been cancelled because of the wind."

Putting his hands behind his back, Charles let out a little sigh. "Cici, may I say, you're looking—"

A loud *pop* made Felicity wince. It was followed by a whoop and a cheer. A compact, athletic man with a wide fun-loving smile had opened a bottle of champagne in spectacular foaming fashion and was pouring it into the glass at the top of a pyramid of coupes, the pale golden liquid splashing liberally on the shining wooden tabletop below. Among the man's entourage was Helen, but also two women Felicity was quite certain she recognised as the Bourgoyne twins.

"If you'll excuse me," said Felicity to Charles and Edwin. "I shouldn't like to miss out on the champagne."

It was an abrupt and rather weak pretext to split from her cousin and his friend, but a glance at Alex spurred Felicity on with her investigation. Alex was listening to a discussion between Leonard and the monocled man and looked more than a tad bored. Catching up with family and friends was something Felicity could do in her own time. It wasn't Alex's fault Felicity hadn't kept up with her people.

As Felicity approached the champagne pyramid, the foxtrot stopped. Helen cantered across the room to oversee the selection of a new disc record. Leonard watched her carefully, as did

Jambo. In the relative quiet between songs, the wind shook the windows behind thick pale-green curtains. Even if Felicity were to identify the letter writer forthwith, was driving home through the dark in the freezing wind any kind of option?

"Clemency? Patience?" enquired Felicity, side-stepping a puddle of champagne that had gathered on the carpet.

The Honourable Clemency Bourgoyne and her sister, the Honourable Patience Bourgoyne, typified what periodicals and newspapers across the Empire referred to as 'society beauties'. Although twins, they were not identical. Clemency had honey-blonde curls, a willowy frame, and a rounded pixie-like nose. Patience's hair was dark brown, her figure more rounded, and her facial features were slender and elegant. Both girls had amber-brown eyes.

Clemency wore a blue frock covered in tiny slices of blue mirror. Patience's dress was a rich red spattered with gold beads. Both girls' outfits were augmented with showy jewellery, sparkling at wrists, necks, upper arms, and ear lobes.

As the sisters turned towards Felicity, generous feathers in colours matching their clothes bobbed on their headbands. Clemency looked at Felicity with innocent curiosity. Patience's icy gaze bordered on hostility.

"Emerald, are you?" said the dark-haired sister in a challenging tone.

Felicity blinked. "I-I'm sorry?"

"The theme. For the ball?" Patience sighed with exasperation. "Although it's not much of a ball when the musicians have cancelled, only a fraction of the guests have arrived, and no one's allowed in the ballroom."

"I'm sapphire," said Clemency with a playful giggle. "Pat's ruby. You simply must be emerald. Oh, say we've got it right."

"Yes, I'm emerald," confirmed Felicity, for there seemed little point in resisting. How to bring matters around to uncovering a motive for sending Helen threatening letters? Felicity wished she'd had more time to herself to think. She only knew the Bourgoynes through Helen. There wasn't much common ground between them.

"What happened to the ballroom?" It was all Felicity could muster.

"Branch came down on a skylight. Floor's covered in glass." The hint of a smile creased Patience's lips. "I say. You write for one of those local papers these days, do you not?"

"That's correct." Felicity was eager to grab any thread that would keep their conversation going. "Are you a reader of the Western Daily News?"

Patience laughed, an elegant hand raised to her chest. "Please. The idea of it."

Felicity raised her eyebrows. "Is the reading of newspapers so ridiculous?"

Patience sighed. "Oh, darling. I read The Times or The Telegraph or whatever Papa leaves lying around. Listen. We only came down from London because Hel promised us a party to end all parties. And yet here we are, treading on each other's toes in the North Drawing Room like absolute paupers. I'm only sorry I didn't send across a last-minute decline like practically everyone else."

Helen threw a scathing look towards Patience from where she was still sorting through disc records. While Felicity was saddened by the quality of friend with which her cousin surrounded herself, it seemed unlikely the person responsible for the threatening letters would indulge in open hostility towards the victim. Otherwise, why go to the trouble of anonymity?

Had she her notebook to hand, Felicity would have struck a decisive line through Patience's name.

"Whoops, sorry!" The sporty-looking man who'd poured the champagne appeared at Clemency's elbow, sloshing the golden liquid out of two coupes. "There we go."

He handed one glass to Clemency, which she gracefully accepted. The other glass he offered to Patience, which she refused with a haughty lift of her chin. Shrugging, the man then offered it to Felicity, which she declined with a gentle head shake and a polite smile. The man shrugged again and took a gulp from the coupe himself. "We've not met, have we?" he said after his drink, extending a hand to Felicity with a dashing smile. "Rex Debenham."

Felicity shook Rex's hand and introduced herself. "Indeed, we've not met, yet your name is familiar."

"Rex is a rather successful equestrian athlete." Clemency's amber-brown eyes blinked puppy-like at the sportsman as she tucked a hand into the crook of his elbow. "Aren't you, darling?"

Rex's jaw tightened slightly, though his smile remained. "Polo, showjumping, steeplechase. If there's a horse involved, I want in. I say, Hel mentioned you're a journalist. Has she got that right?" His green eyes twinkled with interest.

"I'm afraid I'm off duty this evening," Felicity clarified with a heavy dose of equivocation. She was, of course, actively investigating the letters. Was there a way Clemency's potential for involvement might be as quickly assessed as her sister's? "And what keeps you both busy these days?" Felicity enquired of the twins.

"Pat's writing a book," said Clemency, although Patience shrank a little from the comment. "And Rex and I are engaged to be married." The blonde-haired twin clung harder to her fiancé's arm.

Rex placed a hand on Clemency's cheek, drew her to him, and kissed her forehead. "That's right. That's quite right."

"How lovely." Felicity was still looking to link or exclude Clemency from involvement in the letters, but it was proving difficult. "And when is the special day?"

"Lady Felicity?"

The interruption came from a doll-like girl with pale wisps of blonde hair and bright, intelligent, periwinkle-blue eyes. Large sea-green sequins rippled across the length of her dress, and her gold-coloured velvet gloves were pulled above her elbows. The tall feather in her headband had been dyed to match her outfit precisely.

"Lady Ariadne." Without wanting to, Felicity guessed the stone she represented to be aquamarine. "What a pleasure to see you again."

"May I speak to you for a moment?" While Helen's step-sister, Lady Ariadne Carrington, was not yet eighteen, she clearly had a talent for style. Her use of jewellery was subtle, yet beguiling. Her perfume was rich and musky.

Felicity glanced round, but there was no need to excuse herself. Rex had spilt champagne on Clemency, and Helen had joined in the laughter while Patience wore a look like thunder.

"Of course," said Felicity.

Reaching a chintz sofa at the side of the room but without time to sit, Ariadne said, "I know why you're here." She spoke confidently but not loud enough for anyone else to hear above a warbly number from a musical playing through the gramophone. "So I'd like to confess. I did it."

Felicity wasn't sure she understood what Ariadne was saying. The butler passed by, offering canapés of oysters au gratin, which both Felicity and Ariadne politely declined.

"I'm sorry, but you did what?" asked Felicity, confused.

The periwinkle-eyed girl folded her arms impatiently over her sea-green frock. "I sent the letters to Helen. That's what you're here to investigate, isn't it?"

Felicity's breath caught. Was there a chance she and Alex might leave Grimstow House before the night was through?

Chapter Three

With her investigation abruptly over, and Helen, Rex, and Clemency having begun dancing, with some confusion over who was to dance with who, Felicity was disturbed that while her career as a sleuth — if that's what it was — had barely begun, she'd already gained enough notoriety for her undercover work to be jeopardised.

"I read the papers," said Ariadne sharply, in answer to Felicity asking how she'd uncovered the investigation. "I know what you do. And I've not seen you at Helen's gatherings before."

"I see," said Felicity, imagining the girl before her sitting down at a typewriter to create the malicious letters. There was a straightforwardness and absence of drama about the messages that matched Ariadne's manner.

"You can tell Helen she'll get no more letters," continued Ariadne. "But I shan't apologise to her. Not yet." There was an edge of anger in her tone. "The matter is cleared up now, isn't it? Helen can call off her hunt."

Felicity didn't consider herself any sort of hunter, but she knew better than to argue with a young woman simmering with acrimony. "May I enquire why you did it?" she asked.

"It was a stupid, childish trick. That's all. I shan't send any more. The matter is closed."

Ariadne's eyes flicked to the other side of the drawing room. Alex was still there, listening to Leonard. Was there really a chance they might leave that same evening?

"I'm telling you this because I don't want a scene," Ariadne added.

Felicity wasn't one for creating a scene. Perhaps Ariadne had read detection novels in which the suspects are gathered and the sleuth unmasks the guilty party in front of everyone.

"In the letters, you spoke of something you would reveal about Helen. Do you intend to carry out the threats made?" Felicity could at least be thorough even if she couldn't take much credit for the solving of the crime.

Ariadne shook her head, the feather on her headband dancing. "I made it all up. It was just stuff and nonsense." Again, her eyes darted away.

Felicity didn't press for more information. She was there to investigate the letters, not her cousin. "Would you not like to inform your step-sister yourself?"

Ariadne tightened the cross of her arms over her chest. "I told you I don't want a scene."

Felicity nodded. "Very well. I shall inform Helen of your confession and that she'll receive no more letters. Shall I tell her you've the intention to make amends in due course?" Family was, after all, family. Through the marriage of Helen's mother to Ariadne's father, Ariadne herself was now a relative of sorts of Felicity's.

A flash of anger passed across Ariadne's doll-like features. "I can't promise that."

The gong sounded from the entrance hall. Ariadne hastened away. Felicity let her go, her work at Grimstow House done. If she was to inform Helen of the developments before everyone sat down to dinner and make an early exit with Alex, Felicity would have to be fast.

"That little…"

Helen had been on Leonard's arm and was making her way to the dining room when Felicity asked for a quiet word. They'd found a spot in an alcove by a portrait of a young man in military uniform typical of the Great War, tucked out of earshot but in view of the stream of guests advancing towards dinner.

Helen was no longer recognisable as the vigorous horsewoman in jodhpurs. Her lashes were mascaraed, her cheeks rouged, and her hair was elegantly swept into shining, even waves. Several lengths of jewelled necklaces lay across her chest. Layers of tassels made from tiny purple glass beads covered every inch of her dress and gently clattered whenever she moved. Unable to help herself, Felicity guessed amethyst.

At first, Helen had been excited and pleased that Felicity had an update. When Felicity told her about Ariadne's direct and self-confident confession, Helen's mood changed.

She shook her head angrily, the long purple plume attached to her headband shivering. Felicity felt almost embarrassed at being yet another woman with a feather on her head, but it was clearly some popular London vogue she'd missed out on.

"The gall of it," growled Helen, her voice raising uncontrollably. "To not have a shred of regret. My mother insists I invite the little shrew to all my gatherings. I said from the start, Ariadne and I would never be friends. But to treat me like this?" Helen stamped her foot with rage.

"If there's anything further I can do to assist," said Felicity half-heartedly, for her mind was on Alex. She'd not seen him pass yet. If they were to leave before dinner, she needed to reach him before he was seated, otherwise they would be trapped. Standing up to leave the dinner table would have been intolerably rude.

Helen sniffed and straightened, the feather on her headband bobbing. "No. You've done quite enough, and I'm extremely grateful."

"I didn't really do—" began Felicity.

"You must relax and enjoy the gathering."

"It's really too kind of—"

"Cici, I absolutely insist." Helen reached out and squeezed Felicity's hand. "You're my guest. And my cousin. We're going to have rather jolly amounts of fun. You'll see."

On the cusp of attempting another protest, Felicity watched as Alex passed along the corridor towards the dining room. He was accompanied by Rex and didn't look Felicity's way. Would he forgive her if they didn't leave Grimstow House till the morning? It was an opportunity for Felicity to spend more time with her family, and there was the danger posed by the ice and the steep hills to consider.

"Thank you." Felicity smiled. The situation wasn't ideal, but at least it was decided. "I shall do my best to enjoy myself."

"Marvellous," purred Helen. She looped her arm through Felicity's, and Felicity allowed herself to be escorted to the dining room.

Whether Felicity would enjoy herself was highly uncertain. It was as uncertain as Alex's forgiveness, which would be the only thing to remove the knot forming in Felicity's stomach.

Chapter Four

The styling of Grimstow House's dining room, with its dark wood panelling, thick tapestries, and sturdy high-backed chairs, was austere. It was offset by effusive displays of white flowers, twinkling chandeliers, and an ice sculpture cut to resemble a diamond that sat in the centre of the long oak table.

Alex was already seated between Leonard and Rex, meaning Felicity's apology to him would have to wait, and dinner would have to be forced down despite the tension in her stomach. As Helen tucked herself into a chair next to Leonard, Felicity took a seat between Ariadne, who was incredibly cool and collected, and Edwin, who was seated at the end of the table opposite a woman Felicity hadn't yet seen.

From across the table, the man with the monocle smiled slyly at Felicity and introduced himself. "I don't believe we've had the pleasure. Sir Vernon Adams." Sir Vernon was certainly over fifty but had likely been handsome in his youth. Like Edwin, he also wore a tailcoat, only he did so with a nod to classical elegance rather than a refusal to move with the times. He still had a champagne coupe in his hand.

Felicity introduced herself, raising her voice above the raucous atmosphere of the party that had been transported wholesale to the dining room. Rex had half the table in stitches at some extravagant tale that involved him leaping out of his seat every ten seconds. Even Jambo, who was seated at Leonard's side, joined in with a bark or two.

"I'm an old friend of Leonard's," continued Sir Vernon. "Well, of Leonard's father's, although he's no longer with us, of course. Leonard's doing an excellent job picking up just where he left off."

Felicity nodded politely to Sir Vernon as service of the first course cut short their conversation. The butler and footman were careful to circumnavigate Rex's extravagant gestures as they placed soup plates in front of the guests. Leaning to look past the ice sculpture, Felicity caught Alex's gaze. He was laughing at something Leonard had said, his dark blue eyes twinkling with gaiety. The knot in Felicity's stomach loosened.

"You've not yet been introduced to Miss Fairchild, have you, Felicity?" enquired Edwin, his freckled cheeks turning pink as they tucked into a delicately flavoured consommé. From the colour in his face and his attempt to appear somewhat off-hand about the introduction, Felicity suspected Miss Fairchild might be of some romantic importance to Edwin.

The woman seated opposite Edwin gave a timid smile. "Pleased to meet you, your ladyship." She was only a little older than Felicity, but Miss Fairchild's gauzy cream frock with its frills and draped sleeves was from another era. Even her fashionable feathered headband looked dowdy somehow. Miss Fairchild might have been dressed as opal, or she might not have been aware of the ball's theme at all.

Felicity returned Miss Fairchild's smile as she introduced herself, polite nods acting as a proxy for handshakes across the table.

"Felicity is a cousin on my father's side," added Edwin.

"How lovely," said Miss Fairchild with restrained but genuine interest.

Felicity was about to enquire further about Miss Fairchild when Sir Vernon leaned an elbow on the table.

"Your father also going in on the Central American mines deal, is he, Lady Felicity?"

"My father is no longer with us, Sir Vernon," said Felicity dispassionately.

"Oh." Sir Vernon's face threatened to lose its grip on his monocle. Quickly regaining his composure, he addressed Ariadne. "I say, Ari, old girl. Where's that brother of yours? Is he not interested in coming in on Leonard's latest deal? It's a once in a lifetime opportunity, what?"

Ariadne, who had also been enjoying the lively action at the other end of the table, turned her attention towards Sir Vernon with the calm steadiness of someone much older than her years. "Which brother?" she said.

Again, Sir Vernon looked confused, the champagne in his coupe slanting perilously towards the glass' edge.

Patience, who was seated on the other side of Ariadne and who had been rather stiff and quiet throughout the dinner so far, turned to Ariadne. "There's someone I know who might help you in that regard," she said, her amber-brown eyes alight with interest. "It's absolutely possible to contact loved ones no longer with us. In fact, I guarantee it. I'd be more than happy to make the introduction."

Ariadne turned away from Patience without giving an answer, the arrival of the fish course providing a distraction. Ariadne's self-control was intriguing, especially considering her youth.

But as fascinated as Felicity was by the assortment of personalities gathered for dinner, she turned her attention to her cousin. "Tell me, Edwin. Just what have been the most recent advances in eye surgery?"

"Well." Edwin dabbed excitedly at his lips with his napkin as Miss Fairchild beamed from the other side of the table. "Where does one begin?"

Felicity listened with as much interest as she could muster and asked prompting questions as Edwin extolled the virtues of recent advances made in procedures for cataracts and listed the achievements of specialist surgeons — himself included — in treating war veterans still afflicted by sight problems. He expressed his intention to one day hold the post of professor at University College Hospital.

His interests were limited to a very narrow yet extremely deep field, but Edwin was Felicity's cousin, and that's what mattered. It saddened Felicity only slightly that Edwin didn't ask her anything about her work at the newspaper. If she made the effort to see Helen and Edwin more often, perhaps conversations with them would take on more balance in time.

A main course of aromatic pheasant with Golden Pippin apples arrived, and as Felicity pondered how to enquire about Edwin and Miss Fairchild's association with one another in a way that wouldn't prompt awkwardness, the lights in the chandeliers above the dining room table flickered and dimmed. Gasps and nervous laughter went up.

"It's quite normal," said the imperturbable Ariadne.

Although knocked off his stride in talking about his work at the hospital, Edwin, too, was unfazed by the dipping lights. "Grimstow generates its own power from the river at the bottom of the hill," he explained. "The connection often plays up when it's windy."

Sir Vernon raised the eyebrow above his unmonocled eye. "How much does such an installation cost?"

"You'll have to ask my father," said Ariadne with a sigh. "My brother designed it, but Papa paid for it."

"If I were him, I'd want my money back," mumbled Patience, apparently still hurt by Ariadne's earlier snub. "But then money can't buy everything, can it?"

With a chuckle, Helen turned her attention away from the men at the other end of the table for the first time during the dinner. "Money helps, though, darling, doesn't it?" she said to

Patience as she rose from her seat. "You and Clem of all people should know that. Having had it and then lost it."

"What?" said Clemency, leaning forward from her seat at the far end of the table. "What should I know?"

Patience seethed but said nothing. Her eyes went to Leonard then darted away. Helen was moving towards the head of the table, the purple tassels on her dress gently clattering, the room quietened besides the sounds of flatware on china and the wind buffeting the windows beyond the shutters. Alex observed Helen carefully. Felicity accidentally caught Charles' gaze, and he gave her a smile. She politely returned it before looking away.

Helen looked at the guests with mischievous, glinting eyes that were precisely the same shade of hazel as Felicity's. "I propose a round of toasts." Helen lifted a half-finished glass of Bordeaux in her fiancé's direction, the feathers in her headband bobbing as the butler and footman moved rapidly to top up glasses. "First, to Leonard." The speech-giver grinned impishly. "Our engagement has been a passionate affair. I only hope he doesn't realise he's made his first poor investment till after we've tied the knot."

Felicity looked around the table. Sir Vernon was chuckling. Even Charles was smiling in amusement. Helen appeared to be making a joke, although Leonard didn't seem to find it funny. He blinked at his fiancée, stony-faced.

"Thankfully, my betrothed has a better nose for money than for brides," continued Helen. "May those Central American mines make all who invest in them very wealthy indeed."

Leonard solemnly raised his glass.

"Hip, hip!" Rex cheered as more glasses were raised.

"Here, here," agreed Sir Vernon.

Patience was the only guest who didn't react.

"Next, a toast to my cousin, Cici."

As all eyes swung to Felicity, she did her best to appear calm and gracious. How she detested being thrust centre stage. It was a relief to meet Alex's gaze. The twitch of his brow seemed to say, *Bit much isn't it, all this?*

Helen sighed loudly. "Cici hasn't chosen a classically female path through life, preferring the world of work to the role of wife and mother."

Felicity swallowed and attempted to remain gracious-looking. Exactly when had she said she'd renounced marriage altogether?

"But that's precisely why I admire her," continued Helen. "May you find your own meaning and success in life, Cici. You truly are a wonder."

As glasses were raised enthusiastically in her direction, Felicity nodded politely. She hoped no one noticed the tremble in her lower lip. Was Helen aware of the power words had to hurt?

"To Lady Felicity!" echoed Rex in his booming, playful voice.

Charles raised his glass, though he looked rather serious.

Helen allowed the butler to top up her wine. "My last toast is for someone new in my life but still very dear to me."

Felicity crumpled with relief as the gazes and glasses around the table shifted away from her.

Helen's smile was as beguiling as a tiger's maw. "Lady Ariadne Carrington."

Ariadne's periwinkle-blue eyes widened with alarm.

Helen continued. "I haven't known my dear little step-sister very long, my mother and her father being married not much longer than a year. But my goodness, what an impression this delightful young woman has made."

A chill passed through Felicity. Alex looked at her questioningly. For Felicity, it was clear what was happening.

Helen went on. "For the longest time. I imagined dear little Ari didn't care a fig about me. Then I started getting letters."

Felicity raced through her thoughts. Was there a way to put a stop to things? It was Helen's party. It was Helen's show.

"These letters told me I'd be punished," said Helen. "They told me I'd be brought down a peg or two. Naturally, I wondered who'd sent them."

Unease spread around the dinner table, the guests shifting in their seats. Ariadne sat still, her cheeks ghostly pale.

"Please, Helen," said Leonard in a low, calm voice. "Sit back down."

Helen ignored her fiancé. "Then tonight, I found out. These threatening, anonymous letters were sent by no other than my darling little step-sister."

Rex let out a laugh of disbelief. "Is this some kind of joke?"

Clemency looked confused and worried. Patience's expression was cool, but her eyes glinted with interest.

"Helen, what is this?" challenged Edwin.

Colour had risen in Ariadne's cheeks. Anger was replacing her fear.

Alex shook his head slowly. But what could Felicity do?

"Come on, now, Hel," said Charles. "We were having such a splendid time, weren't we?"

"I propose a toast." Helen raised her voice and her glass above the dissenters. "To Lady Ariadne. I'm flattered by your attentions, but perhaps next time you want to destroy me, you'll find a manner of doing so that doesn't destroy yourself in the process."

Leonard stared hard at Helen, his thin moustache twitching, but her eyes were locked on her step-sister. Rex was the only one in the room with his glass raised for the toast when Ariadne stood up. Her chair fell backward as she thundered out of the dining room, almost colliding with the bespectacled footman. The violent slam of the dining room door was followed by a scream so full of hate and frustration it threatened to shatter glass. Then there were Ariadne's footsteps, running away along the stone corridor.

"Really, Helen." Edwin's pale eyebrows were lowered in reproof at his sister. "I don't know what she's done, but Ariadne is barely more than a child. Show some compassion for once in your life."

Miss Fairchild kept her eyes on the tablecloth before her. Based on knowing only Edwin, this was unlikely what she'd expected of his family.

Helen shrugged. "She got what was coming to her."

"Did Lady Ariadne really send such nasty letters?" asked Clemency, blinking in disbelief. "How absolutely horrid."

"Rather mean-spirited, I must agree," said Sir Vernon to no one in particular while taking a slurp of wine.

Leonard said nothing. He stared at his plate. Jambo whimpered.

The butler and the footman stood stiffly beside the buffet, the butler's expression impassive, the young footman's a little less so.

"Should someone check if she's all right?" The suggestion came from Charles, but no one ventured to act upon it. There'd been no one else from the Carrington side of the family at the dinner table.

Felicity's heart was still pounding from what she'd witnessed. From Alex's leaden expression, he would have rather walked across hot coals than spend another moment at Grimstow House.

As an awkward silence descended on the gathering, the wind rattled the windows, and the lights dimmed again for a moment.

"Now," said Helen. "Who's up for games?"

Chapter Five

Only Rex protested the skipping of dessert as the gathering decamped from the dining room under Helen's lively chivvying. Their footsteps echoed in the draughty stone corridor as Felicity did her best to manoeuvre herself towards Alex. As she slowed to allow Helen to pass her, Leonard caught his fiancée by her gloved elbow, the chain attached to the Ridgeback's collar gripped firmly in his other hand.

"I'd prefer to take brandy in the library," Leonard hissed.

Helen's smile twisted into something unpleasant. "You said it was my party. I told you there'd be games."

"Having fun?" asked Alex brightly as Felicity fell into step beside him, keeping more than a respectable amount of distance. They weren't supposed to know each other, although after Ariadne's confession and Helen's performance, everything felt topsy-turvy.

"Certainly not after that scene," replied Felicity grimly as they passed another portrait of the same young man seen painted before, this time in slightly different military attire.

The man pictured was Ariadne's brother, Lord Archibald Carrington, whom Felicity had met only once, at the wedding of Earl Carrington to Helen and Edwin's mother. Archibald had seemed painfully shy, although Felicity had opened up gentle conversation, and they'd found common ground on the subject of dogs. It hadn't been a surprise to find Archibald absent from Helen's party.

Felicity lowered her voice further. "Are you suffering unbearably? I can't tell you how sorry I am."

Alex sighed deeply. "Did you know your cousin could be that way?"

As they passed windows upon which a thin layer of white ice was forming, clearly visible against the coal-black night beyond, Felicity was quiet. From squabbles over toys as small children to unkind comments when they were of school age, there'd always been an edge of meanness to Helen. However, as much as Felicity trusted Alex, to criticise one's own family to an outsider wasn't good taste.

Felicity checked there was no one within hearing distance. "Ariadne confessed to me about the letters, and I told Helen. She was upset, of course. I didn't quite realise how upset."

The corner of Alex's mouth hooked upwards. "Talk about a gift. Your mere presence elicits confessions from the guilty." His smile dropped. "It wasn't exactly kind what Helen said about you."

"Shall we leave?" It was a silly, desperate suggestion, but Felicity was keen not to be reminded of Helen's hurtful words.

"And chance the journey in the dark, on roads covered in ice?"

Through inattention, they'd split from the group and were heading down a narrow hallway with a vaulted ceiling.

"Goodness." Felicity stopped and looked around. One stone corridor looked very much like another. "I fear we're lost."

"Retracing our steps shouldn't be difficult," suggested Alex, as unflappable as ever.

Scritch, scritch, scritch.

On the stone floor further along the corridor, in front of a glass-paned door that afforded a view of the darkness outside, lay a large Borzoi with slightly shaggy silver-grey fur, who was using a hind paw to scratch her ear. The itch dealt with, the dog trained her long elegant muzzle on Felicity and Alex, twitched her folded ears, and blinked.

From an adjoining corridor appeared a man in loose-fitting tweeds and a large, old-fashioned moustache, which was striking given the man's youth. His ash-blonde hair was parted on the side but not slicked down. He had ruddy cheeks and nervous periwinkle-blue eyes. He held a voluminous bag in worn, tan leather.

"Lord Archibald," said Felicity, advancing along the corridor. "How delightful to see you again. This must be Mina."

The Borzoi's ears pricked at the sound of her name.

Archibald nodded in acknowledgement. "Lady Felicity." His voice was flat and gruff, his eyes darting quickly away. "Come," he commanded, and with a dignified gait, Mina followed Archibald as he disappeared through another doorway.

Alex frowned. "Polite of the fellow to have introduced himself."

"Archibald is Ariadne's brother," explained Felicity, stopping short of apologising for his behaviour. Her blood relation's performance was enough of a burden to bear. "He's been a recluse since the war, as I understand it."

Alex's demeanour changed. He nodded with understanding. He hadn't escaped the Great War unscathed either. What man of their generation had?

"Lady Felicity." The housekeeper approached from behind. "I'm terribly sorry to interrupt, but Miss Quick awaits you in the billiard room."

Felicity smiled weakly. "Of course." She looked apologetically at Alex.

Leaving Grimstow House was no longer an option. The journey over frozen hills was potentially lethal. They would have to go along with things, hoping for as smooth a ride as possible along the way.

With the blue-green expanse of the heavy-set billiard table taking up most of the floor, the billiard room was already a snug space, with room to swing a cue but not much else. The addition of Helen, her party guests, and an array of servants gathered to assist with the proceedings — namely the butler, housekeeper, footman, and a little brown-haired maid who'd helped dress Felicity — made it uncomfortably cramped.

The only seating was a set of button back chairs in red leather, of which only Sir Vernon so far had taken advantage, a wine glass still in his hand. A row of lamps hanging low over the baize lit everything with a glaucous glow.

There was an uneasy silence as Helen glared at everyone, her eyes glinting with mischief.

Miss Fairchild stood timidly beside Edwin, who looked positively unamused by his sister's behaviour. A combination of trepidation and excitement defined Clemency's wide-eyed expression. Standing next to her, Patience seemed deadly bored. Rex smiled knowingly, his arms folded in a satisfied manner as he leaned against the dado. Charles stood relaxed, his hands in his pockets. Leonard lowered himself into the chair opposite Sir Vernon and lit a cigar, the earthy scent of the smoke spreading through the room. The Ridgeback, still on his chain, shifted anxiously at Leonard's side.

Felicity and Alex stood next to one another, so she couldn't quite read his expression. Not that it would change much. It was now simply a case of getting through the evening.

Helen clapped her hands, the tassels on her dress gently clattering. "This isn't quite the ball I had planned, but that doesn't mean we can't have fun. Indeed, I've arranged a surprise for you all. We're going to play—" Helen paused for dramatic effect "—murder in the dark."

Clemency gasped. Miss Fairchild's hand flew to her chest. Even Patience's eyes widened with surprise.

"I say," said Charles, his eyes searching the gathering, as though keen to gather the overriding sentiment of the room.

"Oh, Hel, what fun," chirped Rex.

Sir Vernon flapped a dismissive hand as if to say he wanted no part in it. Edwin also frowned. From what was visible through the clouds of his cigar smoke, Leonard was as impassive as the servants.

Felicity and Alex glanced at one another. Neither of them were in the mood to play games and — given everything they'd been through together — particularly not with murder for a theme. But what choice was there? As much as Helen had done to make Felicity feel uncomfortable, that didn't give Felicity the right to behave impolitely and refuse to take part.

"Horrocks," commanded Helen. "If you please."

The butler dutifully stepped forward, a selection of playing cards splayed face-down in his hands.

"You'll each take a card," continued Helen. "No one else must see it. If you've got the joker, then lucky you. You're the murderer. It's your job to kill."

Felicity winced. There was absolutely no joy in murder.

Helen went on. "If the murderer approaches you and says you're dead, then I'm afraid that's it. You're a corpse."

"Come on, Hel. Just turn the lights out. We all know how to play," jeered Rex good-naturedly, running a hand over his shiny dark brown hair.

The butler edged around the thick-legged billiard table as each person selected a card.

"I don't know how to play," whispered Miss Fairchild to Edwin.

Helen smiled at Rex and continued. "Should the murderer wish to stash your body in a cupboard or some such, you must comply. And if you got the king's card—"

It was Alex's turn to take a card. Felicity watched for his reaction. He pressed his card to the satin lapel of his dinner jacket and gave her a little smile.

"—then you're our detective." Helen gave Felicity a sly look. "It'll be up to you to fathom who did it."

"Thank you," said Felicity quietly as she took a card from the butler. She hoped desperately it was neither the joker nor the king.

"And what if the murderer kills the detective?" The question came from Charles.

"Then whoever gets the queen is our sleuth," answered Helen.

Clemency piped up. "What if the queen also gets killed?"

Felicity took a deep breath and looked at her card. It was the two of clubs. Her shoulders dropped with relief. She was utterly done with sleuthing for the evening.

The butler approached the leather chairs. Leonard turned to face his friend, pulling on his cigar. "Vernon."

Sir Vernon sighed loudly. "If I must." He took a card.

"Let's just play the game, shall we?" said Helen.

Clemency nodded uncertainly.

"But let me warn you—" Helen reached into the front of her dress and withdrew something. "I'm armed and unafraid to use it. So if you've got the joker, don't come after me." It took a moment to register that Helen was brandishing a tiny black pistol with a glinting pearl handle.

Rex laughed, thoroughly entertained.

A chill ran through Felicity.

Colour rose to Edwin's freckled cheeks. "Helen. This is sheer recklessness."

An enigmatic smile appeared on Leonard's face as the Ridgeback whined and wagged his tail. Was Leonard impressed by his fiancée's gesture or at his wit's end with her?

Patience narrowed her eyes. "Is it real?"

"It's real enough," said Sir Vernon with a chuckle. "But is it loaded?"

Even Horrocks couldn't control his reaction. "Miss Quick, I believe we discussed the matter of firearms before the party—"

The butler's reaction riled Helen. "I am the lady of the house this evening, am I not? Now. The lights, please. And if Horrocks refuses to do it, then Mrs Rudd will see to it."

The housekeeper nodded perfunctorily and started towards the door.

"I-I shall do it," said the butler, and he promptly left the room.

"When the lights go back on," continued Helen, "those of us still living shall regroup here in the billiard room."

Felicity turned to Alex. Concern flickered in his dark blue eyes. Then the lights went out. Gasps, nervous laughter, and a few oaths went up around the room. Felicity blinked. It was so dark she could see nothing at all.

"When do the lights go back on?" The thin, worried voice sounded like Miss Fairchild's.

"When someone's found dead," came the answer in unidentifiable masculine tones.

There was a click as the door to the billiard room opened — the corridor beyond had also been plunged into darkness — then it slammed shut. This was followed by footsteps running and distant laughter.

From within the room came a thud. "Blast that blasted billiard table!"

"Are we allowed to roam about?" The question was perhaps Clemency's.

"Clearly," came a flat, feminine reply.

The door to the billiard room opened and closed again.

Tap. Tick. Tap.

There came a series of wooden and metallic noises. Then the outline of the billiard table appeared, cast in silvery light. Alex was at the window, folding back the wooden shutters, allowing the brightness of the moon to flood the room.

Felicity laughed with relief and delight at his ingenuity. "Do I take it you're not the murderer, then?" she asked Alex.

Alex rocked back on his heels and arched a thick eyebrow. "I take it you're not either?"

"Well, that's rather spoiled the game, hasn't it?" On the other side of the billiard table, Clemency folded her arms over her sparkling dress, which looked silver rather than blue in the moonlight.

Everyone else, the servants included, had already left the room. The door to the dark corridor stood open. There was laughter and a sound like heavy furniture being shunted across the floor in a neighbouring room.

"The game's not spoiled," insisted Felicity, although personally, she didn't care if it was. "Everywhere else in the house is still dark. The murderer must be out there somewhere."

Clemency harrumphed and tightened the fold of her arms like a disappointed child. "And what if I'm the murderer? What then?"

"Well," said Alex. "You could kill us, if you like."

With another harrumph and a violent tinkle from the slithers of mirror on her dress, Clemency left the room.

Felicity flopped into a button back chair, relieving her throbbing feet. Alex eased himself into the seat opposite. He had the familiar scent of fresh meadows about him.

"So I suppose Clemency isn't the murderer either." It was a relief to hear a hint of amusement in Alex's tone.

"I'm not yet sure how," said Felicity earnestly, "but I promise I'll make this whole mess up to you."

"It's not your fault your cousin delights in chaos. And please excuse me if I cross a line by saying that."

Felicity wasn't offended, but neither did she feel absolved. "I sincerely hope the ice thaws early tomorrow."

"It's not entirely your fault we're stuck here."

"I should have been firmer with Helen."

Alex frowned at Felicity. "Are you suggesting I'm unable to look out for myself?"

The comment made Felicity sit up straight. Born to a greengrocer, Alex had fought to rise through the ranks of Fleet Street. Felicity, meanwhile, had practically everything handed to her on a silver platter. "That's not what I—"

"Everything all right in here?" Charles poked his head cheerily around the door, but his face dropped. "I say, Cici. Are you feeling all right?"

Felicity blinked. "I-I'm quite well, thank you. The moonlight makes everything look pale."

"Oh dear, I didn't mean to..." Charles looked anxious. "Well, if you say it's all right, then it must be. I'm off to get murdered. Or to murder someone." He gave an exaggerated wink.

Felicity nodded stiffly. Alex smiled politely. Charles withdrew from the doorway.

Alex crossed his legs at the knee and leaned back in his chair. Aside from Charles' footsteps tapping away and the wind occasionally rattling the windows, the house had become quiet.

"If I were writing for the society pages, I'd be rather pleased about being here this evening." As he spoke, Alex looked out at the moon.

Felicity frowned. "Why? The evening's been a disaster so far."

"All the tension and intrigue."

"Argh!" An exaggerated manly yell went up from the hall, followed by laughter.

"You mean between Ariadne and Helen?" Felicity grimaced. "You'd like to see that in a newspaper column?"

It was Alex's turn to frown, emphasising the scar on his forehead. "You've not noticed the rest of it?"

"I was rather focused on making the most of the opportunity to spend time with my family," admitted Felicity.

Alex leaned forward in his chair. "All's not well with the Bourgoyne sisters. And I'd wager there's something not quite right about that Rex fellow."

Another masculine shout went up from a nearby room, this time without an ounce of comedic overplay. The Ridgeback barked ferociously. Alex winced at the sound.

"Do you suppose—" began Felicity, but her question was cut short.

Crack! Crack!

The sound of the gun was unmistakable, as was a terrible crash of glass. A woman screamed. The shrill noise was long and chilling. Then the lights went back on, flickering a moment and dimming, before glowing strongly.

The butler dashed past the door of the billiard room, quickly followed by the footman.

Felicity stood up as Alex rose to his feet, apprehension tightening like a belt around her chest.

They looked at one another.

"We ought to see what's going on," she said.

Chapter Six

Felicity and Alex hurried in the direction in which they'd seen the butler and footman both running, the heels of Felicity's shoes clicking rapidly along the stone floor. Sobbing, growling, and whimpering drew them to turn off the main corridor and step through an open door into a morning room decorated with pale yellow soft furnishings. As they entered, the footman almost knocked them over, hurrying in the opposite direction. At the far end of the room was a large bay window with a set of French doors.

"Is everything quite all right?" enquired Felicity as she approached the gathering standing in the bay, although she could already see it wasn't.

His face creasing with strain, Leonard used all his power to keep control of Jambo. The Ridgeback lunged and snarled towards Sir Vernon, who stood with his back to the French doors, cradling his hand and whimpering, his monocle gone. Clemency stood to one side, hugging herself, her eyes fixed on the butler, who was crouched low on the carpet.

No one spoke as Felicity and Alex approached. Gusts of freezing wind hit them as their feet crunched over broken glass. Again, the lights flickered. Then they saw her.

Sprawled on the floor before the butler was Helen, her face in the carpet, the tassels of her sparkling purple dress splayed chaotically, a dark stain on her back. Her face was pale and expressionless. At her neck, her strings of gems had been broken, the precious stones scattered among shards of glass from a broken panel in the bay windows, through which the freezing wind was howling.

A short distance from Helen's hand lay the pistol, its pearl handle glinting.

"Upon my soul," said Alex.

Felicity felt cold to her bones. "Is she…"

"Miss Quick." The butler gently shook Helen's lifeless shoulder. His voice trembled. "Miss Quick."

Alex stood aside as the footman returned with Edwin. He had his black leather medical bag with him, but he almost dropped it, his mouth going slack at the sight of his sister laid out on the floor.

Tossing his cane to the carpet and kneeling beside Helen, Edwin tore open his medical bag. "I told her not to play with that blasted pistol."

"I tried to warn her, sir," said the butler.

"Have it locked up," commanded Edwin.

"Will do, sir."

Clemency held a hand to her forehead. Her complexion was ashen. "She's not… I mean, Helen's not… Is she?"

Alex's expression was extremely grave. He'd come to the same dreadful conclusion as Felicity.

Edwin dropped his sister's lifeless wrist to the ground and sat back on his heels. He stared hard at Leonard. The Ridgeback responded with a ferocious bark.

Leonard's eyes darkened, both hands on Jambo's chain. "Don't look at me. This isn't my fault."

The electric lights overhead flickered.

"Horrocks, have that hound locked away in the stables," commanded Edwin.

The butler turned purposefully towards Leonard and the Ridgeback. The footman went to the butler's side, but neither servant dared move closer to the angry dog.

"Clem? Hel? What's going on?" Patience had entered the room.

Clemency ran to her sister. "It's too ghastly to be true. Oh, please say it isn't true."

Patience looked around, confused. "What's not true?"

The bespectacled young footman took a step forward, but a bark from the Ridgeback sent him several paces backwards.

Edwin looked up from his sister's side. "Helen's dead. She's been shot."

"Edwin," said Felicity. She could only imagine the pain of losing a sibling. "I'm so very sorry."

"My condolences," said Alex solemnly.

Patience shook her head, the feather on her headband trembling. "So, do we go back to the billiard room to guess the murderer?"

Clemency burst into tears on her sister's shoulder.

"It's not a game anymore," shouted Leonard above his dog's snarls. "It was never a game. Now, show me where I can lock him up. I'll do it myself."

The butler nodded briskly and led Leonard out of the room, the dog pulling on its chain the whole way.

Patience put an arm around her sister. Her lower lip trembled. "Helen's… Dead?"

Edwin was still kneeling at his sister's side, the tails of his jacket hanging over the soles of his shoes. Sir Vernon sniffed, the corners of his lips drawn down. Untethered from Horrocks' oversight and guidance, the young footman shifted nervously. The freezing wind continued to blast through the broken window.

Felicity stepped forward, keen to shield Edwin, whose shock and grief must have been acute. "Very sadly, that appears to be the case," she said gently to Patience. "Helen is no longer with us."

Hurried, purposeful footsteps approached from the corridor.

"But how?" Patience swallowed as she glanced at her friend's body. "I mean, who would do this? Wait. I know people who specialise in exactly this sort of thing. Contact can be made with the deceased. We can ask Helen herself who it was that—"

"Stop," said Edwin firmly. "I won't stand for mumbo jumbo."

"It's likely to have been a tragic accident," said Felicity as reassuringly as she could. A gun for parlour games in the dark had indeed been reckless.

"What's all this about an accid—" Rex had come to a stop with his hands in the pockets of his fashionable suit. Noticing the body, he flew to Helen's side, skidding on his knees. "Helen?" He put a hand on her shoulder and shook it violently. "Helen!"

"Enough." Edwin stood up, his freckled cheeks bright red with emotion. "I want everyone to leave."

Rex remained knelt beside the body. He clutched Helen's hand, tears rolling down his cheeks. He had mud on the soles of his shoes.

Edwin tugged at Rex's shoulder, forcing him away from the body and almost tossing him backwards onto the floor.

"Out, I say!" growled Edwin, all trace of his usual gentle manner gone. "Everyone!"

Felicity hesitated for a moment. She'd never seen Edwin like this. She signalled to Alex that they should leave.

Rex wriggled backwards and climbed to his feet. "This can't be real though, can it? I mean, she can't really be dead? It's part of the game. Isn't it?"

Looking more angry than sad about the passing of her friend, Patience was already at the door to the corridor, her arm around her sister. "Come on, Clem."

Clemency wept and craned her neck towards the bay where Helen still lay sprawled.

"Clem!" called Rex as he chased after the twins, wiping his eyes.

Still cradling his hand, Sir Vernon stepped away from the

French doors, his patent shoes crunching on the broken glass. "I… Um." He seemed confused.

Alex went to his side. "This way, Sir Vernon."

Sir Vernon shuffled obediently alongside Alex towards the morning room door, where Felicity waited.

"We need to telephone to the police," said Edwin, addressing the footman.

Felicity swallowed, but her throat felt awfully dry. Even if Helen's demise had indeed been an accident, one would still telephone to the police.

"Telephone, sir? I-I'm afraid that won't be possible, sir."

"Upon my word. There's a telephone in this wretched castle, isn't there?"

"Y-yes, sir."

"Then use it!"

Rattled by Edwin's shouting at him, the footman went tearing past Felicity and Alex, jostling Sir Vernon's elbow as he passed. Sir Vernon gasped in pain and stumbled. Alex caught him.

"That ruddy—" Sir Vernon cut himself off.

"Edwin?" Miss Fairchild had arrived. Stepping past Felicity into the morning room, she looked as pale as a bedsheet.

"Ruth," said Edwin. "Thank goodness you're here. Close the door, would you?"

Miss Fairchild did as Edwin bade her, blinking nervously and apologetically as she shut Felicity, Alex, and Sir Vernon out in the draughty stone corridor.

Felicity let out a slow, shuddering breath.

"Are you all right?" asked Alex, his eyes searching hers.

Helen, her cousin, was no more. The horrible truth of it was only just sinking in, but if Edwin needed her, Felicity would be ready to help. She would be strong.

She straightened. "I will be."

Alex gave a firm nod, taking Felicity at her word. "You've injured your hand, have you not, Sir Vernon?"

"A scratch is all it is," he said as Alex gently insisted Sir

Vernon allow him to look under the handkerchief wrapped around his palm. "It'll heal."

"It's a dog bite," said Alex. "It needs seeing to."

Sir Vernon shrugged a little uneasily. "I was hoping Doctor Quick might see to it, but I suppose there's little chance of that now."

"I'm sure the butler will have the necessary supplies. Let's start by getting the wound cleaned up." Alex looked enquiringly at Felicity. "What would you say to that, Lady Felicity?"

"That sounds like a very reasonable plan," she replied, still a little too stunned to do much else than follow the flow of things.

Alex guided Sir Vernon along the corridor with Felicity in tow. Again, the lights flickered. It made Felicity's heart leap. Was Helen really gone?

"As soon as it's safe to travel, we'll need to get you to a hospital," said Alex. "Dog bites can be a nasty business."

"To a hospital?" Sir Vernon frowned. "But I came down from London to attend Leonard's ball." The poor man was confused.

"Sir Vernon," said Felicity. "I'm afraid the party is well and truly over." A horrible new chapter had begun, and Felicity still couldn't quite believe it.

What exactly had happened in the dark?

After a few wrong turns in the tangle of Grimstow House's stone corridors, Felicity, Alex, and Sir Vernon found their way below stairs. News of the incident had reached the servants' hall. The little maid who'd helped dress Felicity and a rotund, frizzy-haired cook were among those weeping. A kitchen maid and a pair of estate workers stood by, looking stunned. The butler and the footman must still have been upstairs.

Mrs Rudd, though pale, was among the most composed of the servants. She maintained her upright posture as she examined Sir Vernon's hand. "Oh, dear," she said, "that indeed looks nasty." With Felicity and Alex in their wake, the housekeeper led Sir Vernon to her sitting room.

"I'm sorry there's not more space, your ladyship," said Mrs Rudd as she took one of the two straight-backed chairs in the little room in order to tend to Sir Vernon, who sat in the other.

"That's quite all right," said Felicity as she positioned herself before a radiator, thankful for the warmth.

Alex remained by the door. "Has contact been made with the police?" he asked.

Sir Vernon winced as Mrs Rudd gently peeled back the handkerchief wrapped around his hand. The housekeeper's hands trembled slightly, her professional countenance not enough to conceal every hint of emotional reaction to the events upstairs. "I'm afraid the telephone isn't in service weekends and evenings," she said without looking up from Sir Vernon's wound.

"Heavens," said Felicity. At Bradley Court, the telephone line was in operation every hour of every day, but she supposed her brother's position as editor-in-chief of the region's biggest newspaper explained that. "Then how shall the police be summoned?"

Mrs Rudd began cleaning Sir Vernon's hand. "I should expect it'll mean a trip to Cheriton St Mary, your ladyship. I believe the telephone lines in the village are connected to the main exchange."

Alex threw a glance at Felicity. "The roads are iced over, are they not?"

Felicity grimaced. "It's not just the police. Earl Carrington and my aunt must also be informed." She imagined their pain and their questions. As yet, there was so little information.

Grim-faced, Mrs Rudd shook her head, her eyes still on her patient's wound. "Such a terrible accident, but there's no undoing it now. No way to bring poor Miss Helen back. We don't yet know Lady Carrington awfully well, your ladyship, but the Earl is such an incredibly kind man. One would like to shield him from any suffering, if one could."

"Edwin, too," said Felicity, her stomach tightening at the thought of her surviving cousin's agony at the loss of his sister.

Mrs Rudd nodded in agreement. She made neat work of the bandage on Sir Vernon's hand. Sir Vernon blinked as he inspected the dressing. The housekeeper busied herself clearing away the basin and medical kit, a slight tremble to her gestures.

"Sir Vernon," said Felicity gently. "Were you in the room when the gun went off?"

Sir Vernon swallowed and then nodded.

"I realise it was dark," continued Felicity, "but might you have any idea what happened?"

Sir Vernon's mouth gaped and then closed. "I-I was the murderer, you see."

Mrs Rudd looked up and froze, eyes wide. Alex frowned.

"You mean as part of the game?" clarified Felicity. "You drew the joker?"

"That's right," said Sir Vernon. "I'd already done away with one chap, then I followed the noises into the morning room. A whole number of people were gathered there."

"Who?" pressed Alex. He hadn't a notebook in his hand, but a reporter's instinct couldn't be stifled.

"Will that be all, your ladyship?" asked Mrs Rudd.

Felicity confirmed it would be, and the housekeeper withdrew, closing the door gently and moving silently away from the little sitting room.

Sir Vernon squinted, as if trying to re-imagine what he had seen. "Leonard was there with that deuced dog of his. I rather underestimated how obsessed the hound is with him." He looked angrily at his bandaged hand. "It was foolish of me to make Leonard my victim."

"Who else was there?" asked Felicity.

Sir Vernon thought for a moment. "Difficult to say. There was only a little moonlight from the windows."

It seemed possible the morning room faced a different aspect than the billiard room. Felicity had been distracted, certainly, but she couldn't remember seeing the moon in the bay windows.

"There were perhaps as many as six of us gathered," continued Sir Vernon. "If I had to guess, I'd say three men and three women, but I can't be sure. I could see the outlines of the feathers all the women seem to wear these days."

Felicity pulled awkwardly at the feathered headband still wrapped tightly over her auburn curls. "Can you tell us what happened?"

Sir Vernon paused. He squinted. "I say. You're a journalist, aren't you, your ladyship? Am I being interviewed for the papers? And may I ask what Mr Cooper's involvement in this interrogation is? I wasn't aware you knew one another."

They were all fair questions, but Felicity wasn't on newspaper business, and her engagement as a sleuth had ceased with Ariadne's confession. "Helen was my cousin, Sir Vernon. I should like to understand how my relative met her untimely end. And Mr Cooper is a friend." Felicity glanced at Alex to ensure she wasn't over-stepping any boundaries by referring to him in this way.

Alex nodded his confirmation. "Are you able to provide Lady Felicity any further information about what happened to her cousin?"

Sir Vernon sighed. "As I said, I approached Leonard. His dog bit me. There was some kind of tussle, then the gun went off. When the lights came back on, there was just Leonard, myself, and… You know. Lying on the floor and all that. I can say for certain that I wasn't involved, and neither was Leonard."

"A tussle?" asked Felicity.

A knock came at the door. It opened to reveal the young bespectacled footman looking flustered. "My apologies. I was looking for Mrs Rudd." He went to withdraw.

"Your name, please?" enquired Felicity.

The young man paused in the doorway. "W-Wilkinson, your ladyship."

"Mr Wilkinson, has anyone been sent to Cheriton St Mary to telephone to the police?"

"Not yet. The driver was on his way, but then… Th-there's rather a to-do, your ladyship."

"A to-do?" asked Alex.

The footman looked uncomfortable. "A disagreement, sir."

"Not Leonard?" Sir Vernon winced as he stood up, nursing his injured hand.

Felicity took a steadying breath. If there was an opportunity to help, she would take it. Edwin had already been through so much. She looked at Alex. "Shall we return upstairs?"

Chapter Seven

"You let this happen!"

"What the deuce are you implying?"

Angry voices echoed along Grimstow House's chilly corridors as Felicity, Alex, and Sir Vernon hurried towards the commotion. Felicity didn't know the guests well enough to recognise the shouts. Was it Leonard? Rex? More than one man was involved.

"Thank goodness. There you are." Charles appeared suddenly from an adjoining corridor, striding purposefully towards Felicity. His approach blocked her from following Alex and Sir Vernon, who continued towards the raised voices.

Felicity smiled politely. "There's no need to worry about me, Charlie." She was keen to keep moving.

"Well, I'm relieved you're in one piece. But just what the blazes is going on? I'm told I'm dead and stuffed into a cupboard. When I finally emerge, I learn about this terrible accident. And to think I was in a cupboard the whole time. I feel like an absolute ruddy fool. I've let Edwin down terribly."

"It's far from certain we'd have been able to avert the course of events," said Felicity, reassuring herself as much as Charles. It had been Helen's decision to carry a loaded pistol, after all. There was no point criticising her now.

Charles' brow wrinkled. "But what about the threatening letters? Leonard said they rattled Helen so deeply that she engaged you to look into the matter for her."

Felicity blinked. She'd been outed as a sleuth. Given the circumstances, it was perhaps both inevitable and forgivable.

"And one can't shoot oneself in the back," added Charles. "Someone must have taken Helen's gun from her."

"Helen was shot from behind?" The unwelcome image of Ariadne creeping through the dark for deadly revenge on her step-sister flew into Felicity's mind. Yet despite her self-possession, Ariadne was barely more than a child. Could someone so young be capable of such malice?

Angry voices continued in the distance. The wall-mounted lights flickered momentarily.

"Oh, dash it all," muttered Charles. "I ought to be there for Edwin." He hurried towards the argument.

Felicity was about to set off in the same direction when a rustling drew her attention. She turned.

Further down the corridor stood Lord Archibald, his silver Borzoi at his side. He wore a heavy greatcoat and had a dimly glowing lantern in one hand and the same large leather bag seen earlier in the other. He stared for a moment at Felicity, saying nothing, then disappeared outside. Freezing air swept along the stone floor as the door opened and closed.

Felicity shivered. Where was Archibald going?

The raised voices hadn't abated. "If you're not willing to do anything about it, then I shall find out myself!"

Taking a fortifying breath, Felicity went after Charles. If she could help prevent matters at Grimstow House spiralling further out of control, then that would be her priority.

The lights dimmed in their brass fittings, then returned to full power as Felicity arrived in Grimstow House's entrance hall. A large red Persian carpet, carved oak doors, and the buttery grey of its chiselled-smooth walls created a welcoming atmosphere, but there was no hospitality among those gathered.

"Don't tell me I have no right to care. I cared more about her than you ever did." Rex bellowed these words at Edwin, who stood firm, his hand gripping the top of his cane. Beside him lingered Charles, as though unsure whether to take action. Miss Fairchild cowered in the background.

"You're talking to her brother, you pathetic fool." Leonard stepped forward. He was without his dog, big-knuckled fists balled at his sides. Sir Vernon hovered behind him, cradling his bandaged hand.

Alex kept his distance from the dispute but observed every move. Also present were the butler, footman, and some other men Felicity recognised from the servants' hall. Horrocks, in particular, looked concerned by the goings on.

Rex turned to Leonard. "I'm the fool?" He jabbed his finger at the lapels of his own black dinner jacket. "You were right there when she died and did nothing to prevent it. Yet I'm the fool?"

"Enough!" Edwin dragged Rex back by his shoulder. "Or I'll have you all locked up till the police arrive."

Alex caught Felicity's gaze, widening his eyes as if to say, *Wow*. All trace of gentleness had left Edwin.

Rex stepped back. "You wouldn't—" he began shakily.

"Oh, I would." Edwin span around, addressing everyone in the room. "Because my little sister didn't put a bullet in her own back. One of you did it."

Miss Fairchild appeared frozen with terror. Felicity was on the cusp of approaching Edwin when Charles put a hand on his shoulder. "Let's try to keep calm, shall we?"

Leonard tugged at the collar of his dress shirt. "I appreciate we're all upset, but there's no point jumping to conclusions. The police are being summoned, are they not?" Leonard directed his question towards the gathering of servants.

Horrocks lowered his brow. "I'm afraid there's been a complication. Mr Gibson?"

A thin man in chauffeur's livery stepped forward. "Driveway's frozen solid, and it's so steep. I did my best but…" Mr Gibson wrung his hat in his hands. "I-I lost control of the motor, sir. Hit a tree."

"You did your best, Mr Gibson," said the butler reassuringly. He returned his attention to the guests. "It appears we're unable to leave the grounds by road, and we've not yet reached the lowest temperature for the night."

The flush of anger drained from Edwin's freckled cheeks. "You mean there's no way to contact the police?"

"There may be a chance, Doctor Quick," said the butler. "The stable master has a proposal. Mr Jarvis?"

A man of around sixty in corduroy, with metal-grey hair and weathered skin, cleared his throat. "I've a couple of horses might be up to the job. Mr Peabody says he's willing to try."

A younger man with a square jaw and in similar workwear nodded decisively. "I believe I can make it down to Cheriton St Mary."

"Mr Peabody knows which paths to use," said Jarvis. "It'll take time, of course, but it's quicker than waiting till morning."

"I'm going, too." Smoothing a hand over his hair, Rex moved decisively towards the older stableman. "I'm the best rider we've got."

"No, Mr Debenham." Edwin spoke firmly, the colour returning to his cheeks. "I'll not have it. Perhaps you were dear to my sister, but I barely know you from Adam. And from your behaviour up to now, you are not to be relied upon."

Rex spun towards Edwin. Charles stepped forward.

"I'll go," said Charles with a brief glance in Felicity's direction. "It's indeed better to have two men."

"The weather's perilous." The stable master looked with concern at Horrocks. "Mr Peabody knows the land."

"I shall follow young Mr Peabody's lead," assured Charles.

"Charles can be trusted to behave responsibly," said Edwin

Horrocks nodded. "Mr Jarvis, equip Lord Lorrimer with a horse. He'll ride alongside Mr Peabody."

"You'll be all right while I'm gone?" enquired Charles of Edwin.

Edwin glanced at Miss Fairchild, who still looked too terrified to move.

Felicity saw her chance. "I'm here for anything my cousin might need."

Charles looked relieved. "I'll be back as soon as I can." He left the entrance hall with the two stablemen.

His breath coming hard through flared nostrils, Rex returned his gaze to Edwin. "You've already announced I'm not to be trusted. Why not say what you're really thinking?"

Before Edwin could respond, the tapping of heels along a corridor off the entrance hall drew everyone's attention. With purpose in her stride, Patience arrived, leading Clemency by the hand. They wore long fur-collared coats over their party dresses, their feathered headbands bobbing as they walked. Behind them hurried the little maid, struggling with two travel bags.

The distraction was but brief.

"You think I murdered her, don't you?" Rex snarled at Edwin.

"Mr Debenham," began Felicity, advancing towards the two men. "My cousin has had an awful shock."

Patience stopped abruptly. "Murder?" Her sister knocked into her back. The maid managed to stop without a collision.

Clemency blinked, as though dazed. "Rex?"

Rex spun towards the twins, his expression switching from anger to deep chagrin. "Clem. Oh, Clem." He rushed towards the blonde-haired sister, but Patience came between them.

"No one's mentioned murder except Mr Debenham," said Edwin coolly.

Rex twisted away from the twins. "Well, she bally well didn't shoot herself in the back, did she?"

Edwin's face darkened. Had Helen been in grave danger, and Felicity hadn't even noticed?

"It still could have been an accident," Felicity suggested.

Rex whipped towards Felicity. Alex stepped forward.

"Really?" said Rex with a strange laugh. "What makes you the expert? You weren't there when it happened."

"But you were, Mr Debenham?" replied Felicity.

Rex's face hardened. He pressed his lips together. Felicity noticed that the lapel of his jacket was torn. She was desperate to know what exactly had happened when the lights went out, but the situation in the entrance hall was too tense. It wasn't yet time to push for answers.

"Let's keep calm," said Alex soothingly, "and avoid making accusations." He eyed Felicity without chastisement, but Alex was right to rein her in. The best course of action was to wait patiently for the police.

The wind screamed like a banshee at the front door. Again, the lights flickered.

"Do what you like," announced Patience. "We're leaving."

Rex took long steps to catch Clemency by the arm. "Don't go. Not yet," he implored. With Patience still holding her other hand, Clemency was now stretched between her sister and her fiancé, like a toy between squabbling children. Her bewildered face bordered on tears.

Leonard cleared his throat and withdrew a cigar case from the inside of his dinner jacket. "Lady Felicity, while we wait for the police, might you be able to assist us?"

Felicity turned to the businessman. "Me?"

Alex's dark blue eyes narrowed with concern.

"Her?" Patience dropped her sister's hand.

"Doctor Quick?" prompted Leonard.

Edwin furrowed his brow. "Mr McQueen mentioned you came to Grimstow on a matter of… Of private business for which Helen engaged your services as a…"

"A private detective." Leonard lit a cigar.

Patience's mouth fell open a little, then closed.

"I thought you were a journalist." Sir Vernon sounded betrayed.

Miss Fairchild continued to search the room with wide, frightened eyes.

"I'm sorry. Just what exactly is going on?" No one responded to Clemency's question. Rex had also dropped his fiancée's hand, his gaze now fixed on Felicity.

Being exposed as a sleuth in a manner beyond her control wasn't pleasant, but Edwin deserved the truth. "Helen asked me to look into the letters as a personal favour," Felicity added quickly. "Not in a professional capacity."

Rex slapped his thigh. "Now we're getting somewhere. The letters. Of course. Where's the little minx who sent Helen those threats? The investigation should start with her."

"The police's investigation, you mean?" said Felicity.

Alex looked deeply sceptical.

"Might you gather some facts before the police arrive, Lady Felicity?" suggested Leonard with a puff of smoke.

The request was flattering, but false hope could not be encouraged.

"I'm not in any position to investigate," said Felicity apologetically. She was an exceedingly amateur sleuth. Anonymous letters were about the limit of what she would agree to, and she hadn't even solved that matter.

"Mr Cooper can assist you, of course," added Leonard.

Rex frowned. "Mr Cooper?"

So Alex's cover was gone as well. He looked uneasy but said nothing.

"Mr Cooper is a colleague," clarified Felicity. *And still a friend*, she hoped, for more than just professional bonds were required to forgive the mess in which they were now entwined.

"Aha." Sir Vernon perked up. "Now I see it."

Pallor had returned to Edwin's freckled cheeks. He leaned on his cane. "Felicity, might you be able to... To put things together in a manner that spares my sister embarrassment?"

At last, Miss Fairchild unfroze. She went to Edwin's side and placed a hand on his arm.

"I'm not sure I follow," said Felicity, buying time as she considered her cousin's request. Taking a loaded gun into a parlour game played in the dark under the influence of champagne had been extremely ill-advised, whichever way one looked at it.

"Fine." Rex twitched with pent-up irritation. "If you won't act, then I will. I'll find that little letter-writing minx and make her pay. And what about that barmy brother of hers?" He strode towards a corridor, but Clemency caught his sleeve.

"Rex," she pleaded. "Don't."

A wash of disgust passed over Patience's features. Still holding the twins' travel bags, the little maid looked both confused and exhausted.

"What about it?" Leonard eyed Felicity as he continued to smoke his cigar. He leaned towards her. "I'll pay whatever you want to keep my Helen's name clean," he added with limited discretion. "I know you aristocrats aren't as rich as you once were."

Felicity swallowed. The comment made her feel unclean. She would never discuss money so openly, and it had nothing to do with her motivations.

"We're not asking you to solve anything," said Edwin, his voice trembling, "we're just asking you to... To... Present things in a manner that might..."

Edwin was asking for their help, not just as investigators, but as journalists.

Alex raised his eyebrows at Felicity. If newspaper work was involved, then it was a different matter.

Felicity straightened, the feather in her headband quivering. "I believe I understand what you're asking of us. Mr Cooper and

I should like to offer our assistance, but I'm afraid I must stipulate a condition."

Chapter Eight

Grimstow House's study was a comfortably snug room. A large desk with a deep red leather inlay stood at its centre, and two elegantly carved swivel chairs upholstered in red leather matched the desk. On the walls were electric lights behind frosted glass, and under foot was a dark blue carpet with a deep pile. Heavy curtains in rich burgundy damask kept freezing draughts at bay. The scent of wood polish hung in the air.

Felicity took a seat in the chair on the commanding side of the desk. Her condition for offering her help had sounded simple — that the house be returned to some semblance of order — but multiple steps were required. The morning room where Helen had been found was to be secured, with no one to enter until the police arrived. All firearms in the house were also to be locked up. Felicity and Alex were then to interview each person in turn, with everyone requested to wait patiently and quietly, preferably in their rooms, until they were each called into the study.

As the most senior family member present, Edwin had issued the necessary orders in alignment with Felicity's vision for how the rest of the evening would proceed. The goal wasn't to draw solid conclusions about what exactly had happened in the morning room. That would be left to the police. Felicity's aim was to gather information useful to the newspaper — an activity Alex was naturally keen to be involved in — that would set a respectful tone for the coverage of the incident.

For there was no question about it. The Western Morning News, through no deliberate action of Felicity's or Alex's, would once again have the scoop.

Another aim, and perhaps the more important one at this stage, was to calm the household with a sense of something being done. For Edwin's sake, more than anyone else's, Felicity hoped a series of orderly interviews would keep the volatile situation at Grimstow House under control till the police arrived.

Standing beside Felicity, Alex flicked through his notebook, occasionally scribbling something down. The agreement they'd made was that Alex would be the scribe and Felicity would lead the questioning, to ensure the right tone of reassurance was struck.

"And you're quite sure you're comfortable with this whole arrangement?" Alex asked without looking up from his notes.

"Comfortable is a stretch." Although seated, Felicity's feet still hurt from her ill-fitting shoes. She also didn't relish the thought of the discussions ahead. Helen had been her cousin, and Felicity certainly hadn't yet come to terms with the loss. Waves of guilt hit her as she recalled her focus on her cousin's less favourable attributes only shortly before her demise.

Her own discomfort didn't matter, however. Felicity would do whatever she could to help Edwin.

"I realise Miss Quick was your relative," continued Alex, "and I'm sure Jasper will be upset by the news, but you must have already realised. This story's going to be big." He looked up from his notebook. "And that's before we know all the details."

Felicity wasn't offended by the observation. "I'm relieved you're keen," she said, and she meant it. Now that he was engaged in the role of journalist, the responsibility Felicity felt for Alex's discomfort lifted.

Alex tucked his notebook into the inside pocket of his dinner jacket. "Were Helen and Edwin close?"

Felicity considered the question for a moment. "I believe they were fond of one another, even if they had very separate interests."

Alex nodded thoughtfully. "Do you believe murder to be a possibility?"

Felicity shifted uncomfortably in her seat, the beads of her dress pressing into her. Another wave of guilt hit as she considered how Helen was far from universally liked. "Besides my glaring lack of true expertise in criminal detection, my relation to Helen clouds my perceptions. No one wants a member of their own family done away with in such a fashion."

Alex's eyes twinkled with amusement. "How many cases have you unravelled now? And still you insist you're a dilettante."

Felicity sat up straighter. "It's been a run of coincidences and nothing more. I was simply there when things came to a head. At Wolborne House, in Lower Diddleton, at Langton Manor, and in Ippleford." She spoke confidently, almost believing the claim herself.

Alex shook his head some more and shrugged. "If you say so." He rocked back on his heels. "What do you make of Sir Vernon's version of events?"

Felicity reflected on what they'd heard in the housekeeper's sitting room as the wind shook the windows beyond the curtains. "I noticed a tear in Mr Debenham's lapel," she said. "That could corroborate the tussle Sir Vernon said he witnessed, except I can't say if the damage to the jacket was there before the lights went out." Felicity had already made one rather clumsy insinuation in the sportsman's direction. It was her aim to keep the peace, not rile the household with accusations.

"You've an enviable eye for detail."

Felicity shrugged dismissively. "One can't help noticing things."

Alex reached again for his notebook. "The fellow who went

with the horses to summon the police." He leafed through the pages. "Lord Lorrimer, is it? Do you know him incredibly well?"

"What, Charlie?" Felicity tried to imagine him responsible for Helen's passing. The idea almost made her laugh. "He's a dear friend of Edwin's and a thoroughly good egg. He also told me he was in a cupboard till the lights came back on."

"I see," said Alex flatly, continuing to flick absent-mindedly through his notebook.

There came a knock at the door. The footman's shiny bespectacled face appeared in the doorway. He'd been charged with bringing the interviewees to the study, while the butler had the task of locating Ariadne, whom no one had seen since dinner. Felicity had also requested an audience with Lord Archibald, but none of the guests had spoken to him, and the servants reported difficulty locating him at the best of times. He was known to roam across Grimstow's expansive estate in all weathers.

"Doctor Quick and Miss Fairchild are here to be interviewed, your ladyship," said the footman.

Felicity shifted in her seat. It wasn't the one-by-one interview process she had in mind, and her own doubtlessly innocent cousin wasn't where she would start an investigation. Yet it wasn't an investigation, was it?

"Please, Mr Wilkinson," said Felicity. "Bring them through."

Alex took up his post beside her chair, his notebook at the ready, and a frisson of excitement passed through Felicity, which she immediately tamped down. There was to be no unbridled curiosity, no thrill of the chase. Felicity's sleuthing instincts were to be kept firmly at bay. The priorities were calm, order, and the preservation of Helen's reputation.

"So, in summary, neither of you were in the morning room at any point while the lights were out for the game," said Felicity. "Is that correct?"

Miss Fairchild, still in her frilly, outdated party frock with ostrich plumes in her hair, was seated straight-backed and wide-eyed on the other side of the desk from Felicity. Behind Miss Fairchild paced Edwin, his brow drawn low, the tap of his walking cane deadened by the carpet. The wind gusted viciously beyond the heavy curtains.

The pair had been keen to be interviewed, which could be misconstrued as suspicious, but a motive for wishing Helen harm was, of course, entirely absent. Despite their differences, Edwin had been fond of his sister, and Miss Fairchild had encountered Helen for the first time that evening. Not that motives were Felicity's business. That was a matter for the police.

Alex waited for Edwin's and Miss Fairchild's reactions, his pencil poised on his notebook. Edwin had awkwardly admitted to using the cover of darkness to enter the off-limits ballroom with the intention of smoking a pipe in peace. Miss Fairchild, who wasn't acquainted with the layout of Grimstow House, had done her best to follow Edwin but had got lost. She'd stumbled into a chair in an alcove by a large potted plant and had waited there for the lights to come back on.

Miss Fairchild shook her head emphatically, deeply unnerved by the deadly drama. "I arrived in the morning room only after the lights had gone on."

"We already told you the way of things," said Edwin impatiently. He'd not stopped pacing since arriving in the study and was becoming more agitated. "You arrived before us, Felicity. You saw both Miss Fairchild and I enter the morning room."

Felicity nodded. "Naturally." Repetition for clarity was a journalistic technique, but further unsettling her cousin defeated the purpose of the interview. It was time to move the focus of the questions away from Edwin and Miss Fairchild.

"How long have you known one another?" The question was Alex's.

Felicity shot him a confused glance, but he was looking intently at the interviewees, his notebook at the ready. As a reporter, Alex was hard-nosed and unafraid of tough questions. Felicity admired his expertise and was even, on occasion, inspired by him to take a detour from her usual tactful, organic approach to questioning. Edwin was Felicity's bereaved cousin, however. There was no need to take a firm hand. She might have made it clear to Alex that she would be the only questioner rather than simply in the lead.

Felicity frowned apologetically at Edwin. "Of course, there's no need to answer should you not want to. Your association with one another is unlikely to be of importance for the reporting." While Miss Fairchild was Edwin's guest at the party, the precise nature of their relationship hadn't been articulated. Edwin was in many ways behind the times. He had perhaps taken advantage of his sister's looser and more modern ways to get closer to Miss Fairchild, but that didn't mean he would be comfortable talking about it.

Alex gave a little shrug, apparently unfazed by Felicity undermining his questioning.

"No, no." Edwin stopped pacing. "I've nothing to hide. It's important we're all honest here." He cleared his throat. "Miss Fairchild is here at my invitation. We met some months ago, when she was accompanying an elderly relative to my clinic."

Felicity raised her eyebrows. Perhaps her cousin was more open-minded than she gave him credit for.

Miss Fairchild's cheeks flushed a little. She lowered her gaze demurely.

"I realise it's not the most traditional way of doing things," continued Edwin, "and I'm immensely sorry to Miss Fairchild for what she's witnessed this evening." He glanced bashfully at his female companion. "By bringing Miss Fairchild to my sister's event, I hoped to get to know her better." Edwin paused momentarily, again making eye contact with Miss Fairchild. "I still hope to get to know her better."

Miss Fairchild blushed more deeply but remained silent. Indeed, Edwin's earnestness and his open display of emotion even made Felicity a little uncomfortable. It was almost too intimate.

Shifting in her seat, Felicity raised an eyebrow at Alex. Was his interrogation over? He returned a subtle nod. It was.

Felicity returned to the line of questioning she had intended. "Is it your feeling that Helen's passing was indeed an accident?"

Edwin resumed pacing. "I'd like to make one thing clear. I don't know her awfully well, but my step-sister, Ariadne, cannot be considered an adult. She might be at ease in adult company, and she may have sent those silly letters to Helen, but I'm quite certain she did nothing more than that."

"That's my impression also," said Felicity. She hoped the butler could locate Ariadne and that her account would confirm this view.

Edwin continued to pace. "Of course, I realise my sister didn't always behave graciously, and I dare say there are people here tonight who had reason to dislike her from time to time." He stopped, his face taut with grief, his hand gripping his cane. "But put an end to her life?"

Miss Fairchild trembled at Edwin's words. Felicity grimaced. She hadn't intended to jump to discussing potential murder suspects. Alex continued to write everything down. Felicity knew she could trust him to act in her family's interest — her brother, Jasper, was a close friend of his — but his idea of a scoop hopefully didn't involve an exposition of suspects and potential motives.

"Do you consider a deliberate act a possibility?" Felicity asked this gingerly of her cousin.

Edwin went back to pacing. "Helen had a sharp tongue, but she wasn't the sort to go for blackmail or anything like that. Why would she? Even before Mother remarried, we were comfortable enough. Then she met Mr McQueen." Edwin's pale eyebrows drew together.

Felicity remembered the stare Edwin had given Leonard in

the drawing room. "What was Helen's relationship with Mr McQueen like?"

Edwin sighed. "Helen was dazzled by the fellow's extreme wealth, and Mr McQueen was shrewd enough to spot an opportunity in Helen, with her connections to the aristocracy. The match was fast and convenient for both of them. That said, they were alike in their tastes for expensive purchases and foreign holidays and seemed content enough together. As best as I could, I wished them well."

Felicity considered her next question. Composure and reassurance were required. "If a coroner deemed the situation an accident, would you accept the ruling?"

Again, Edwin ceased pacing, coming to a stop beside Miss Fairchild's chair. He pressed both hands on top of his cane. "Even if it wasn't the intention to do away with Helen, someone pulled that trigger. She jolly well didn't do it herself. That none of them have confessed is something I find very difficult. Take that Rex fellow with his dramatic gestures."

The torn lapel flashed through Felicity's mind.

"Perhaps I'm just old-fashioned," continued Edwin, glancing at Miss Fairchild, "but I don't like it. A gentleman ought to conduct himself with decorum." The colour was rising in Edwin's cheeks. "I'm not insinuating he did anything on purpose. Why would he? Why would anyone? But a man should have the common decency to confess to his mistakes."

Miss Fairchild placed a hand on Edwin's. Seemingly embarrassed by her own gesture, she trained her eyes on the carpet, but her hand remained pressed on Edwin's.

Felicity's opinion of the woman softened. Miss Fairchild must have cared for her cousin.

Edwin sighed deeply, his anger receding. "In my profession, one grows accustomed to death, but I find it difficult to accept I'll never speak to Helen again."

Alex had stopped writing.

"I know," said Felicity. She, too, felt Helen's loss, yet she experienced Edwin's suffering even more keenly than her own. Not knowing exactly what had happened was torture for him. Might a confession provide solace for Edwin? Would it be appropriate for Felicity to make that her aim?

The door to the study flew open.

Edwin stiffened and turned, Miss Fairchild quickly withdrawing her hand.

"Sir Vernon," said Alex, with both irritation and concern as the grey-haired tail-coated man stumbled into the room.

After a moment's surprise, Felicity reacted. "Would you be kind enough to wait—" she began in a chastising tone, but Sir Vernon lurched forward.

"I've remembered something," he said, holding his bandaged hand aloft. "I've remembered something important."

Chapter Nine

The smell of alcohol emanating from Sir Vernon was so pungent that had his movements not been clumsy and his speech not slurred, Felicity would have surmised he'd tipped a bottle of brandy over himself before coming to the study.

Edwin suggested he might stay to hear what Sir Vernon had to say, but Felicity gently urged her cousin and Miss Fairchild to leave the room, reassuring them she would continue to look into matters in a most thorough and serious manner. Whatever the outcome of the interviews, dragging Edwin through the weeds of the discussions would bring him no peace, and Edwin's comfort was Felicity's priority.

Edwin and Miss Fairchild having left the study, Sir Vernon flounced down into the chair on the other side of the desk from Felicity and Alex. His bandaged hand seemed to pain him much less. The bib front of his shirt was slightly askew under his tailcoat.

Felicity rearranged the green organza sash at her waist as Alex readied his notebook, eyeing the unexpected interviewee carefully.

"What is it you'd like to tell us, Sir Vernon?" asked Felicity.

Sir Vernon leaned forward, putting an arm on the desk. "I

remember what happened after the gun went off." He lowered his voice, though there was no one else to hear him. "A man and a woman went outside. Through the French doors in the bay window."

Felicity blinked. This was indeed new information. "Who?"

Sir Vernon shook his head. "Afraid I couldn't say. Only saw their outlines in the moonlight. First, the gun." Sir Vernon held up two fingers of his unbandaged hand in a firing gesture aimed in Felicity's direction. "*Bang. Bang.* Then the woman went outside. The man went after her."

"Might you describe them?" probed Alex.

Sir Vernon thought for a moment. "The man had brilliantined hair, rather like yours, Mr Cooper."

Alex raised an eyebrow. His hair, dark blond, parted on the side, and slicked back, would indeed have shone in the moonlight, but then so would have every other man's, from Edwin to Leonard to the servants. There was scarce variety to the way men wore their hair.

"And the woman had feathers on her head," added Sir Vernon. "Just like you, Lady Felicity."

Felicity smiled tightly. While there was nothing in Sir Vernon's tone that indicated he considered Felicity and Alex suspects, his testimony hardly narrowed things down. Ariadne, the Bourgoyne twins, Miss Fairchild. Even Helen herself. All were victims of the craze for feathered headbands.

So far, they were no closer to a resolution for Edwin.

"Did you notice any other details?" pressed Felicity.

Sir Vernon exhaled slowly, the smell of drink wafting across the desk. "The woman ran out of the room. No, wait. She started running when the man went after her. Oh, and the man wasn't Leonard. Leonard stayed with that blasted dog of his. And it wasn't me, either, but you know that already, having come upon us as you did."

Felicity nodded slowly as she digested Sir Vernon's inebriated phrasing. If the testimonies heard so far were true, there was only one man in attendance at Helen's party who could have gone through the French doors after the gun went off. Ought she pursue it? Or would it result in the opposite of restoring order to Grimstow House?

Alex turned a page in his notebook. "Sir Vernon. How well do you know Mr McQueen?"

It wasn't where Felicity would have taken the conversation, but she allowed it.

"Known him all his life. I was a friend of his father's. Went in on every investment Leonard's father ever made." Sir Vernon leaned back from the desk. "Why do you ask?"

"I'm simply curious," said Alex without a shred of apology.

Sir Vernon looked from Alex to Felicity. "I say, just what is it you're both up to? I came here to help. Am I now a suspect?"

"Not at all," said Felicity reassuringly. A discussion with Alex about the role of lead questioner was required, after all. "Our purpose is to collect information to write a respectful newspaper story in an orderly fashion."

Sir Vernon's face grew dark. "Now look. This whole thing needs clearing up with minimum fuss."

"I quite agree," said Felicity.

"Leonard's been through enough," continued Sir Vernon. "He doesn't need his name dragged through the papers."

"Neither Lady Felicity nor I have ever dragged a person's name through any paper." Though Alex's voice was calm, he'd clearly found Sir Vernon's comment abrasive.

"Is that so?" Sir Vernon narrowed his eyes at Alex. "Well. Just remember this. I'll not allow anyone to hurt Leonard's reputation. I've friends in high places, and don't you forget it." He stood up. "I'll see myself out."

Knocking awkwardly into the chair he'd been sitting in, Sir Vernon slammed the study door behind him, leaving only a faint smell of alcohol lingering in the air.

Felicity turned to Alex and raised her eyebrows. Sir Vernon's dramatic exit had been anything but peaceful.

Alex flicked between pages in his notebook. "What was that about, do you think?" he asked without looking up.

Felicity stood up. She had other matters on her mind. "Which of us did we say would lead the questions?"

Alex closed his notebook and drew back his chin. "My apologies for imagining we were a team. You'll not hear a peep out of me in the next interview."

"We are a team," said Felicity quickly, her cheeks flushing with embarrassment at her own outburst. She very much valued working with Alex. "And you can ask questions. I'm not saying that. Just try not to rile anyone."

"What do you make of Sir Vernon?" asked Alex, either unwilling or unable to make any promises about his questioning style.

"I believe he wants to help, but I'm not sure I understand his motives for doing so. His allegiance with Mr McQueen is clearly strong."

Alex smiled with satisfaction. "You're quite incapable of preventing yourself from fathoming things out."

Felicity tipped her head to one side. She was mildly vexed. "You asked me what I thought."

"You might have thought nothing at all."

Felicity drew a breath to reply, but her response was curtailed when the lights flickered and went out. With the study's curtains drawn, there wasn't even a slither of moonlight by which to see. It was a blackout.

"Modern devices aren't quite the answer to everything, are they?" observed Alex with amusement.

"I hadn't classified you as a Luddite," replied Felicity with a hint of frustration, both at Alex and being plunged into darkness.

Felicity began edging around the desk, keen to throw open the curtains. Apparently, Alex had a similar idea, and they collided.

A warm chuckle drifted through the dark. "My apologies," Alex said. The fresh smell he always had about him invaded Felicity's senses. Her cheeks flamed, thankfully unseen.

There was a knock at the door. The butler appeared, breathless and with a lantern swinging in his hand, which cast a dim, roving glow around the room. "Awfully sorry about the lighting situation, your ladyship. We'll make arrangements forthwith. We don't want to keep your next interviewee waiting."

Chapter Ten

Horrocks left his lantern in the study — for which Felicity was thankful, considering what had happened the last time the lights had gone out for any significant amount of time — and quickly returned with a tin of candles, a box of matches, and a large candelabra, which he placed towards the edge of the desk.

"Did you succeed in locating Lady Ariadne?" enquired Felicity as the butler added the long, ivory-coloured candles to the silver sconces, which gleamed in the lantern's soft glow.

"Not yet, your ladyship," replied the butler. "Although our search of the house hasn't finished. As I'm sure you've noticed, Grimstow is rather large with many a nook and cranny. I am, however, confident we'll be able to locate Lady Ariadne."

"Who's our next interviewee?" enquired Alex.

The butler struck a match. "It's Mr McQueen, sir. Like Doctor Quick, he was eager to speak with you both. I asked him to kindly wait while we made the necessary preparations here in the study."

Standing beside one another on the commanding side of the desk, Felicity and Alex exchanged looks. What was playing on Leonard's mind?

With the candles burning, a warm, intimate light filled the

study, shadows dancing on the walls as the flames flickered. The slightly sweet scent of beeswax hung in the air. Straightening, the butler cleared his throat. "I shouldn't like to delay your interviews any further, your ladyship, but may I speak freely for a moment?"

"By all means," said Felicity. The evening's events could surely not be any further confused by the butler's opinion.

Horrocks lifted his chin, his sagging yet dignified features taking on a hint of pride. "The suggestion to Miss Quick — may her soul rest in peace — to summon your services was mine, your ladyship. I follow the local papers diligently, you see." The butler glanced at Alex as if to include him in his admiration. "On behalf of all the staff here at Grimstow, if there is anything we can do to aid you in improving our current situation, then you have our full support. All of us, even young Wilkinson, have been with the Earl for many years, and we are, without exception, unconditionally dedicated to his lordship. We'd not known Miss Quick terribly long, of course, but she was a most striking presence. None of us wished upon her what has happened."

Felicity was touched by Horrocks' sentiments. It wasn't the first time she'd heard the staff proclaiming their dedication to Earl Carrington. She wasn't sure she could live up to the confidence placed in her, but would there be any harm if Felicity were to expand her remit slightly?

"There is something you might do to help, Mr Horrocks," she said.

"Please, your ladyship. The other servants and I would be glad to assist."

"I believe it would be helpful if everyone below stairs reported what they witnessed when the lights went out last time," continued Felicity. "That might help us get a clearer picture of what exactly happened." Wider testimony might help encourage a confession, a confession that would settle Edwin's mind and shorten the involvement of the police, allowing the family more privacy in their grief.

"Of course, your ladyship," replied the butler. "I'll get to it right away."

Alex gave a firm nod of approval. "If any of the staff would be willing to give a statement for the newspaper, I'd be glad to hear it."

"Of course, sir."

"Will the lights be coming back on soon?" enquired Felicity. She asked this nonchalantly, and the light from the candelabra was soft and welcoming, but the situation felt safer with every corner of the house well lit by electric lighting.

"We've been searching for Lord Archibald," said the butler, "with no luck so far, your ladyship."

Alex frowned. "Why Lord Archibald?"

"His lordship has a keen interest in engineering," explained Horrocks. "We refer to him for matters pertaining to the running of certain systems. He has a deep understanding of the electricity supply here at Grimstow, for example."

Felicity remembered the large bag Archibald had had with him. Had it been for transporting tools? "You're hoping to find Lord Archibald to fix the lights?"

"Precisely, your ladyship."

Felicity nodded but said nothing. It didn't seem prudent to announce she'd seen Archibald leave the house. It might be interpreted as the guilty taking flight, while there might be a perfectly innocent explanation. The throwing around of accusations wouldn't help keep the household calm.

"Is there anything further I can do for you, your ladyship? Sir?" enquired the butler.

Felicity confirmed there was nothing further required. The wind moaned beyond the curtains.

"Then I shall bring Mr McQueen through to you," said Horrocks.

It was time to hear from Leonard.

Taking a seat, Leonard waved an unlit cigar, his face sullen. "Mind if I smoke?" he said in his clipped South African accent.

Felicity was in the chair on the other side of the desk, Alex standing beside her, his notebook readied. "Not at all," she said.

As blue-grey smoke spread through the study, the businessman crossed and then recrossed his legs, seeking a comfortable position in the interviewee's chair. Felicity watched him in silence. Leonard seemed more agitated now than he had done earlier. Alex waited patiently for Felicity to start the interview, respectful of her role as lead questioner.

"I understand you're anxious to share your testimony with us, Mr McQueen," said Felicity.

"Anxious?" Leonard laughed a little. "That butler's a bit over-sensitive, isn't he?" From Leonard's behaviour till now, it wasn't surprising to find him still stony-faced. Still, his laugh was jarring. Felicity had to remind herself that grief manifested itself differently in everyone, and Helen's demise had been an incredible shock. Judging Leonard for his behaviour wouldn't help matters.

Leonard pulled on his cigar. "But I'll admit I'm worried. I've a lot on my mind. And I wanted to speak to you about one thing in particular."

"Oh?" said Felicity.

"I want to apologise to you for the behaviour of Sir Vernon."

Alex raised his eyebrows.

"Sir Vernon's done nothing to offend us," Felicity confirmed.

"Forgive me for being blunt, but Vernon's a drinker. Most of the time, it's under control. This whole nasty business with Helen, and we were both there when it happened…" Leonard trailed off. "Vernon's a good man. I'm sure he's trying to help, but it will be difficult to take for granted anything he tells you." Leonard winced at Felicity through the smoke.

Felicity blinked. "You're aware of what Sir Vernon told us?"

Leonard jiggled his foot, his leg crossed at the knee. "Perhaps you'll enlighten me."

Alex flicked through his notebook and came to the right page. "According to Sir Vernon, there were perhaps six people in the morning room when the gun went off. He can't confirm anyone's identity besides yours. He told us there was some kind of physical altercation."

A ripple of discontent passed over Leonard's brow. He said nothing.

Felicity spoke next. "Sir Vernon also said a woman left through the French doors after the gun had gone off. She was followed by a man."

Leonard remained silent. His foot continued to bounce. Which elements of Sir Vernon's testimony was he keen for Felicity and Alex to discount?

"That's everything he told you?" asked Leonard.

Felicity nodded.

"He mentioned to you nothing about my work?"

Alex turned a page in his notebook. "Sir Vernon said you picked up where your father left off and are doing a fantastic job of it."

Leonard's thin moustache twitched. He seemed relieved.

"What were you worried Sir Vernon might have told us?" enquired Felicity carefully.

Leonard shook his head. "Oh, nothing. Vernon's a drinker, that's all. I thought you should know."

Felicity waited for a moment. "Can you tell us who was in the morning room when the gun went off?" The directness of the question surprised even herself. It wasn't just answers for Edwin pushing her forward. There was something about Leonard's behaviour that bothered Felicity.

The businessman's jaw stiffened. "I'm able to confirm Vernon's presence. And Jambo's, of course. For obvious reasons, we can say Helen was there as well."

"Who else?" pressed Alex.

Leonard rolled his cigar between his fingertips. "I can't say who else."

Can't or won't? Felicity didn't voice the question. As intrigued as she was, her purpose was to keep the peace, not stoke the flames. "Did you or anyone else handle Helen's gun while the lights were out?" she asked.

"I certainly did not."

"Then someone else must have done so," continued Felicity. "Might you know who?"

"I've no clue." Leonard's foot jiggled.

"Who was there when the lights went on?" asked Alex. Felicity wholeheartedly approved of this line of questioning.

"Myself, Jambo, and Sir Vernon." Leonard swallowed. "And Helen."

"What about Miss Clemency Bourgoyne?" asked Felicity. "She was there when Mr Cooper and I arrived in the morning room."

Leonard frowned. "Clemency is the blonde-haired Bourgoyne sister, is she not?"

Felicity nodded.

"She arrived on the scene just after the lights went on," confirmed Leonard.

Felicity paused to think as Alex continued to write. "May I ask what my cousin's passing means for you, Mr McQueen?" she asked.

Leonard lowered his cigar. "Naturally, I'm upset. Helen was extremely dear to me. Just because I'm not in floods of tears doesn't mean my heart is untouched." He frowned. "I do have my concerns about the Earl, however."

At last, there was a hint of selflessness in the businessman's demeanour. "Was Earl Carrington particularly keen on his step-daughter?" enquired Felicity.

Leonard looked confused. "I'm talking about the investment. Gem mines in Central America. Helen was very excited about it all, and I still plan to move ahead with it, but I'm not sure what effect this development will have on Earl Carrington's position.

He's not experienced with this type of investment. A shock like this can cause a person to wobble."

Sadness stabbed Felicity's heart. She could contain herself no longer. "Mr McQueen. I'm aware Helen perhaps wasn't always the easiest of people with whom to get along, but did she truly mean so little to you?"

Leonard huffed. "Lady Felicity. I came here to assist with your interviews, and I fully trust your abilities to keep any nasty business out of the papers. But I don't see why you're treating me like this. I told you, I cared for Helen. What more proof do you want?"

Felicity took a deep breath. While she couldn't separate her feelings for her family from the work she'd promised to do, she ought to have done better at controlling her emotions. But a question stood out that she almost dared not ask. To what 'nasty business' was Leonard referring?

Alex stepped in. "What we're trying to understand, Mr McQueen, is the nature of the incident with the gun."

Leonard's brow creased with thought. "You mean whether it was an accident?"

"That's right," confirmed Alex.

Leonard examined the tip of his cigar. "Helen provoked a certain amount of envy, particularly among women. We're now aware it was Ariadne behind the letters. I dare say those so-called twins also had their moments of wishing Helen misfortune. But desiring her death? I'm sorry, I simply can't see it."

"Helen's demise must have been an accident, in your view?" asked Felicity.

Leonard nodded. He and Edwin were in alignment on that point.

"Is Sir Vernon involved in the Central American mines investment?" enquired Alex.

Leonard huffed. "Sir Vernon is... Sir Vernon's a man of business. But I don't see what that's got to do with anything."

The topic indeed seemed rather removed from the task Felicity and Alex had promised the household they would perform. "Mr McQueen," she said before Alex could get in another question. "We're extremely grateful to you for everything you've shared with us." It seemed prudent to end the conversation before further offence was caused. Leonard had likely divulged all he would. "My apologies if any of our questions seemed heavy-handed."

Leonard lifted his chin. "Who will you speak to next?"

"I'm not sure," said Felicity, looking up at her colleague.

Tucking his notebook away, Alex crossed the study and opened the door. After a brief muffled exchange, he returned to Felicity's side of the desk. "The footman says there's no one else lined up for us. We shall have to locate our next interviewee ourselves."

The electric lights mounted on the study's oak panelling flickered back on, glowing hard with a surge of power before returning to normal brightness.

"Well," said Leonard, standing up briskly, "if you don't need me." He left the room, trailing cigar smoke and closing the door behind him.

Alex went to the other side of the desk and sank into the chair opposite Felicity. "What are you thinking?"

Felicity put the gloved tips of her fingers together. She was disappointed her plan for an orderly set of interviews wasn't going as smoothly as hoped, but many paths remained still to be explored.

"I believe I know who we should speak to next," she said.

Chapter Eleven

Rex Debenham had last been seen venturing outside. The butler had enquired where he might be going, to which he had reportedly replied, "To get myself a horse."

While there was some risk Rex had already ridden off across the frozen moors — an ill-advised journey but not out of the question for the impulsive sportsman — Felicity was keen to attempt to catch him. More protection was needed against the freezing conditions outdoors than just her flimsy borrowed party frock, however.

The footman, Wilkinson, escorted Felicity and Alex from the study to a cloakroom off the entrance hall. Having helped Alex into his overcoat, the footman became flustered when Felicity asked if there was perhaps a fur stole or some thicker gloves she might borrow, her own wrap-style brown wool coat and brown leather gloves having been suitable for a motor ride during daylight hours but not for sub-zero temperatures and Arctic winds. Baffled by the specificities of the feminine wardrobe, Wilkinson dashed off to summon support.

"The first Lady Carrington kept these furs precisely for this kind of weather," said Mrs Rudd, as she carefully presented a long coat in dark-brown mink and a stole in the same fur. "The

Earl has always ensured everyone is well prepared for all conditions. Even us servants. Isn't that right, Mr Wilkinson?"

The young footman nodded in enthusiastic agreement.

Sparing a thought for the poor creatures who had donated their pelts, Felicity slipped into the fur coat. Cool and heavy at first, it warmed to her body's temperature and soon felt like a second skin.

"There's a hat to match, your ladyship," said Mrs Rudd, proffering a fur-lined toque.

Alex and the footman watched as Felicity gratefully slid her feathered headband off and replaced it with the winter hat, which flattened her curls in much the same way as the headband. Briefly, Felicity examined her appearance in a narrow, full-length mirror in the corner of the cloakroom. Satisfied, Felicity thanked the housekeeper for her help.

"Which is the shortest route to the stables?" Felicity asked.

"The quickest way would be via the steps at the side of the house," said Mrs Rudd. "It's not far, but given the ice, it might be best to take the front drive and follow the sweep of the road to the right. The gravel shouldn't give you too much problem."

"I-I can guide you, if you like," offered the footman. His wincing as he spoke betrayed an understandable lack of true willingness to venture out into the cold.

Keen to use the walk to the stables to discuss matters with Alex, Felicity declined the offer.

All hope of a meaningful consultation was, however, dashed when a freezing wind as sharp as daggers stole Felicity's breath upon stepping outside Grimstow House's front door. The ice in the air stung her face, and a dim light above the front entrance swung on a heavy chain, the lamp's glass thick with ice.

"Everything's frozen solid," said Alex, the wind coming in gusts and attempting to take his words. "I hope our two riders are getting on all right."

Felicity considered the bravery of Charles and the young

stablehand. "I knew the weather would turn bad tonight. I had no inkling it would be as bad as this."

Alex had thought to bring a lantern with him, although it was not yet needed. An elegant multi-lamped outdoor light on a smooth cast-iron frame lit the sweep of the front drive, making the gravel sparkle like quartz.

"This way?" Felicity gestured as she raised her voice above the gusting wind, tugging the thick collar of the mink coat across her mouth and nose, which already stung from the cold.

Alex nodded, and they set off. As the drive wrapped around the side of the house and began a gentle incline, the strength of the freezing wind eased off. Lights on the outside of a smattering of buildings appeared, and as they followed a further twist in the drive, the wind blew keenly into their backs.

"You think Rex went out the French doors, don't you?" said Alex, the lantern swinging at his side in his leather-gloved hand, his grey Homburg hat pulled low.

"How could it be anyone else?" asked Felicity, bracing herself against a gust.

"What about Lord Archibald?"

"I've entertained the idea," said Felicity as they trudged through the freezing gravel, "but the detail Sir Vernon provided about the shining hair didn't fit. Archibald must be one of a handful of men in England not to follow that fashion."

"He might have changed his appearance?" suggested Alex.

Felicity shook her head. "I find it doubtful. I saw him again just before I joined you in the entrance hall. His hair wasn't greased then either."

The lights on the buildings ahead grew steadily closer. Felicity sincerely hoped the stables were heated.

"What was Archibald up to when you saw him, do you think?" asked Alex.

"I saw him go outside."

Alex turned to her and raised his eyebrows. The sharing of

that detail had indeed triggered the assumption of the guilty taking flight.

"He was with his dog," Felicity added, as if that was proof of innocence. For some reason, she couldn't picture Lord Archibald doing anyone harm.

Alex tugged on his overcoat's collar. "He might have been in the morning room in the dark, though, mightn't he?"

Felicity set her gaze on the buildings ahead. "It strikes me that given Rex's closeness to many at the party and his enthusiasm for the game, between him and Lord Archibald, Rex is the more likely candidate to have been in the morning room when the gun went off."

"And if we don't find Rex in the stables," added Alex, "I suppose they'll find him frozen somewhere on the moors in the morning."

With the image of Rex saddling up an unwilling ride hanging in her mind, Felicity crunched faster through the gravel.

"Although I hope even Rex wouldn't be that foolhardy," said Alex, matching his pace to Felicity's.

As the gravelled drive continued its sweep down the side of the hill upon which the main house stood, Felicity and Alex arrived at the first of the lit buildings. It appeared to be constructed from the same pale stone as the main house, but instead of medieval-style battlements and crenellations, it had a tiled roof and generous timber-framed eaves.

The building was, however, not part of the stables.

Large, thin-framed iron doors inset with glass panels and flanked by wall-mounted electric lamps in robust metal casings made up the building's front facade. One of the doors had been folded back, offering a view of a neat row of cars parked on a smooth stone-slabbed floor. An engine could be heard turning over.

"Drat. Double drat!" The woman sounded angry.

Another woman could be heard sobbing.

Felicity halted outside the garage doors. One motor had

already slid off the steep, tarmacadamed portion of the driveway, which was the only way off Grimstow House's grounds.

Felicity looked with concern at Alex. As though able to tell exactly what Felicity was thinking, he nodded, and they went into the garage.

Being out of the freezing wind was welcome, but the garage wasn't exactly warm and cosy. Large grey flagstones were scuffed with tyre marks, electric lighting overhead comprised metal shades with bare bulbs, and the cool smell of oil mingled with the rich scent of leather upholstery.

Among the tightly parked vehicles two rows deep, Felicity spotted her white two-seater Alvis, still in pristine, restored condition. Further along the line, tucked between Bentleys and Rolls Royces, was a burgundy Model T Roadster, rather an economical choice of vehicle compared to the others in the garage. It was from the Model T that the sobbing and cursing emanated.

Felicity and Alex approached.

Clemency was seated in the Model T's passenger seat, her eyes ringed with red, a large bag on her lap. The blue feathers in her headband had been crushed by the motor's canvas hood, the gems of her necklace still glittering at her throat. Patience stepped out from the driver's seat and paced about, looking angry. Her glamorous dark brown waves fell before her eyes as she inspected the vehicle. Her feathered headband protruded from the pocket of her kimono-style coat, where it had been unceremoniously stuffed. In the crook of her arm was a bag that appeared to be crammed full of papers.

Getting annoyed with the encumbrance, Patience threw the bag onto the driver's seat, causing a sheet or two of paper to flutter out.

"They must be barmy," muttered Alex, as Patience climbed

back behind the wheel and attempted to get the motor running. Thankfully, all that came through was a ticking noise.

As eager as Felicity was to speak with Rex, it would not have been right to ignore the Bourgoyne twins. One should never underestimate a woman's capabilities, but the house's driver had already had an accident and declared Grimstow House's steep, frozen drive impassable. What chance was there for the two city-dwelling sisters to get off the hill intact?

"Not leaving, are you?" Felicity's voice echoed through the garage.

Her gloved hands gripping the steering wheel, Patience leaned forward to peer past her sister. Seeing Felicity, she grimaced. "And if we are, what is it to you?"

"I can't, Pat," sobbed Clemency. "I can't do this. He needs me." Leaving her travel bag on the seat, Clemency climbed out of the Model T and hurried towards the garage's open door, the edges of her coat sweeping over headlights as she went.

"Oh, for goodness' sake." Patience jumped out of the driver's seat and chased after her sister, catching her by the wrist. "We've been through this a thousand times." She jerked the blonde-haired twin around to face her. "Clem, we are leaving."

Clemency sobbed again, her arms limp, her crushed feathers trembling.

"Leaving by road simply isn't possible," said Felicity. She and Alex continued a slow approach towards the sisters between the parked vehicles.

Patience tutted, highlighting her disregard for Felicity's assessment.

"The ground's frozen solid," added Alex. "You won't make it down the drive."

Patience span towards him. "I'm sorry, but who are you, exactly? And what business is it of yours what I do?"

Alex held up his hands as if to say he would meddle no more, but he didn't apologise. Felicity was glad he didn't. Patience was being unspeakably rude.

"Might you continue to the stables?" suggested Felicity quietly to Alex, conscious of the possibility of Rex's imminent departure on horseback. Alex glanced at the twins, nodded at Felicity, and departed, his footsteps echoing across the oil-stained flagstones.

Patience shook her head. Her grip remained tight on her sister's limp wrist. "What sort of woman invites a colleague to a ball? Or even has a colleague to bring? Helen was of the same opinion, you know." A haughty smile spread across Patience's lips. "There's something undeniably queer about you, Felicity."

Felicity lifted an eyebrow. She was thoroughly unimpressed.

Clemency sniffed and chastened her sister half-heartedly. "Patience."

"Something very queer indeed," added the dark-haired twin.

The image of the Model T with Patience at the wheel ploughing headlong into a sturdy tree suddenly brought great pleasure to Felicity, but only for the briefest of moments. Taking a deep breath to steady herself, Felicity kept her emotions in check. There was not just Patience but also Clemency to consider, and Edwin's peace of mind would not be helped by the bodies of two society girls pulled from the wreckage of a motoring accident.

"Attempting a potentially life-ending escape is a rather queer decision," Felicity said, running a nonchalant finger over the shining bonnet ornament of a nearby Rolls. "Although whether the risk is worthwhile, I suppose depends on from what one is running."

Clemency sobbed and tugged uselessly at her wrist. "I need to go to him."

Patience's eyes narrowed. "Just what are you insinuating, Cici?" There was venom in her spitting of Felicity's nickname.

Felicity sighed as though bored. "Even if you make it off the moors in one piece, I shan't be the only person to find it suspicious that you attempted the escape at all."

Patience kept her eyes on Felicity. Her jaw tightened.

Felicity didn't seriously consider Patience or Clemency guilty of murder, but she was quite certain one of the twins must have been the woman who left through the French doors.

"I thoroughly resent what you are implying," said Patience in an acidic tone.

Felicity narrowed her eyes. "Were either of you in the morning room when the lights went out?"

Patience turned and pulled her sister towards the Model T. "We're leaving."

Clemency resisted. "Please, Pat. You don't understand. I love him."

"Did Rex follow Clemency outside?" It was a bold play on Felicity's part, but it served a dual purpose. "Or was he following you, Patience?" She wanted to know what happened to Helen. She also wanted to keep the twins talking.

Patience's desperate gaze flew to her sister, then to Felicity. "Neither of us were there. Neither of us saw anything."

"Where were you then?"

"We don't have to answer your idiotic questions."

"Indeed, you don't, but you'll need to answer the police's. And you'll need a better story than what you're telling me."

Patience stamped her foot and let go of Clemency's arm, which flopped to her side. "After the lights went out for the game, Clemency went after Rex but lost him. I'd intended to go up to our room, only I got rather lost and didn't find any stairs. More's the pity. It was only after the lights came back on that we went to the morning room."

Felicity blinked. If Sir Vernon's recollection had been correct, what Patience was saying can't have been entirely true. As Felicity saw it, one of the sisters must have gone through the French doors. Then again, Leonard had warned against relying on Sir Vernon's testimony.

Patience smiled and shook her head. "It's painfully obvious what's really going on here, and I'm not even pretending to be a journalist or a detective. Nor do I need to seek guidance from any of my connections in the world of spiritualism to draw the correct conclusion." She sniffed. "Not that their wise counsel would be appreciated here."

Felicity skipped over Patience's boasting about her supposedly powerful friends. "What's really going on here, in your opinion?"

Patience lifted her brow. "Did anyone check if Helen's jewellery was all still there?"

"Her jewellery?" Felicity remembered the broken necklaces, the gems scattered among the shattered glass from the bay window. "You suspect someone robbed Helen?"

Patience scoffed. "And I'm not the one running around pretending to have a career."

Clemency sniffed. "When we went to collect our belongings, someone had been in our room. The bracelet Rex gave me…" She sobbed again.

Patience sighed with frustration at her sister. "That worthless thing is the least of it. They took every piece we weren't wearing, and do you think we'll be able to afford to replace them?"

Clemency's lower lip trembled. "But Rex gave the bracelet to me when he—"

Patience waved an angry hand at her sister and turned towards Felicity. "While the lights were out, someone went upstairs and robbed us."

Chapter Twelve

While Patience's efforts to belittle hadn't entirely met their mark, the mention of theft went through Felicity like a hot poker. How could she have missed it? Robbery would explain Helen's broken necklaces. Robbery would also explain the struggle that — surely, by accident — ended Helen's life.

Because if the intention in the dark had been theft, the goal surely wouldn't have been to kill.

The wind howled through the garage door. The metal lamps hanging from the ceiling swung gently, flickering briefly.

"Have you told anyone else?" enquired Felicity.

"What good would that do?" said Patience sharply. "We'll talk to the police, but we're not waiting here till morning to have more of our belongings stolen, and perhaps even end up dead in the course of it."

Clemency had fallen to weeping uncontrollably. "But the bracelet was the only thing he ever gave to me."

Felicity wasn't entirely insensitive to Clemency's distress, but considering Helen's passing, the matter of a bracelet seemed rather trifling, and the new information about the thefts needed to be acted upon.

"If you're honestly worried about your safety and that of your belongings," said Felicity, "then lock yourselves in your room. Don't let anyone in till the police arrive. That's the best advice I can give you, but please, don't drive anywhere. You'll be risking your lives."

Clemency looked wide-eyed at her sister. Patience looked back at her.

Felicity turned towards the garage doors. *One can lead a horse to water*, she silently told herself, her jaw set.

"I didn't ask for your advice," Patience called out.

Felicity didn't look back. There had perhaps been a time when she would have invested more in pleading with the Bourgoyne twins, ensuring they were safe in their room before moving forward with her own activities. Was Felicity becoming less patient? Or was she simply keen to focus her efforts where it mattered, where she knew she could make a real difference? She was loath to admit it, but Patience's hurtful remarks had likely aided Felicity in her decision to leave the garage.

As she stepped outside into the bracing cold, the stars twinkling above, the gravel crunching beneath her feet, and her breath torn away by the biting wind, Felicity faced a conundrum. It was imperative that Edwin be informed of theft as a possible motive for the tussle that ended his sister's life. Helen's necklace had clearly been broken. Might the thief have grabbed a fistful of gems before the gun went off? This could be checked.

But as much as Felicity wanted to return to the main house, she also wanted to continue to the stables. Rex was still someone with whom she needed to speak, and discussing everything she'd learned from the Bourgoyne twins with Alex was an unmissable step. Together, they were stronger.

After a brief pause, Felicity turned towards the main house, pulling her fur-lined toque low on her brow and burying her hands in the pockets of the mink coat. Edwin had to be her priority.

"No!" The wind carried snippets of a man's shouts from further down the hill. "I'll not have it!"

If there was a set-to at the stables, Alex could handle it, couldn't he?

"Come any closer and I'll—"

Felicity turned her back on the main house and hurried down the hill.

The stables were a squat set of buildings organised in a U-shape around a central cobbled courtyard. Slate roofs sparkled white with ice and vaulted across sturdy timber eaves. The styling was approximately the same as the garage's, but while the garage seemed crowded with the house's and guests' motors parked inside, the stables were at least six times the size. Earl Carrington's passion for horses was clear. He had also perhaps underestimated the advances the motor car would make in a few short years.

"I don't suppose you've had many people tell you 'no' in your life, have you?"

The shouting from within the stables grew louder as Felicity hurried towards the buildings. Of the two male voices in play, neither was Alex's, but it wasn't of tremendous reassurance to Felicity. A life had already been lost that evening.

Foolishly disregarding the risk of unstable footing in favour of rapid progress, Felicity continued apace onto the frozen cobbles. Both her feet slipped immediately from underneath her, causing her to do a desperate, quick-footed dance to regain her balance.

Bang, bang!

A horse kicked a stable door and followed up with a long, withering neigh. Felicity wasn't horse-mad like Helen had been, but it wasn't possible to grow up on a Devonshire estate and not have spent time around the large, elegant creatures.

"You're upsetting my horses. I tell you, I'll not have it!"

In Felicity's experience, horses were indeed emotionally rather sensitive.

Her footing restored, Felicity trod cautiously to the stable wall, where the roof's overhang provided drier, less icy cobbles across which she could stride decisively, her borrowed heels tapping a swift rhythm, her feet numb with cold. A long canine howl went up from somewhere within the stables. So this was where Jambo had been locked up.

As she reached the archway of the stables' main entrance, its double doors standing open to the cold, Alex dashed out and halted her progress, his Homburg hat in one hand and the lantern in the other. His dark blond hair was mussed, and he held up his hands to slow Felicity's progress. "The situation in there is rather tense."

Felicity halted. "What's going on?"

"Rex is present. As is the stable master."

"They're the ones arguing?"

"It's as we thought. Rex wants a horse…" Alex looked over his shoulder as there came more shouting, followed by another thunder of hooves against stable doors. The Ridgeback let out another howl. Then came the sound of a man crying.

Felicity pressed her lips together. She had wanted to instil calmness and order at Grimstow House. So far, she had failed, but she wouldn't give up. "Thank you for the warning," she told Alex. "I'll do my best to settle the situation."

As she went to pass Alex, he touched her shoulder. "He's got a gun."

Felicity's eyes widened. "Rex?"

"No. The stable master."

Chapter Thirteen

Moving ahead of Alex through the arched entrance into the stables, Felicity's heels tapped across the stone flooring of the entryway. She would have preferred a stealthy approach, but there was little to be done as the sound of her footsteps carried into an expansive indoor exercise area with a sandy floor. A mingled scent of hay, manure, and leather tack hung heavy in the air.

In the middle of the great expanse of the exercise floor, between practice jumps and under electric lights strung from the roof beams, Rex lay on the floor propped up on an elbow, his dark dinner jacket and trousers dusty. There was sand in his chocolate-brown hair, and his eyes were brimming with tears.

Standing above Rex, a bolt-action rifle trained on the sportsman, was Jarvis, the grey-haired stable master. Behind him stood a refined-looking white-and-grey dappled mare, her ears pricked and her tail twitching.

"I'll not have you endangering the Earl's horses." The stable master's growl was forceful. His gun was aimed steadily at the helpless sportsman, with no hint of a tremble. A grim disagreement had clearly got out of hand. "And I'll use force if I have to. Don't think I won't." The wind howled around the roof and the electric lights flickered.

Felicity cleared her throat, the sound of hers and Alex's footsteps not having served as the distraction she imagined it would. A horse somewhere in the stabling block whinnied. Jambo let out another mournful howl.

With tears rolling down his cheeks, Rex blinked up at Felicity. "Lady Felicity. Please. Help me."

Haltingly, the stable master shifted his focus from Rex to Felicity. "Your ladyship." He relaxed the aim of his weapon. "I can explain."

Alex had no doubt already done his best to defuse the situation. Was it the mention of Felicity's title that made the difference to the stable master? While she preferred not to lean too much upon it, her position could occasionally prove useful.

As the stable master lowered the barrel of his rifle, Rex slithered backwards across the sandy floor, stumbled to his feet, and ran to Felicity and Alex, cowering behind them. "He said he would blow my head off. The man's out of control. He's a lunatic."

"Calm yourself, Mr Debenham," said Alex, watching somewhat helplessly as Rex covered the shoulders of his overcoat in dusty handprints.

"Would you indeed care to explain the situation, Mr Jarvis?" asked Felicity.

It was reassuring that the stable master had put his rifle on its strap over his shoulder. He approached the dappled mare, making shushing noises. A servant discharging a weapon at a defenceless house guest was, under normal circumstances, unthinkable. While Felicity was glad to have helped soothed the tension in the stables, the danger had perhaps not yet passed.

Jarvis held the horse's bridle and stroked the creature's elegant, powerful neck, the horse's long-lashed eyes still nervous. "I was with the work horses in the stables' east wing, your ladyship, when I heard a commotion coming from the part of the building where the Earl's thoroughbreds are kept. I went to investigate and found that rascal attempting to saddle up poor Pearl here."

"Me? A rascal?" Rex dared to step out from behind Alex. "You've no proper understanding of the situation, man."

"We'll come to your account in a moment, Mr Debenham," urged Felicity calmly. "Go on, Mr Jarvis."

The stable master continued stroking the mare. "I enquired what it was he was doing, and he told me to mind my business. I informed him that the welfare of the Earl's horses is precisely my business."

"What's the welfare of a horse compared to Helen's murder?" Rex took a step towards Jarvis. "It's as if no one gives a fig!"

Fearing him becoming worked up again, Felicity turned her attention to the sportsman. "What were you planning on doing with the horse, Mr Debenham?"

Rex looked at Felicity as if she were an imbecile. "I want to ride out and find someone to help. Someone to settle this whole blasted situation." He raised a finger and stabbed at the air before Felicity's face. "To find whoever it was killed Helen and bring them to justice!"

Alex stepped forward, his arms outstretched. "Whoa, there." Without touching him, Alex prevented Rex from advancing any further towards Felicity.

The dappled mare whinnied and shook her mane. "Easy, Pearl," said Jarvis, stroking the horse's neck.

Felicity stood up straighter. "Mr Debenham. You're surely aware that Lord Charles Lorrimer and a member of Grimstow House's staff—" Felicity broke off and looked towards Jarvis.

"Mr Dennis Peabody, your ladyship," said the stable master. "He's a stable hand and also an excellent cross-country rider. Very familiar with the Earl's horses and with the territory around these parts."

Felicity nodded her thanks. "Lord Charles and Mr Peabody

are, as we speak, making their way on horseback to summon help, Mr Debenham. Why do you find it necessary to launch your own outing? Do you not trust the capabilities of the two riders already sent out?" As she spoke, Rex's shoulders slumped. His expression went from anger to despair. Felicity continued. "You came down from London for the ball, didn't you? It would be your first time navigating the surrounding area, would it not?"

Again, tears gathered at the corner of Rex's eyes. He brought the flat of his palm to his forehead with a slap. "I want to do something. Anything. I want to help. I want to make things right!"

Felicity glanced at Alex. His eyes were bright and wary.

"It's all right, my girl." The stable master continued to soothe the dappled mare. There was no need to subject the poor creature to any more of Rex's outbursts.

"You may return to your work, Mr Jarvis," said Felicity as Jambo could again be heard howling. "I don't think Mr Debenham will have any further requirements from the stables this evening."

"Your ladyship." Jarvis gave a stiff bow and gently coaxed the worried horse away, leading her out of the exercise area.

Alex gave Felicity a brief nod, as if to say, *Nicely done*. But Felicity didn't feel her work was finished yet. She still wanted to question Rex.

The sportsman wiped his eyes with the heels of his dusty hands. He was in a sorry state, his powerful shoulders hunched and his dark suit creased and dusty. He had no coat on, and although sheltered from the freezing wind, the exercise arena wasn't heated. Rex's bare fingers were red and trembling with cold. As a celebrated equestrian, he must have understood the risk to both himself and the horse in his plan to venture out. What was making him so irrational?

"Mr Debenham—"

Rex sniffed loudly, interrupting Felicity's interrogation before it even began. "I'll tell the truth," he said. "I'll tell the truth of it to anyone. There's no point lying about it. Not now."

Alex narrowed his eyes at the sportsman. The lights overhead flickered.

"The truth?" urged Felicity. Was it to be the confession Edwin hoped for?

Rex let out a long exhale, violently puffing his cheeks. He shook some of the sand out of the back of his hair. "I loved her. I loved Helen. That's the truth of it." He allowed his hands to fall to his sides. He looked at Felicity, suddenly puppy-like. "I can't state it plainer than that."

Felicity nodded cautiously. "We all loved Helen, Mr Debenham."

Rex smacked the air in Felicity's direction. "No. Not like that. I desired her. I was obsessed with her. Don't you see? And now she's gone." He kicked at the sand underfoot, sending up a spray.

Felicity swallowed. The situation was incredibly delicate.

"And Helen... Loved you in return?" enquired Felicity carefully.

Rex wiped both hands over his face. "Oh, what does it matter? What does any of it matter now? It's all too late. She's gone."

Alex watched Rex intently as the sportsman began pacing about. It was unclear what he might do next.

Felicity cleared her throat. She would come to the crux of the matter. "Were you present when Helen left us, Mr Debenham?"

Rex stopped pacing. Tears again welled in his eyes. "I was." The sportsman's voice trembled. "I was, but I didn't know it. First the gun. Then that lunatic of a dog. And I went after Clem." He bowed and shook his head. "I didn't know. I didn't know that Helen was hurt. That she was..."

Felicity's heart skipped a beat. She flashed a glance at Alex. So the twins had lied. "Clemency Bourgoyne was in the morning room while the lights were out?" asked Felicity. Was that the real reason the sisters were so keen to escape?

Again, Rex shook a hand through his hair. "Oh, what does it

matter now? Dash it. Dash it all." Agitation was replacing his despair.

"It matters a great deal, Mr Debenham," said Alex stiffly. "The woman you proclaim to have loved is dead."

"I did love her!" Rex stabbed a finger at Alex. "More than that blasted businessman ever could!"

Felicity manoeuvred herself between Rex and Alex. "Could you describe your movements after the lights went out, Mr Debenham?"

Rex retrained his attention on Felicity, his eyes wide. "You think I did it?" He was becoming shrill.

"I, too, cared deeply for Helen," said Felicity firmly. "She was my cousin. I also care an awful lot for Edwin, and I dread to imagine my aunt's reaction when news reaches her of her only daughter's passing. Knowing what happened won't mend their pain, but it will help."

Rex breathed heavily, his nostrils flaring, but he remained still. He seemed less challenged by Felicity than by Alex.

Felicity went on. "To understand whether someone meant Helen harm or whether her end was some terrible accident will make all the difference to my family's suffering."

Rex sniffed and looked at the ground. Alex rather judiciously remained silent.

When the sportsman at last spoke, he did so without looking up. "When the game started and the lights went out, I followed Helen to the morning room. We'd agreed upon the meeting earlier in the evening." Rex's jaw tightened. "We weren't alone for long."

"Who else was there?"

"McQueen was the first to arrive. I know it was him because of that blasted hound and all his panting and whining. Then another man arrived. It was too dark to see who. Everyone was very…" Rex glanced at Felicity. "Agitated. That was when Clemency arrived. I've never seen her so upset."

"How did you recognise Clemency?" asked Felicity. "It was too dark to identify people, was it not?"

The wind gusted against the roof above the exercise arena, and the electric lights swung slowly on their chains.

Rex regarded Felicity sternly. "A man can recognise his own fiancée."

With his proclaimed love of Helen, Rex had not been fully dedicated to Clemency. Still, Felicity knew better than to challenge the volatile man's version of events openly. Might the twins still be in the garage for Felicity to cross-question them with Rex's account?

"What happened upon Clemency's arrival in the morning room?" asked Felicity, the idea of challenging Patience's testimony an appealing prospect.

Rex exhaled shakily. "Must I put words to the deeds? Has Helen not been shamed enough?" He shot a wary look at Alex.

A gust of icy wind swept through the stable's open doors.

Alex moved away, his hands in his coat pockets, kicking lightly at the sand of the exercise yard floor, as though suddenly uninterested in Rex. His timing was excellent.

"Mr Debenham," said Felicity quietly. She spoke briskly and as reassuringly as possible. "I am Helen's cousin. Whatever you say to me will be treated with the utmost respect and discretion. I'm not sure what I can say further to convince you that you can trust me in this matter."

Rex's eyes threatened tears again. "Helen and I were innocents. We couldn't help how we felt. Love is intoxicating. It's like a drug. It changes everything. You must know what I mean."

Felicity wasn't sure that she did, but she nodded.

"Everything was so new, and we were eager to explore one another." Rex shook his head. "Somehow McQueen found us in the morning room, and he ripped me away from her. He cursed me, and his dog was snarling and barking. I thought he was going to have it bite me. I don't know how he found us out. We'd been so discreet."

Felicity reflected on what she was hearing. Rex was describing Helen's complicity in what, by some measures, could be referred to as an illicit affair. She thought back to Edwin and Leonard's pleas for Felicity and Alex to keep any 'nasty business' out of the papers. Is this what they'd been referring to?

"Nothing had happened between us," continued Rex despairingly. "Almost nothing at all."

It was difficult for Felicity to gather her thoughts on what this meant for Helen's reputation or even her own opinions about her cousin. One thing, however, was clear. It wasn't just the twins who'd lied under questioning. Leonard hadn't been entirely honest in his interview with Felicity either.

Felicity glanced at Rex's jacket. "Did Leonard tear your lapel in the morning room?"

Rex looked down. "Y-yes. I suppose he did. I hadn't noticed." Leonard must have been quite rough with Rex. His jacket, though now extremely dusty, was of good quality and wouldn't have been easy to rip.

"What happened after Leonard separated you from Helen?" asked Felicity. Was she close to finding out who held the weapon that ended Helen's life?

Rex wiped his hands over his face. "Another man arrived. I couldn't say who. That lunatic dog got even more agitated. Leonard was holding the beast away from me. No. Wait. Clem came before the other man. Helen tried to get Leonard off me. Clemency, she… She tussled with Helen. But how did she know? She can't have known about Helen and I. We'd been so discreet."

His liaison with Helen perhaps hadn't been as discreet as Rex imagined. Although Felicity herself had suspected nothing, hadn't Patience been rather off with the sportsman? And was the affair what Ariadne had been alluding to in her letters?

Rex put a hand to the back of his head. "Oh, it was such a mess. Such a blasted mess. Then the gun went off, and Clemency fled. She ran outside. I didn't know that Helen was… That she was hurt. I thought Helen had pulled the trigger to get Clemency off her. So I went after Clem, thinking I could somehow make things up to her." He shrugged. "I lost her at the side of the house. I almost slipped, and when I regained my footing, she was gone."

Felicity thought back to the shock and distress displayed by Clemency at the sight of her dead friend in the morning room. Clemency's reaction had seemed genuine. Had she fled through the French doors in a panic, then come back inside to inspect the damage she'd done? If Clemency had been involved in pulling the trigger on Helen's pearl-handled pistol in the dark, it would be very difficult to distinguish intention from misfortune. Either way, a torrid case of deception and infidelity seemed to be at the root.

But what of the robbery? Or was that simply the Bourgoynes' pretext for their escape from Grimstow House?

Alex remained at a distance from Felicity and Rex, creating the impression of privacy. From the concentration on his face, she could tell he was doing his best to listen in.

"The man who entered the morning room after Mr McQueen. Was it his friend, Sir Vernon?" Feeling rather certain of this, Felicity was curious to hear Rex's reaction.

Rex wiped a hand over his mouth. "I honestly couldn't say for sure. I'm not familiar enough with the chap to recognise his shadow, and he didn't speak to me. At the time, I imagined it might have been Helen's dark horse of a step-brother. If you're looking for someone wanting to harm Helen, speak to those step-siblings. They're a queer lot. Ariadne wrote those letters after all, didn't she?"

Felicity narrowed her eyes. Was there indeed a chance Lord Archibald had gone into the morning room? And although Helen hadn't seemed to take the threats in the letters seriously, had she been bluffing so as not to seem intimidated?

"How many people were gathered in the morning room?"

Rex huffed out an exasperated sigh. An undercurrent of agitation was welling up in him again. "I don't know. Four? Five?" This wasn't the only point on which Rex's and Sir Vernon's testimonies differed. "Look. I've told you what I know. I trust you to be discreet about it. But I also trust you'll do something with the information, for Helen's sake."

There were so many leads. Betrayal. Jealousy. Theft. Which thread to tug on first? How could Felicity best help Edwin? Perhaps it was more intuition than logic driving her forward, but it was clear to Felicity what she had to do next.

Chapter Fourteen

The climb back up the gravel drive felt longer and more arduous than the descent from the house to the stables, as it was both uphill and facing into the freezing wind. Felicity had convinced Rex to return to the house. She'd told him that waiting quietly in his room until the police's arrival was the best course of action with regard respectful behaviour towards the deceased. At first, he'd seemed calm and willing. Then he stalked off towards the house at a much brisker pace than Felicity, whose heels insisted on sinking into the gravel.

Alex kept alongside her, his hat pulled low against the wind. "That was rather a close call," he said once Rex was out of earshot.

Felicity pressed her hands into her pockets. "I don't believe the stable master had any real intention of using his rifle." The wind stung her lips as she spoke.

"Perhaps not, but Rex would have ridden away on that horse if Jarvis hadn't picked up a weapon."

As they passed the garage, the lights were still on, but the Bourgoyne twins were no longer there. Their Model T, however, remained in place.

"The sisters must be back at the house," said Felicity with some relief.

Alex smiled. "You've a talent for defusing situations."

Felicity shrugged. She knew she struggled to take compliments, but this one was genuinely doubtful. Patience had been angered by essentially everything Felicity had said to her. She told Alex as much, recounting to him the exchange she'd had with the sisters, including the talk of theft.

As they approached Grimstow House's front entrance, Alex frowned. "If the tussle in the morning room was an attempt to rob your cousin, it doesn't quite square up with what Rex was telling us."

"And what he told us doesn't perfectly match Sir Vernon's account." A powerful gust of wind blasted Felicity's words into the freezing night. Tugging at her collar, she continued. "We can't even be sure how many people were in the morning room, let alone who they were. Perhaps the butler will bring us some corroborating accounts from the servants, and we'll get a clearer picture that way."

Alex pulled on the chain by the front door. "But that's not our aim here, is it?"

Felicity turned to Alex. "What isn't?"

"Fathoming out exactly what happened to your cousin."

"It wouldn't hurt, though, would it?"

"You said we were to keep the peace and gather input for our article. Or have I got that wrong?"

Alex was right, of course. Was it inappropriate of Felicity to allow a widening of their remit, for Edwin's sake?

She was considering how best to position this for Alex when the front door was opened by the footman. As he assisted Felicity and Alex in shrugging out of their cold, heavy coats, Edwin arrived in the entrance hall. He was closely followed by the butler and by Miss Fairchild, who'd added a gauzy shawl to her opal outfit but continued to tremble.

"Felicity, I can only apologise," said Edwin as he approached, pressing hard on his cane. He seemed to stand taller than he had done earlier. "It wasn't at all the intention for you to go chasing outside in this awful weather. Clearly, I overestimated our guests' willingness to comply. I also underestimated your tenacity."

Horrocks bowed his head somewhat sheepishly. It had been the servants' responsibility to gather the interviewees.

"Please," said Felicity, glowing faintly with pride at being considered tenacious, "there's no need to apologise."

The lights flickered. Miss Fairchild cast a worried, wide-eyed gaze around the entrance hall. Edwin muttered an oath. "Another spell in the dark would be all we need. There must surely be more reliable sources of power than the river." He sighed. "Have you uncovered anything further?" There was a glimmer of hope in his eyes as he searched Felicity's and Alex's faces.

"Well," began Felicity, glancing at Alex and buying herself time to consider what exactly to say. Delivering an update to her cousin was what she'd had in mind to do when she'd left the garage, but considering the delicate nature of what Rex had revealed, she couldn't share everything, could she? "I hope it's not too insolent a detour," she continued, "but I should first like to hear from Mr Horrocks, if he has completed his enquiries among the household staff."

The butler's noble face flinched almost imperceptibly.

"My apologies, Mr Horrocks," said Felicity earnestly, "to spring the request upon you."

"Not at all," replied the butler, his composure fully regained. "I've spoken to all the domestics who were in the house at the time of the accident. None of the servants were in or even near the morning room. Cook believes she might have seen someone moving about outside, but she admits it might equally have been a tree waving in the wind. Other than that, there are no witness statements of any significance."

Felicity nodded. "Thank you, Mr Horrocks." She'd hoped for more. She turned to Edwin. "I suppose the most significant development from our investigations would be a report from the Bourgoyne twins that some of their belongings have gone missing."

"Missing? As in stolen?" Edwin turned to the butler, whose mouth fell open. Miss Fairchild and the footman turned pale. "Did you know about this, Horrocks?" asked Edwin.

"N-no, sir. I shall send Mrs Rudd to attend immediately to the Misses Bourgoyne. We shall catalogue whatever is missing and do our best to locate it. Having interviewed all the staff already, we have the details of their whereabouts for the whole evening. Everyone's presence in the proper places is accounted for. I can, of course, speak to everyone again, sir, but I would like to stress that all the servants, even young Mr Wilkinson here, have all been in the Earl's service for years. Some of us for decades. We're all extremely loyal to his lordship."

Edwin held up a hand. "No one's making accusations, Horrocks. Not yet. That is correct, is it not, Felicity?"

Felicity nodded. "It does, however, raise another possibility." She glanced at Alex. "Might Helen have been a victim of theft?"

The blood drained from Edwin's freckled face. Miss Fairchild put a hand to her throat. "Horrocks," Edwin commanded. "I want the items on my sister's person checked. If there is anything missing, even a single gem from one of her necklaces, I want to know about it. Is that clear?"

"Quite clear, sir."

"I don't—" Miss Fairchild stumbled.

Edwin was just in time to put a hand under her elbow. "I've got you, Ruth. This is too much for any of us to bear. Come, let us sit you down." Edwin escorted Miss Fairchild to a carved wooden bench at the side of the entrance hall. That he had the strength to offer succour to his companion was a sign of his own hardiness in the face of adversity, was it not?

The butler stepped towards Felicity. "If I may, your ladyship. I have an update on the whereabouts of Lady Ariadne."

Felicity flashed an eager glance at Alex, who lowered his brow sceptically. "Is she willing to speak to us?" Felicity asked the butler.

"She appears to be in the attic, your ladyship. At least, that is the impression we've formed. Whoever it is, they won't open the door."

Chapter Fifteen

As Felicity and Alex climbed towards Grimstow House's uppermost floors, the sweeping shallow stone steps of the main staircase gave way to narrow stairs carpeted in an unfussy grey, denoting that the upper floors of the house weren't intended for general use.

"Is Ariadne on your suspect list?" asked Alex. He was a little ahead of Felicity and seemed completely untaxed by the climb.

Felicity found the stairs hard work. The throbbing of her feet was hard to ignore. "I don't have a suspect list." She and Alex had committed to interviewing everyone, but they hadn't agreed to investigate Helen's demise.

"Oh, come on." Alex frowned, amused. "Of course you do."

Felicity frowned back at him without a hint of amusement. "We don't yet know if it was an accident, and I'm afraid that without a confession, we shan't know."

Alex sighed. "Do you consider Ariadne capable, then?"

"Of harming her step-sister?" Felicity's instinct was that she wasn't. Her hope was that Ariadne's own account of her whereabouts would contribute to clearing her of any involvement in the altercation in the morning room. Still, Felicity's instincts had been wrong before.

Alex stopped on a landing as the lights dimmed and flickered. "Do you consider Ariadne dangerous, is what I'm asking."

With a sigh, Felicity stopped, a hand on the bannister, glad of the opportunity to catch her breath. "Is this about my declining the butler's offer of a firearm?"

Before their ascent to the top of the house, and out of earshot of Edwin, who remained occupied with reviving Miss Fairchild from her near-faint, Horrocks had quietly suggested taking a pistol upstairs as a precaution. Felicity had declined on the basis that carrying a loaded weapon had been integral to Helen's untimely end.

"I'll admit a weapon would help me feel more confident in my ability to react to whatever we face," said Alex.

"Heavens." Guilt flooded through Felicity. Somehow, she hadn't considered Alex as someone capable of being afraid. "I ought to have asked you. I'm sorry. I'm sorry about everything that's happened. If I'd known, I wouldn't have brought you here. I honestly thought we would just peruse some letters and advise my cousin accordingly."

Alex cut Felicity off gently. "You don't need to apologise. None of this is your fault. And you were right to turn down the gun. I suppose I'm just..." His brow wrinkled, the scar on his forehead showing. "I'm feeling a bit useless."

The wind's howling could be heard. They were nearing the roof and the top of the house. Felicity shook her head. "Useless?"

Alex smiled. "You would handle this situation with the same aplomb were I not here. I'm sure of it."

Felicity scoffed. "Nonsense."

"Is it?"

Felicity's heart raced. When her mind got busy, her first thought used to be: where's my notebook? Her urge was to write down her thoughts. Now, it was: when will I speak to Alex? She'd grown quite dependent on him. Yet all Felicity could say was, "It took both of us to handle the situations in the garage and the stables, did it not?"

Alex shook his head. His smile remained, although there was a sadness to it. "No, Felicity. It didn't. You solved them both."

Felicity's heart battered in her chest. She hated that she'd somehow made Alex feel useless. "What do I do for you, then?"

"I'm sorry?"

The question Felicity had accidentally blurted out had thrown her companion, but there was no taking it back.

"You say you feel useless around me," said Felicity. "But what use am I to you?"

Alex laughed awkwardly. "Are you serious?"

Felicity nodded, her gloved hand tightening on the bannister. "Quite serious."

There was a pause. The wind groaned against the house's battlements. Alex put his hands in his pockets and looked at the carpet on the landing, his lips pressed together. Then he turned his dark blue gaze on Felicity. "May I speak frankly?"

Felicity's stomach tightened. "Always."

"When I worked for the newspapers on Fleet Street, it was every man for himself. The atmosphere was cut-throat, and I saw nothing wrong with it. To build a career, you have to be hard-nosed. So when Jasper asked me to come to Devon and work for him, I'll be honest. I found the idea ridiculous. It seemed too easy. Where was the struggle? He convinced me to at least give it a try." He shrugged tightly, his hands still in his pockets. "You're the first person to hear this, and it's been difficult to admit, but being down here suits me better. I thought I'd miss London, but I don't." Alex smiled. "I honestly don't."

The tension within Felicity dissipated. Her heart lifted. "Truly?"

Alex nodded. "After the war and everything, I just… I really struggled to feel part of something. But I feel at home here." He blinked. "And you've had significant influence on that."

A flush of crimson raced up Felicity's neck. She swallowed and shifted, but she couldn't stop the colour blooming hot in her cheeks.

"I-I've said too much." Alex was unusually tongue-tied. "I ought not have—"

"No, not at all. I appreciate your honesty." Felicity's voice felt strangled in her throat. She fixed her gaze on the carpet and started again up the stairs. As Felicity passed Alex, she couldn't ignore the comforting, familiar smell of him. The burn in her cheeks grew. "If you feel at home here in Devon, then I'm happy for you." It was almost a mechanical thing to say, a cover intended to disguise how her own emotions had been sent flying all over the place. "I feel rather at home here, too." She gave an empty little laugh. Having been born in Devon, of course she felt at home in the county. It was a rather blockheaded reply. "Shall we see if we can indeed speak to Lady Ariadne?"

Continuing up the stairs, Felicity dared not turn to see Alex's response. He'd shared something personal, and her answer had been trite, yet her cheeks still burned red.

It was marvellously reassuring when Alex's footsteps resumed their climb up the stairs behind her.

Chapter Sixteen

The attic landing of Grimstow House's east wing was unprepossessing. Painted mainly dull grey, the area was apparently used for storage and maintenance, the servants' accommodation being at the top of the house in the west wing. Incongruously, a hint of musky perfume hung in the air.

To her disappointment, Felicity noticed for the first time the caged doors of a lift that appeared large enough to carry people. Had she known of the lift's presence in the building, she would have chosen it above what must have been at least a dozen flights of stairs.

Having attacked the remaining flight with such zeal that her breath came fast, Felicity knocked at the only door on the landing, which was unadorned wood besides a shining black knob. Alex arrived on the landing beside Felicity, and they stood in silence, the wind gusting angrily at the roof not far above their heads, as the knock on the door went unanswered.

Alex gave Felicity a brief but hard gaze — whether a comment on the lack of response at the door or on their earlier exchange, Felicity couldn't tell — then stepped forward and gave the door a more forceful knock.

Faintly, beyond the raging of the wind, there came a sound

from the other side of the door. It was as the butler had said. There was indeed someone in the attic.

"Lady Ariadne?" Felicity spoke gently but loud enough to be heard beyond the door. "It's your step-cousin, Lady Felicity. I was hoping I might speak with you."

The wind continued to howl. Alex folded his arms over his dinner jacket, a look of displeasure on his face. Felicity knew why. What if whoever was on the other side of the door wasn't a confused young girl but someone capable of killing? Had Felicity indeed been hasty in dismissing the butler's offer of a weapon?

Felicity swallowed, her throat dry. "You're not in any sort of trouble," she reassured through the door.

There came another muffled noise. Then a voice. "Everyone thinks it was me, don't they?" The words through the door were cracked with despair. It was unmistakably Ariadne. "But I didn't do it. I swear I didn't. I didn't actually want to see her harmed."

Felicity looked at Alex. They were both able to relax a little.

"I know you didn't," said Felicity soothingly through the wood of the door. "This isn't about accusing you of anything. I just want to ask some questions about what—"

The door opened slowly.

Ariadne's periwinkle-blue eyes shone through rings of red. She stood small in stockinged feet and had a woollen blanket draped around her shoulders. Her pale, frizzy hair was like a halo around her head. Her feathered headband had been removed, but gems still glittered subtly at her throat and neck.

Sniffing, Ariadne looked up at Felicity with a mixture of relief and sadness. Upon noticing Alex's presence, she stiffened.

"Mr Cooper is my colleague," reassured Felicity. "He is eminently trustworthy, and we are aligned on wanting to get closer to the truth of the matter. For the family's sake. For our family's sake." Felicity hoped the fact that she and Ariadne could be considered relations would incline the young woman to trust her.

Ariadne blinked warily, then stood aside, allowing the door to open further. Perhaps she took Felicity at her word, or perhaps it was possible simply to look at Alex and know he was a dependable person. Or perhaps she was too tired to protest.

The attic room was vast. The walls were hung with neat rows of tools and machine parts, while a series of work surfaces along the walls and on tables in the middle of the space overflowed with pieces of machinery. A smattering of multicoloured rugs covering the floorboards were — Felicity was embarrassed to notice — rather unswept, and oddly, at the centre of it all, was a divan. The room smelt not unlike the garage.

Ariadne flopped onto the divan's dark, untidy coverlet, took a cigarette from a box on an overflowing side table, and exhaled a long plume of smoke into the air. She dabbed at her eyes with a knuckle. Her shoulders remained hunched, the sea-green and gold sequins of her dress shimmering dully. She appeared simultaneously old enough to be tired of life and young enough to need comforting on her mother's lap.

With his hands in his pockets, Alex approached a table and inspected the clutter.

Ariadne watched him. "I would offer you a seat, but as you can see, my brother isn't in the habit of receiving guests."

"This is Lord Archibald's room?" enquired Felicity, doing her best to conceal her surprise. The attic room looked more like the abode of a caretaker or handyman than the eldest son of an earl.

"I suppose some might consider my brother unconventional," said Ariadne between long, comforting draws on her cigarette. "But then you would understand what that feels like." The smile Ariadne gave to accompany this comment wasn't unkind, but Felicity felt the sting. Felicity's lack of convention had been something of a focus since her arrival at Grimstow House, but she could put her discomfort to one side. Creating a clear picture for Edwin of what had happened to his sister was the priority, and with the report of theft being investigated downstairs, a conversation with the writer of the threatening letters would fill in the picture even further.

After a brief search, Alex found a metal stool tucked under one of the cluttered work surfaces and brought it over for Felicity to sit upon, which she gratefully accepted after sweeping away a few dog hairs.

Ariadne smiled. "My apologies. My brother has a layer of Mina's sheddings on absolutely everything he wears. The domestics are too sweet on us to say anything about it, and Archie certainly doesn't seem to mind."

"Mina's a Borzoi, is she not?" asked Felicity, as Alex readied his notebook.

Ariadne nodded. "A good number of them were done away with during the Russian revolution. Associated with the tsar and all that. Mina's stock came over several generations ago." She looked up at Alex between drags on her cigarette. "Is this for the newspaper?"

Alex held the notebook away from himself. "Not if you don't want it to be."

Ariadne looked from Alex to Felicity but said nothing further on the matter. Alex returned his pencil to the readied page.

"Could you tell me what happened after we last saw one another?" asked Felicity.

"After Helen's tirade, you mean?" A grimace twisted Ariadne's lips. "I suppose one ought not speak ill of the dead. Especially if one is the prime suspect in the case."

"There's no case," reassured Felicity. "Mr Cooper and I are trying to collect some facts together before the police get here. I'm hopeful we'll be able to confirm Helen's passing as a terrible accident. That would make matters easier on everyone."

Ariadne's eyes flashed. "You mean you're determined to frame it as bad luck even if Helen's death was deliberate? Is the idea of someone wanting her dead so utterly unthinkable?"

The comment left Felicity at a loss for words. She had yet to fully unleash the possibility in her own mind.

"There were certainly times when I hated her," continued Ariadne.

"You didn't want her dead, though, did you?" said Felicity quickly.

The wind howled at the windows. Ariadne was quiet for a moment. She lowered her pale blonde eyebrows as she rolled the cigarette in her fingers. "No," she said. "I didn't."

"After you left the dining room, where did you go?" asked Felicity.

"I came up here. To Archie."

Felicity nodded. "Did you tell him what happened at dinner?"

"I can hardly be sure if he's listening half the time, but yes, I told him. About the letters. About everything."

"Did Lord Archibald seem bothered by it at all?"

Ariadne straightened, the sequins on her dress clacking. "What are you implying? That my brother had something to do with Helen's death?"

"No. Nothing of the sort." Felicity shifted in her seat. Despite having seen Archibald downstairs not long after the gun went off in the morning room, she could have phrased her question more neutrally. "I just want to know what happened."

Ariadne let out a deep exhale. "Archie's reaction was… It was typical Archie. He said he had to go and fix something. He came back up not long after. That's when he told me Helen had been killed."

How might Archibald have learned of Helen's demise? Felicity supposed it wasn't out of the question that he'd heard the news from the servants. Even in a house as big as Grimstow, news travelled incredibly fast.

Ariadne continued. "He told me to lock myself in here and not open the door to anyone. He gathered his tools then left again."

Felicity considered matters for a moment. Archibald was clearly protective of his sister. "Did your brother say where he was going?"

Ariadne shook her head.

"Did he say what had happened to Helen?" asked Felicity.

Ariadne shrugged. "He said she'd been killed with her own weapon. Not more detail than that."

"And since coming upstairs following Helen's speech at dinner, you haven't been back downstairs?"

"No," said Ariadne. "I haven't."

Felicity paused for a moment, meeting Alex's gaze as she did so. He lifted his eyebrows encouragingly. Felicity knew what he meant. "I'd like to speak to your brother," she said. "Might you know where he is?"

"Is he in trouble?" Ariadne blinked wide-eyed at Felicity and Alex.

"It's not about accusations," said Felicity as plainly as possible. Keeping the peace remained firmly among her objectives. "We just want to gather facts. We would like to hear from your brother what he witnessed. Do you perhaps have a notion of what Lord Archibald was going to fix? That may help us locate him."

"I presumed he went to fix the lights because they kept—" The wall-mounted electric lights dimmed, then surged. "—flickering," finished Ariadne. She swallowed nervously. "I don't ask Archie about his work, and he doesn't volunteer the information. He's never been the most talkative of people. When he came back from the war, he was even quieter. I'm not sure if it was the fact Tony never came home or something else."

Felicity furrowed her brow. "Tony?"

"My brother, Anthony." Ariadne dabbed at a red-ringed eye and sat up straight. "Last seen in Ypres."

Alex looked up from his notebook.

"Oh, how terrible." Felicity felt distinctly awkward. Either she hadn't known or hadn't remembered that the Great War had deprived Ariadne of a brother. "I'm extremely sorry for your loss."

Ariadne drew hard on her cigarette. "I'm sorry for yours. I know Helen was your cousin, but I'm compelled to be completely honest with you. Helen didn't like me, and she didn't like Archie. My tears have been purely selfish. I don't want my reputation destroyed by an accusation of murder before I've even debuted. I realise it's an ugly thought to have in the face of someone's death, but I can't help thinking it." Ariadne sniffed. "And I want to be honest with you."

If, as Felicity believed, Ariadne was uninvolved in Helen's demise, then the timing of the revelations around her letters was indeed extremely unfortunate. For all her maturity, Ariadne was still young. A clear outcome would aid her in moving on from the terrible events of that evening, and despite the girl's frankness — or perhaps because of her clear-eyed honesty — Felicity felt inclined to help her.

Felicity thought for a moment. "What's your opinion on Helen's fiancé?"

A faint blush rose into Ariadne's cheeks. Ariadne behaved as if it weren't there, but Felicity knew immediately what it meant. "Leonard's a sensible man," said Ariadne, suddenly businesslike. "I'm afraid Helen wasn't worthy of the match. She had other men. How could anyone approve of it?"

Felicity caught Alex's gaze. He arched an eyebrow. "Other men?" he asked.

"Well, another man," corrected Ariadne. "That empty-headed horse rider. Well-suited they were, too."

Whatever had been going on between Rex and Helen seemed to be some kind of open secret. Was Rex lying when he said nothing had happened between them? Had anyone so far told Felicity the whole truth?

"Is that what your letters to Helen were about?" asked Felicity gently. "Her treatment of Mr McQueen?" A scene flashed through Felicity's mind. Ariadne sneaking through the dark, confronting Helen in the morning room, the gun going off, and Ariadne escaping with Rex in pursuit, the sportsman having mistaken her for Clemency, which wasn't an impossible error in the champagne-fuelled dark.

Ariadne jutted her chin upwards. "Helen's mother married

my father for his money. Not the other way around. If there was any jealousy, it was from Helen towards me."

"My apologies. That wasn't what I intended to imply." Felicity was getting off-track. She cleared her throat. "Are you aware of anything having been stolen this evening?"

Ariadne put a hand to her necklace. "Stolen?"

"There's been a report of theft," said Felicity.

Ariadne looked around, mildly panicked. "I haven't been to my room. I keep my valuables in a locked box. All my mother's jewels are in a safe in the master suite." Ariadne went to stand up.

Alex stepped forward. "It's best if you stay here, Lady Ariadne, as your brother suggested," he said calmly. "The servants are taking all the necessary steps concerning the reported theft."

Ariadne sank slowly back onto the divan. "Did someone try to rob Helen?" Her expression brightened. The letters Ariadne had written were no longer the only factor implying foul play.

"We're waiting to find that out," said Felicity.

Largely satisfied that Ariadne had played no part in the deadly events that took place in the morning room — if not from hard evidence then from the combination of frankness and self-awareness that the young girl presented — Felicity returned with Alex to the plain landing at the top of the narrow stairs, the wind still howling around the roof.

"What will you do now?" asked Ariadne from the doorway.

"Report back to Edwin," said Felicity as she looked at Alex. Alex nodded. From the twinkle in his eye, Felicity knew he'd recognised her partial truth.

"If you do find Archie, please tell him to come to me." Ariadne sounded a little desperate. "I can't stand all this waiting around on my own."

"I shall do that," said Felicity with a nod.

"Oh, and don't use the lift," Ariadne added. "The electrics can't be trusted in this awful weather. You're likely to get stuck in it."

Felicity raised her eyebrows. It had been lucky she hadn't located the lift before ascending to the attic. As Ariadne closed the door and turned the lock, Felicity and Alex had no choice but to set off down the same stairs.

"We need to speak to Leonard," said Felicity.

"You've a soft spot for Ariadne, have you not?" asked Alex.

Felicity was ahead of Alex on the narrow steps. She turned to look at him. "I don't believe she harmed Helen, if that's what you mean."

"You saw what she wrote in those letters."

Felicity returned her attention to the stairs. "You sound like Rex."

Alex sighed. "I'm not saying she's a murderer, but she can hardly be considered an innocent."

Felicity didn't want to argue about it. "Do you agree Leonard should be our next interviewee?"

Alex went to reply but stopped. The sound of raised voices carried up the stairs to meet them.

"You don't care for her. You've never cared for her!"

"I cannot be held responsible for where my emotions lead me."

"Then why did you ask her to marry you, you cad?"

Alex shook his head. "Here we go again."

Felicity quickened her pace. More drama was erupting downstairs, and she had a duty to put a stop to it.

Chapter Seventeen

Involvement in the second argument to take place in Grimstow House's entrance hall that evening wasn't limited to the men. Felicity and Alex arrived to find Patience and Clemency Bourgoyne at the centre of the action, with the butler, housekeeper, footman, and maid all standing by helplessly. The little maid looked particularly upset.

"Pat, don't. Please." Clemency tugged weakly on her sister's arm.

Patience continued to throw a volley of accusations at Rex. "She's besotted with you. She still can't see you for what you really are. As soon as you found someone with a proper fortune, you jumped ship." She jabbed a finger at Rex's lapels to emphasise her words. "You're a scoundrel and a brute!"

Rex brushed Patience's hand aside. "Money's got nothing to do with it. I'll not hide how I feel any longer, but I don't expect you of all people to understand. Your heart is as solid as a rock." He turned to Leonard, who was standing stiffly to one side. "Just like yours."

"Don't come near me," growled Leonard.

"Stay away, Mr Debenham," intoned Sir Vernon, who swayed a little next to Leonard. "I'm warning you."

Edwin and Miss Fairchild arrived shortly after Felicity and Alex.

"Mr Debenham—" Felicity tried to interject, but her approach was ignored.

"Why?" Rex was posturing in front of Leonard. "What will you do? I've put all my cards on the table. I've nothing to lose now. Why don't you do the same?"

Leonard's thin moustache twitched, his jaw tight. Sir Vernon stepped forward unsteadily, his injured hand swinging at his side. "Of what exactly are you accusing my friend, Mr Debenham?"

"Really, I don't think—" began Felicity.

"Horrocks," thundered Edwin. "Fetch the rifles. Our guests cannot be trusted to behave themselves. Order will have to be enforced."

Felicity's stomach dropped like a lead weight. Loaded weapons were the very last ingredient needed in the potent mix of tensions. She was also keenly aware that her plan to keep matters at Grimstow House under control had rather spectacularly failed.

She turned to Edwin. "Perhaps we might smooth things out a different way?"

"You've done your best, Felicity." Edwin leaned hard on his cane. He looked exhausted. "They've had their chance. Some people just won't bally listen."

Miss Fairchild clapped a hand over her mouth, as the butler advanced with the footman towards the gun room. The housekeeper stepped forward. "Should Miss Ingles and I arm ourselves, Mr Horrocks?" Mrs Rudd looked steadfast enough to handle a weapon, but the trembling maid appeared on the brink of tears.

"Not at this stage, Mrs Rudd," replied the butler. "But should the need arise."

Mrs Rudd nodded solemnly. The maid's lower lip quivered.

It came as a small relief to Felicity that the female servants wouldn't yet take up weapons.

Alex approached Rex. "It's best if we all remain calm, Mr Debenham."

Rex laughed. "Oh, I'm perfectly calm." He tightened his fists at his sides and moved even closer to Leonard, who didn't flinch.

"Don't you come another inch further!" The effect of Sir Vernon's challenge to Rex was undermined by the addition of a hiccough.

Alex stepped between the businessman and the sportsman. He put a hand to Rex's shoulder, preventing him from making further progress towards Leonard. While Felicity didn't enjoy seeing Alex put himself in the firing line, he had probably staved off further physical escalation of the tensions. Alex couldn't hold Rex's tongue, however.

"You never loved Helen, did you?" Rex's voice was wild with emotion. "You wanted her for her money. Or rather, you wanted her for her step-father's money. That's right, isn't it?"

Leonard frowned. "The Earl is his own man. He knows a good investment."

"So, the deal goes through?" It was Patience's question. There was disbelief in her voice.

"Why shouldn't it?" Leonard's response was cold-hearted but perhaps not deliberately so.

Patience held her head high. "I swore to Helen I wouldn't bring it up. She promised me you were different. But as she's no longer with us—" there was a tremor in Patience's tone "—I'm not going to stop myself from saying it. Our father made an investment with your father once, Mr McQueen."

Leonard cocked an eyebrow. "Oh?"

"Yes," continued Patience, her face darkening. "He lost practically everything."

Leonard's mouth fell open. "I… I wasn't aware."

Sir Vernon waggled a finger in Patience's direction. "It's the nature of investments, you know. The return isn't guaranteed. The risk is always there."

"Why," fumed Rex, "you absolute beast."

Alex did his best to hold the sportsman back, but he couldn't prevent him from swinging for Leonard. The businessman stepped back just in time, narrowly missing a broken nose. Sir Vernon dropped his hand and stood by, slack-jawed and shocked.

"Rex!" shrieked Clemency, her cheeks streaked with tears. Patience continued to restrain her.

"Leonard!"

Ariadne had appeared in the entrance hall. She dashed towards the businessman.

Alex threw a look at Felicity that seemed to say, *I give up with these people*. Felicity gave a helpless shrug. She hadn't heard Ariadne following them on the stairs, otherwise Felicity would have forced her back up to her brother's room. Was this the first time she'd crept down from the attic?

"I'm fine," Leonard said dismissively, dusting down his dinner jacket as Ariadne buzzed anxiously around him. "There's no need for fuss."

Rex quickly readjusted the focus of his melodrama. "Oh, here she is. We have our murderer. There's written proof of her hatred of Helen. Lock her up. The case is closed."

"Steady on, man." Alex still had a hand on Rex's shoulder and was struggling to keep him away from Ariadne and Leonard. A lock of hair fell onto his scarred forehead.

The butler and footman reappeared in the entrance hall, both now armed with rifles. Horrocks seemed much more confident with his weapon than his younger colleague.

"Edwin, please," begged Felicity despairingly. "Let's not add more loaded guns to the situation." It was her turn to feel useless.

Miss Fairchild stepped forward timidly, wringing her hands. "L-Lady Felicity's right, Edwin. I beg you to reconsider."

"Horrocks, Wilkinson." Edwin spoke firmly, his face a hardened mask, the women's pleas ignored. "Escort these men to their rooms and ensure they remain locked up till the police arrive."

"Very good, sir." The butler turned immediately towards Rex, his rifle at the ready, although not yet aimed. "Come along now, Mr Debenham. You heard Doctor Quick's wishes."

Felicity's chest tightened. Alex remained between Rex and Horrocks, a hand on Rex's chest, the sportsman's wild gaze flicking angrily between Ariadne and Leonard.

"The fellow's an animal," said Sir Vernon from his hiding place behind Leonard. "He needs locking up."

The butler adjusted his grip on his weapon. "Come now, Mr Debenham." The footman's Adam's apple bobbed up and down. There had already been one deadly shooting that evening. Felicity silently pleaded there wouldn't be another.

"Let's do this like honourable men, Mr Debenham," urged Alex quietly.

"Let me go to him!" Clemency was crying and struggling with her sister, the will to fight rising in her.

"Clem, please." Patience's voice shook with emotion. "Do you not see what he's done to you? What they've done to us?"

"You don't understand," sobbed Clemency, thrashing her arms in a bid to loosen her sister's grip. "You don't understand!"

Edwin addressed the housekeeper. His voice was stiff and emotionless. "Mrs Rudd. See that the Misses Bourgoyne are returned to their room and that they stay there."

The housekeeper acknowledged the command. "Come, Miss Ingles. Let's help the Bourgoyne sisters to their room. It's the least we can do for his lordship in his absence." The maid nodded and followed Mrs Rudd's lead, sniffing back tears. The female domestics were at least unarmed, but the indignity of being forcibly locked up was surely throwing oil on the fire.

"Edwin," began Felicity, "I must urge you to—"

Bang, bang, bang!

The heavy front doors jumped in place. Everyone stopped and turned. The groaning of the wind filled the silence.

"Quickly." The voice came from outside. "I need help out here."

Chapter Eighteen

Alex was the first to react to the appeal for help. He rushed to Grimstow House's front doors and disappeared outside. Felicity hugged herself as wind as cold as polar snow whipped indoors. The curtailment of the drama in the entrance hall was a relief, but what did the interruption mean?

Edwin was next to disappear outside, his forehead deeply creased, his walking cane tapping across the flagstones at the threshold. The butler slung his rifle on his back and followed promptly. The footman looked unsure what to do.

Leonard shook his head. "What the deuce…"

Rex put his hands on his hips. He looked both perplexed and amused. Ariadne glanced around, blinking rapidly, as if waking from a dream. Patience released her grip from her sister, but Clemency didn't move. The housekeeper hung back, putting a hand out to indicate to the maid to do the same.

The more seconds ticked by, the greater Felicity's urge to follow Alex grew. Then she made a decision. Crossing the entrance hall, she went to the cloakroom, pulled on the brown wool coat in which she'd arrived at Grimstow House — the furs she'd borrowed earlier having been stowed somewhere out of sight — and strode back across the entrance hall, intent on helping with whatever situation was developing outside.

Felicity's progress was cut short by the front doors flying open. A blast of Arctic air accompanied the reappearance of Charles, who was almost unrecognisable in bulky layers of clothing, a thick scarf and gloves, and a dense bowler hat pulled low on his head. His nose and cheeks glowed bright pink from the cold.

As Charles did his best to hold the heavy doors open, Alex and the butler struggled inside, their feet shuffling on the granite flags, Edwin overseeing their movements. They had something large, heavy, and misshapen in their grasp.

"I say…" Sir Vernon's mouth hung open.

It was the body of a man.

Patience put her arm around Clemency, who no longer fought her sister's touch. Ariadne gripped her own shoulders, shivering. Rex's smile faded. Everyone was stunned into an inert silence as they watched the jumbled form being carried through Grimstow's front doors.

"Take him to the South Drawing Room," commanded Edwin.

The footman awoke from his stupor. Placing his rifle carefully against an oak side table, he raced ahead of Alex and Horrocks, opening a door on one of the corridors leading off the entrance hall.

Ariadne stepped forward timidly. "W-who is it?"

Felicity moved to follow the procession, doing her best to get a look at the man in Alex and the butler's grasp, but Leonard strode quickly forward, Sir Vernon stumbling in his wake, both of them passing before Felicity into the drawing room.

"Who is it?" Clemency repeated Ariadne's question to her sister, but Patience had no response.

"So we've got our man, have we?" said Leonard as Felicity arrived in the South Drawing Room behind him, still wearing her woollen coat. The room had walls of duck egg blue, a sturdy white marble fireplace, a pair of unfussy chandeliers, and twin sofas in beige velvet.

Charles took off his bowler hat and rubbed his wavy gold-brown hair. "Rather looks that way, doesn't it?"

Alex and Horrocks stood aside, both breathing hard, recovering from the effort of depositing the unresponsive man on one of the sofas. The man's ash-blond hair was splayed in all directions, his cheeks were grey, and his heavy overcoat and trousers were scuffed with reddish mud.

Felicity gasped. She recognised him.

It was Lord Archibald.

"Oh, no! No, no, no!" Ariadne surged towards the sofa and flung her arms around her brother's neck, breaking down into sobs.

Edwin, who had been handed his medical bag by the footman, was almost knocked out of the way. He chastised his step-sister. "Do you want me to help your brother or not?" Archibald's lips were tinged with blue.

"On the run, was he?" Sir Vernon peered over the back of the sofa as Edwin got to work inspecting his patient. Felicity couldn't quite believe it, yet the evidence was there.

"Can't say I knew the fellow well," said Leonard, his jaw tight. "But it looks like he removed that big old moustache of his. Come now, Ari." Leonard put a hand on Ariadne's shoulder. "Give Doctor Quick the space he needs."

She looked up at Leonard, her angelic face stained with tears. "No," she breathed. "I don't believe it." But she withdrew docilely from her brother's side.

"He's still alive, isn't he?" asked Alex.

Edwin nodded, untucking a stethoscope from his ears. "He's got the beginnings of hypothermia, and a broken rib or two."

A porcelain clock on the marble mantelpiece ticked steadily, and the wind whistled beyond the pale blue curtains. No one said it, but from their grim expressions, everyone gathered in the

South Drawing Room, from the Bourgoyne twins to the butler, had drawn the same conclusion. Archibald had clearly fled Grimstow House to escape from his involvement in Helen's demise. The calmness in the room was therefore remarkable. Then again, Rex was not present. The housekeeper and the maid had also not followed the group into the South Drawing Room.

Edwin turned to Charles. "Where did you find him?"

Charles sighed deeply. "I'll be honest. I wouldn't have spotted him if it weren't for the young fellow I was riding with. He noticed him lying in a bank of brambles at the bottom of a rather steep slope. Must have lost his footing crossing the field. Easy to do oneself an injury out there. The ground is absolutely frozen solid."

"Did you come across Lord Archibald's dog?" enquired Felicity.

Charles shook his head, confused. "His dog?"

Ariadne sniffed. "Mina." She kept her distance from the sofa, standing alongside Leonard, but her eyes remained fixed on her brother.

Charles looked concerned. "There was no dog."

Felicity nodded gloomily. The Borzoi was a breed suited to freezing weather, but the idea of the graceful hound out on the icy moors by herself was dreadful.

"Where's the other rider?" asked Leonard.

Charles rubbed his forehead where the bowler had left a mark. "Carried on, brave blighter. Excellent horseman. Knows the territory intimately. I know he'll make it to the village. It's just a question of when they'll be able to send someone out to us. There's simply no chance of a motor getting through. The roads are like glass."

Felicity caught Alex's gaze as another silence descended upon the room. He looked grave.

Patience broke the stillness. "At least we now know who did it."

"We do?" Clemency, who had been clinging to Patience's arm, looked up at her sister.

Leonard cleared his throat. "Escaping like a fugitive into the freezing night is rather incriminating."

Patience turned pale. She bit her lip and glanced at Felicity, clearly wondering if anyone else had noticed the twins' trip to the garage.

"Wouldn't you say, Lady Felicity?" Leonard looked at Felicity.

"The situation is highly suspicious," said Felicity carefully, "but evidence linking Lord Archibald to Helen's accident hasn't yet been found."

"Oh, Archie. Archie!" Unable to control herself, Ariadne again flew to her brother's side, stroking his hair and putting her arms around him. "Why? Why did you do it? Why?" She sobbed with her head on his almost motionless chest.

Felicity winced. She could envisage the chain of events. Ariadne fleeing upstairs, humiliated by Helen at dinner, then Archibald stalking through the darkness, ready to avenge his little sister.

Colour rose in Edwin's freckled face as access to his patient was again blocked. The conflict within him must have been severe, his duty as a man of medicine forcing him to assist the very person who did away with his sister. "Your brother's health is extremely fragile." Edwin spoke sternly to Ariadne. "Do you want me to help him or not? If you hadn't written those letters…" He trailed off as he returned his attentions to the unconscious Archibald. "Horrocks, I need blankets."

"Of course, sir." The butler spoke to the footman, who then left the room.

Felicity approached her cousin. "Allow me to help."

Edwin held up a hand. "You've done enough."

Felicity retreated. She'd let Edwin down. It was clear he thought so as well.

"Come now, Ari," said Leonard almost tenderly as he escorted her away from where her brother lay. "No one's happy in this awful scenario, but I can't agree your letters set all this in motion."

Edwin straightened, affronted. "Mr McQueen. Why are you, of all people, defending Ariadne? Your fiancée — my sister — is dead, likely murdered if the evidence before us is to be believed."

Sir Vernon frowned. "Come now, Doctor Quick."

Edwin continued to berate Leonard, leaning heavily on his cane as he moved towards him. "And you choose now of all moments to open your heart and provide succour? To one of the very people who instigated the drama of this whole deadly situation? You were never that caring towards my sister, as I recall. Oh, you bought her jewellery and took her to the French Riviera. But I don't believe you ever truly cared for her."

"Now that, Doctor Quick, is simply offensive," boomed Sir Vernon.

Felicity's heart banged in her chest. Tensions were again rising. Despite her commitment to help, Felicity didn't know how to react. The man responsible for Helen's death had been found without her help. The matter had been wrapped up so neatly, Felicity still couldn't quite consider it true, but that didn't detract from how little she'd done to help matters.

She looked to Alex for a hint of support. He remained calm but watchful. Felicity tried to do the same.

Charles approached Edwin. "Look, old chap. You've had a rough time of it. Perhaps allow the servants to take care of Lord Archibald?"

Breathing hard through flared nostrils, Edwin glanced at his friend but didn't respond to him. "Where's Miss Fairchild?" Again he addressed the butler. "Have her sent to me, please, if she's feeling well enough. I need her assistance."

"Right away, sir," confirmed Horrocks, and he left the room.

"The rest of you may leave as well," commanded Edwin grimly.

"Eddie," said Charles gently, "surely it's better if—"

"No exceptions," said Edwin sternly.

It hurt Felicity's heart to see her cousin in pain and lashing out. She wanted to soothe him but feared any attempt would only agitate him further.

After the butler's departure, Patience and Clemency were the first to leave the drawing room, followed by Leonard and Ariadne. Ariadne kept glancing over her shoulder at her motionless, blue-lipped brother. Alex turned towards the door. Felicity followed him, looking back to see Edwin tending to the welfare of the man believed to have ended his sister's life. Nothing about it seemed right.

"I'm curious to know what you made of all that," said Alex in low tones as they proceeded along the corridor.

As much as Felicity wanted to exchange ideas with Alex, there was something else on her mind. "I'm sorry, do give me a moment." Spotting the butler emerging from a door further ahead, Felicity sped towards him. "Mr Horrocks, is there any news on any other items having been stolen?"

For a moment, the butler looked confused. "Y-yes, your ladyship. The housekeeper has confirmed that gems are indeed missing from the necklaces Miss Quick was wearing. We also found some disturbance to the safe in the master bedroom. It appears to have been emptied of valuables, although we haven't had time to fully investigate how access was gained. We were interrupted by news of the disagreement in the entrance hall." The butler's eyes darted away. He seemed extremely preoccupied. "We shall conclude our investigations and deliver a full report to Doctor Quick forthwith. I must first locate Miss Fairchild, if that will be all, your ladyship?"

"Yes," said Felicity, her mind overflowing with considerations. "Thank you." If Archibald did away with Helen, had he also grabbed a handful of her gems? He was the first son of a wealthy earl. It didn't add up.

Alex. Felicity needed to speak to Alex. Felicity turned to look for him and instead found Charles standing before her, his cheeks and nose still glowing pink from the ride out. His warm brown eyes sparkled.

"Might I have a word, Cici?"

Felicity glanced around for Alex, but she and Charles were the only ones still in the corridor.

She smiled politely at Edwin's old friend. "Of course, Charlie. Of course."

Chapter Nineteen

With her coat hanging open over her sparkling party frock, Felicity followed Charles as they turned and turned again through Grimstow House's warren of corridors. "Only been here a couple of times, so I don't really know the place." Charles smiled at Felicity apologetically. "Just looking for somewhere we might have a bit of privacy."

Felicity nodded and smiled back at him. Delaying a consultation with Alex would surely be worth whatever Charles had to tell her. Charles had found and rescued Lord Archibald. What had he noticed that he didn't want the rest of the household to overhear? The mystery of Helen's passing might have been resolved, but there were still questions that needed answering. Details were still missing.

"This should do it." Charles opened a dark panelled door with brass fittings. "After you."

Charles was an acquaintance from a long time ago, so Felicity didn't doubt her safety alone with him. He had, however, brought her to the house's gun room.

"Oh," she said, unpleasantly surprised by the spectacle of numerous glass cabinets with firearms of all descriptions stored within, mainly for hunting pursuits.

"Oh," echoed Charles a little dismally. "This isn't exactly the setting I had in mind. I shall inform the butler the room ought to be locked." He rubbed his forehead. "In any case. Cici, there's something I need to tell you."

Felicity raised her eyebrows. "Do go on."

Charles fixed his gaze on her. He took a deep inhale through his nose and released it through his mouth. "While I was out in that deuced awful weather, the going was extremely tough. When we came across Lord Archibald, he was so lifeless I mistook him for dead. And what with Helen and…" His eyes went to the floor for a moment. "Look, Cici. I've been thinking things over."

Felicity nodded. She knew where this was going. "The conclusion everyone's jumped to about Lord Archibald doesn't quite add up, does it?"

Charles blinked. "The conclusion about Lord Archibald?"

"That he was escaping out of guilt at having caused Helen's death," clarified Felicity, although Charles had surely already grasped it. "It doesn't quite make sense, does it?"

Charles squinted, then shook his head. He shifted his stance, again locking eyes with Felicity. "What I wanted to tell you, Cici, was that I've been thinking an awful lot about things. Since I saw you earlier this evening, before all the terrible happenings."

It was Felicity's turn to look confused. "Thinking about what?"

"Seeing you again started it off," continued Charles. "The rest of what's happened has just intensified things."

"Intensified what?" Felicity was utterly lost.

"Dash it," said Charles, raking a hand through his dishevelled hair. "I'm going to just come out and say it. Marriage, Cici. I've been thinking about marriage."

"Marriage?" What had marriage to do with anything?

Charles chuckled, happy and nervous all at once. "You and me, Cici. How about it?"

A chill spread through her.

So Charles hadn't wanted to discuss the mystery. His thoughts had been elsewhere completely. How had Felicity not seen it? Her cousin had met an awful end, the household was in turmoil, and now Charles was coming to her with talk of marriage. This wasn't how it ought to happen, was it?

Felicity glanced around at the racks of guns, but the only door was behind Charles.

"This isn't the real proposal, you understand," said Charles quickly, sensing Felicity's unease. "We'll go to Paris or Florence or wherever you want. We'll do things properly. But I just had to say it. Time waits for no man. I've seen that here tonight."

The heat of embarrassment replaced the chill of dread Felicity had felt just moments before. It was real. It was a proposal. "Charlie. Charles." He was such a thoroughly kind, amiable man. "Forgive my reaction. This is so unexpected."

"I don't need your response now," said Charles, almost speaking over Felicity. "Take your time. The last thing I want is to pressure you."

Felicity gave the most awkward smile of her life. Her instinct was to flee. Charles wouldn't have prevented her from leaving, but her flight would have made the situation even more painful than it already was. So Felicity remained still, the awkward smile frozen on her lips.

Charles huffed out a deep exhale. "I haven't felt this alive since surviving Passchendaele."

Felicity's smile gave way to a wince. She would never know what it was like to be at the front, and she never took for granted the bravery of Charles and Alex and all the other men called up to fight. But was it therefore selfish to hope for a marriage proposal to be more romantic?

Alex. Of course. She didn't stop to consider precisely why, but Felicity knew she needed to speak to Alex.

"Charlie..." Felicity considered how she might exit the gun room in a manner that spared further embarrassment for either of them. Instead of a ruse to get to the door, Felicity thought back to what Helen had said about Felicity's queerness and her lack of convention. About her unsuitability for marriage. Yet here Felicity was, with the opportunity to do everything society expected of a woman, and all with a man she knew to be reliable and kind. Felicity had never sworn off marriage, but having debuted in a year when most men were still at the front, and many of them never having come home, she'd not yet been confronted with a suitable opportunity.

Was suitability all that mattered? Felicity swallowed.

"Take your time." Charles spoke sincerely. His warm brown eyes and messy ash-blonde hair were charming and attractive.

Having noticed as much, Felicity blushed. "I-I shall do that, Charlie. Thank you."

Charles rubbed his forehead. "Say, I should get back out there."

Felicity breathed a subtle yet enormous sigh of relief.

"Hopefully Edwin's cooled off a bit," continued Charles, "and will allow me to help him."

Felicity smiled and nodded. "You're a good friend." Charles was a good man.

"I do my best," he said humbly. Then he left the room, closing the door behind him.

Feeling rather overwhelmed, Felicity leaned her back against a tall wooden cabinet built into the wall. She sighed deeply as she swam through the maelstrom of her thoughts, few of which were of an upbeat nature. She sank her hands into her pockets, grateful for her woollen coat, as the gun room appeared not to be heated. There was something in her pocket.

She withdrew a folded piece of paper.

Her coat having been freshly cleaned, the pockets had been empty when Felicity left Bradley Court for Grimstow House.

She unfolded the paper. It contained a short, type-written note.

Keep your nose out. Or you'll be sorry.

Chapter Twenty

When Felicity found Alex, he was outside the South Drawing Room with Rex, who, true to form, was fidgety and highly agitated. While Alex reasoned with the sportsman, the bespectacled young footman — who had taken up a post next to the drawing room door with a rifle over his shoulder — appeared too scared to look at the men, let alone intervene.

"I am doing my best to remain calm," said Rex through gritted teeth, traces of dust from the exercise arena at the stables still evident on his dinner jacket. "But if the man who murdered the woman you love were behind that door, are you telling me you'd do nothing about it?"

"That's not what I said." Alex spoke calmly, although Felicity could tell his patience was wearing thin. Thankfully, Felicity's approach proved a distraction from their tense exchange.

Felicity capitalised on it. "Mr Debenham," she said brightly.

Rex frowned, apparently stunned to be addressed in such a forthright feminine tone.

"It's your intention to help with the situation, is it not?" continued Felicity.

The sportsman looked from Alex to the footman, then back to

Felicity. He nodded with a sinister glint in his eye. "Helen must be avenged."

Felicity lifted her chin. "Then find Clemency and apologise to her."

Rex looked stunned for a moment. "What the blazes are you talking about?"

"You want Helen's name to be honoured, do you not?" continued Felicity.

"Of course."

"Then I suggest you do what you can to make a thoroughly undignified situation as dignified as possible. To begin with, I believe a gentlemanly apology to your betrothed is in order."

Rex again glanced at Alex, who remained firmly and calmly between the sportsman and the drawing room door. Seemingly bolstered by Felicity's performance, the footman dared a look in the sportsman's direction.

"Dashed nonsense," said Rex, and he strode off.

"You never cease to surprise me." Alex's smile was familiar and reassuring.

Felicity let out a shaky breath. "I don't quite know what came over me," she said by way of explanation for her outspoken behaviour, although the statement wasn't entirely correct. An overwhelming sense of powerlessness in the face of an increasing number of tricky situations had driven Felicity's shortness with Rex. What puzzled her was why her normal decorum hadn't held her back. Then again, there was nothing normal about the circumstances at Grimstow House.

"Shall we talk?" suggested Alex.

"Please," said Felicity. They were on precisely the same page.

On their way to find somewhere to speak, Alex explained how the party had broken up after Felicity disappeared with Charles.

Leonard had taken Ariadne under his wing and accompanied her for a stiff drink in the billiard room, and the twins had gone upstairs, although Alex was unsure whether they intended to lock themselves in their room or gather their belongings and attempt another escape.

"Not sure where Sir Vernon went," added Alex. "And I've yet to see Miss Fairchild."

After a few wrongly chosen doors, including the ill-fated ballroom, where the wind gusted through the broken skylight and the shattered glass glittered on the floor in the moonlight, the room Felicity and Alex selected for their much-needed tête-à-tête was the library. Although still wearing her woollen coat, Felicity shivered as she flicked the light switch and revealed the room where Felicity and Alex's initial audience with Helen, Leonard, and Jambo had taken place.

It felt like a lifetime ago.

The shutters hadn't been closed, the servants being understandably preoccupied with other matters. Felicity watched their reflections in the leaded glass of the windows as Alex went to the oval table and leaned back against it. Without wanting it, Helen's comments about Felicity's marriageability sprung into her mind. She almost blushed when this forced her to remember the proposition Charles had assailed her with only moments ago. Thankfully, Alex hadn't yet asked what Charles had wanted to discuss.

To further delay him from doing so, Felicity reached into her pocket. "I found this in my coat just now." She handed Alex the note.

Alex read it aloud. "*Keep your nose out. Or you'll be sorry.*" He met Felicity's gaze, his thick eyebrows knitted together. "When do you suppose it was placed in your pocket?"

"I put my coat on while you were helping bring Lord Archibald inside. The last time I wore it was on arriving here at Grimstow House. I borrowed furs to go down to the stables."

Alex pondered for a moment, his brow still low. "So it could have been placed in your pocket before the party started? Before your cousin's passing, before anything really happened?"

Felicity nodded. It was her hope, too. "I want to speak with Ariadne again."

"It's as good a place to start as any," replied Alex. "But can you trust what she says?"

Felicity let out a little laugh. "Can we trust anything anyone here says?" She sank into the same chair she'd occupied earlier. The memory of Helen pacing beside her in riding gear was so vivid it almost hurt.

"And if it wasn't Ariadne that put the note in your pocket?" asked Alex.

Felicity shook her head slowly, reluctant to consider the alternative. "Let's cross that bridge if we come to it."

Alex sighed. He folded his arms and looked down at Felicity. "So, how are we going to report on this?"

In her eagerness to assist Edwin, Felicity had barely considered the newspaper for which she and Alex worked. They hadn't been on Western Daily News business when they arrived at Grimstow House, but there was no avoiding it. The passing of a society beauty like Helen would be major news across the country.

"If we get our copy in as soon as we get off this frozen hill," continued Alex, his dark blue eyes shining with eagerness, "we'll not only get the scoop, but we'll set the narrative for the whole affair. We can ensure your cousin's dignity is respected and look after Edwin's and your aunt's interests while we're at it."

Felicity bit her lip. Alex was absolutely right. Striking early would make all the difference, both for Felicity's brother's newspaper and for Helen's surviving relatives. Normally a hard-headed journalist, it was touching that Alex considered the reputation of Felicity's family alongside the scoop.

"Are you suggesting we find a typewriter and set to work?" asked Felicity.

Alex smiled, clearly delighted by Felicity's understanding. "Why ever not?"

Felicity blinked up at Alex. "But what about making sense of things first?"

Alex was silent for a moment. The wind whistled at the windows. "This whole situation is rather more than what you agreed to when accepting your cousin's assignment to follow up on the anonymous letters. Is it not?"

Felicity had to admit that it was.

"And what if that note you found is from whoever did away with your poor cousin?"

Felicity remained quiet for a moment. "The idea of leaving things entirely for the police has occurred to me. On multiple occasions."

Alex raised his brows. "There's a 'but' coming, is there not?" He knew Felicity almost too well.

"Would you allow me to speak frankly?" she asked.

"Always," he said.

Felicity adjusted her frock. The glass beads were bothering her. "The butler said that gems had indeed been taken from the necklaces Helen was wearing. This is not the kind of talk that should appear in the paper—"

"Of course," confirmed Alex without hesitation.

"—but Lord Archibald is the first son and heir to the Carrington fortune. What reason would he have to take a handful of jewels from his own step-sister?"

"Perhaps spite? To deface her in some way?"

It was precisely why Felicity had wanted to speak to Alex so badly. He always challenged her, helping her move her thoughts forward. "It seems a rather weak attempt at doing such," she responded.

"What if it were to create a distraction from himself as the murderer?"

Felicity thought for a moment. She still wasn't fully

comfortable with the idea of her cousin being deliberately done away with.

She folded her hands in her lap. "If distraction was the plan, why did Archibald then escape and draw attention to himself? Even if he hadn't ended up unconscious at the bottom of a hill, his disappearance would have been uncovered eventually. No. It makes little sense. Why would a local man with intimate knowledge of the area and its climate go out onto the moors on foot on a night like this? If he wanted truly to escape, why not take a horse?"

"So as not to be noticed?" suggested Alex.

Felicity had more in her. "And why remove one's moustache but not attempt to disguise oneself further? A change of clothes would have made him even harder to recognise."

Alex shrugged. "Perhaps there wasn't time?"

"And where is his dog? Mina appeared devoted to him. Surely she wouldn't have left her master's side."

"You know our canine friends better than I do." Alex rubbed his jaw. "Did your old friend give you any interesting tips?"

"My old—" Felicity broke off as she realised to whom Alex was referring. "Charlie, you mean?" To fight the blush that rushed up her neck, Felicity fussily stood up, took off her coat, folded it over her arm, and sat back down. "He was concerned about my welfare, that's all." Felicity smoothed her coat with her hand. "He wanted to check on me. He had no information to share."

Alex nodded thoughtfully. "I hope you told him what he could do with his concern."

"I beg your pardon." Felicity's blush was cut short by her shock at Alex's reaction.

He smiled somewhat insolently and pushed away from the desk. "I say that as someone who has expressed concern for your welfare in the past. It would be unfair if you treated us differently."

Felicity's mouth hung open for a moment, on the brink of protest. It was a fair point.

Alex put his hands in his pockets and began pacing. "Do we have any confirmation of the woman with the feathered headdress seen leaving the morning room? I think it's fair to say the man who went after her was Rex. He admits as much himself."

Felicity again repositioned herself in her seat. There were so many angles to consider. Archibald, the thefts, and, of course, the tussle in the morning room. Felicity had almost forgotten that she had been quite keen to re-interview Leonard. The twins had more they could say, too.

"I believe there was such a woman," said Felicity. "Sir Vernon and Rex confirm it, but who she was remains doubtful." She tapped her fingers on the armrest of her chair. "We could, perhaps, interview the staff ourselves? The butler may not have asked for the details we need."

Alex ceased pacing. "Don't call me beastly for expressing concern, but you seem to have forgotten the note in your pocket."

The fold of paper lay on the oval table before Felicity. "You're right," she admitted. She had promised Edwin to do her best to keep matters at Grimstow House as calm as possible. While Felicity had fallen short of that in many respects, she could at least take precautions around her own welfare. "I'm sure we'll be able to clear things up with Ariadne. After that, I believe we should speak to—"

Boom!

The windows of the library lit up as an enormous golden chrysanthemum burst lit the sky.

Boom!

Another giant firework exploded before the first had quite faded, the harsh wind carrying the pyrotechnic glitter quickly away.

Fizz! Wheew! Fizz!

"What the blazes…"

Felicity and Alex went to the window, their faces lit by the colourful explosions.

"There must be some mistake," said Felicity.

Boom! Boom! Wheew! Fizz!

Fireworks flew in all directions. The source was somewhere beyond the paved terrace, but the wind whipped the bursts far across the grounds.

"It's not a normal display," said Alex, his eyes tracing the path of several rockets that burst into silver stars. "They shouldn't all be going off at the same time like that."

They watched in silence for a moment, each *boom* thudding in Felicity's chest. It was bizarrely beautiful, even if the tension in her stomach confirmed there was something not right. Something was perhaps even dangerously wrong.

Felicity looked at Alex. "How does one set off a fireworks display by accident on a freezing windy night?"

He turned to her. "One doesn't. Not a display of this calibre, anyway."

Between the booms and bangs came shouting, distant at first. It grew louder.

"Fire! Fire at the stables!"

Alarm shot through Felicity. Could anything else go wrong at Grimstow House that night?

Alex was already moving towards the library door. Felicity was close behind, tugging on her coat. A fire at a remote country house was always an all-hands-on-deck affair, even in good weather. When lives — including those of animals — were at risk, prompt reactions were important. And in the context of everything that had happened at Grimstow House so far that evening, answers to two questions were required without delay. Who had set off the fireworks, and why?

As Felicity and Alex hurried through the house, she feared they would find at least one of the answers very soon indeed.

Chapter Twenty-One

Flames licking at the edge of the stables' roof came into view as Felicity and Alex hurried down the sloping gravel drive.

"Mind if I go ahead?" asked Alex.

"Go," urged Felicity, the freezing wind snatching her breath.

As Alex dashed off, he passed Leonard coming in the opposite direction. He'd collected Jambo from the stables and was leading him back to the house. "Just what we needed," muttered the businessman as he passed Felicity, who continued to move as quickly as she could towards the fire. The Ridgeback was alert but confused and straining at his lead.

The ever-dependable Horrocks came into view. He was at the top of the ladder, throwing buckets of water onto the eaves of the stables, where flames jumped in the wind, threatening to engulf the vast overhang of the roof. The driver and the footman were handing buckets to him, water sloshing over the cobbled yard. With the occasional whizz and pop of a firework still going off overhead, the equally dependable Charles was preparing a water hose that had been attached to a pump above a trough at the side of the yard. Alex ran to the pump to assist Sir Vernon in his rather clumsy attempts to get the water flowing.

"That's it," called Charles, as water began spouting from the hose. "Watch yourself, Horrocks," he called to the butler as the pressure grew and the water sprang up to the height of the eaves.

The driver ceased carrying buckets and went to help Charles steady the hose. It was immensely reassuring to see the arc of water reach the flames. The evacuation of the horses from the wing of the stables affected by the fire continued throughout. Jarvis and Edwin, who limped heavily, his cane abandoned, made quick work of leading the Earl's elegant thoroughbreds across the cobbles to the wing occupied by the estate's working horses.

"It's all right, Duchess," said Jarvis soothingly to a glossy black mare he was leading by the bridle. Her ears flicked, but otherwise she remained calm. "You'll be all right. Don't you worry." Considering the flames, the shouting, and the howling polar wind, the creature's composure was impressive.

Felicity pulled her woollen coat more tightly across her. As Edwin recrossed the yard empty-handed, she ventured onto the cobbles with the intention of offering her help with the horses. She was intercepted by Charles, his dinner jacket wet and his hair all over the place. He'd been relieved by Horrocks in handling the hose's nozzle alongside the driver.

"Don't come any closer, Cici." Charles spoke sternly, holding up his hands, his palms red and raw-looking from controlling the hose. His eyes shone with the golden light of the flames, which no longer leapt as high. "Looks like we've got it under control, but the situation's still dangerous."

Felicity retreated, the heels of her shoes sinking back into the gravel. "I was only going to offer my help with the horses."

"Best leave it to the men." There was a tone of selfless gallantry to Charles' words that was reassuring. Still, it tugged at something uncomfortable within Felicity.

Charles trotted away to offer his own assistance to Edwin. Under the constant barrage of water, the flames were dying. The orange light cast onto the pines of the forest beyond the stables grew dim. Felicity was indeed the only woman to attend the fire. Had it been foolish to dash outside thinking she might help? She hugged herself as she lingered at the edge of the cobbled yard, the wind not easing up for a moment.

"Whoever set those fireworks off is a blasted nuisance." Leonard was still muttering as he strode past Felicity towards the stables, his beloved hound presumably locked up anew in the main house. He headed for the water pump, where Alex and the footman were working hard to maintain a steady supply to the hose. Sir Vernon had stepped back from the water trough. He wavered a little as he stood with his hands on his hips, watching the flames continue to subside.

Still keen to help, Felicity considered ascending to the gardens beyond the paved terrace to inspect the fireworks — which still occasionally popped above but had nearly petered out — for any hint to indicate who set them off. As she turned, blinking into the wind to ascertain the best route, she saw Ariadne making a hasty approach from the house.

"What happened?" asked Ariadne breathlessly as she stopped beside Felicity, a beautiful white fur coat draped over her shoulders.

"A firework must have landed on the roof," said Felicity, for there seemed no way to access the eaves without a ladder.

"But who set the fireworks off?"

Felicity looked at the girl. "That's something we don't yet know."

Ariadne gasped, her eyes opening wide.

Leonard hadn't reached the water pump. He'd stopped alone between the pump and the hose. He was bent over, a hand on his shoulder. Then he went down on one knee.

"Leonard!" Ariadne flew to him. Felicity quickly followed, her feet sliding on the cobbles. Alex looked up from the pump.

Ariadne fell to her knees and cradled Leonard as he sank to the ground. He groaned. His eyelids fluttered, then closed.

Alerted by Alex, who remained at the pump, Sir Vernon hurried in Leonard's direction.

"Oh, no. No!" Ariadne lifted her hand. It was smeared with a dark liquid.

Felicity dropped to the freezing cobbles beside Leonard and Ariadne. In the light of the electric lamps on the stable walls and the dim glow of the receding flames, it was hard to see clearly, but as the dark stain spread from under the shoulder of Leonard's dinner jacket and onto his white shirt placket, Felicity's throat tightened with panic.

"Leonard!" Sir Vernon tumbled to his knees at Leonard's side. "What the deuce is wrong with you?"

Felicity span round. Everyone present was still fully engaged in their fire-fighting tasks. The flames having almost died out, the trees beyond the stables had returned to blackness. Who had done this? Barely thinking, Felicity rose and began running, the ice on the cobbles no match for the urgency of the situation. Charles blinked as Felicity flew past him, a slightly stunned white-and-brown gelding attached to a lead rope in his hand.

Alex backed off from the pump. "Felicity!"

Felicity kept running, her footsteps echoing as she entered the stable block. Edwin emerged from a bay containing two horses. "Felicity," he said, his face growing dark. "What is it?"

"He's been shot," said Felicity, gasping for breath. "Mr McQueen's been shot."

Chapter Twenty-Two

Tick. Tock. Tick. Tock.

The porcelain clock on the white marble mantelpiece of Grimstow House's elegant South Drawing Room had never ticked so loudly nor so slowly. The lights in the chandeliers flickered, but this was no longer a primary concern. On one of the beige sofas, atop blankets spread to protect the furniture, lay Lord Archibald. While his colour looked better, he was still unresponsive, although the precaution had been taken to lock him in the room when everyone went to help with the fire. There was no way he could have fired the shot that hit Leonard, who lay on the matching sofa opposite.

Leonard had passed out before being put on a stretcher at the stables. Upon being carried into the drawing room, he'd awoken to look down at his stained shirt, muttered *Oh dear*, and passed out again. Both men were under the care of Edwin, who was seated on a chair that had been drawn up next to Leonard.

With his brow creased deeply from concentration and worry, the doctor cleaned and dressed the gunshot in the businessman's shoulder. Miss Fairchild dutifully played the role of nurse assistant, handing Edwin items from his medical bag and fresh linens brought by the housekeeper, who remained composed but looked extremely shaken, watching with concern as Edwin tended to Leonard. Miss Fairchild sobbed quietly as she worked, her shoulders shaking and the occasional tear making it onto her cheek before being wiped away with trembling fingers.

She'd clearly not expected the evening to develop the way it had. No one had.

Finishing his work with Leonard's dressing, Edwin straightened. "If we can get him to the hospital first thing in the morning, Mr McQueen will live."

"The two of them are incredibly lucky you're here, Ed." Charles was at the mantelpiece. He'd lit a pipe but was chewing it more than smoking it. "Incredibly lucky." In his belt, Charles had added a leather holster in which a handgun sat. It looked incongruous against the trousers of his dinner suit, with their satin strip down the side, but no one — not even Felicity — had attempted to stop Charles from nominating himself the guard on duty in the drawing room, the male domestics still being occupied with matters at the stables after the fire.

Charles hadn't had yet to brandish his weapon, but it was almost certainly thanks to him that the South Drawing Room remained a restful space. Having been refused entry by Charles, Sir Vernon had taken himself off for a stiff drink, although no one had seen Rex or the Bourgoyne twins since before the fireworks went off.

Felicity observed the proceedings from the side of the room. Despite the calmness and quiet, her mind was exploding with ideas and possibilities. The attack on Leonard changed everything.

Beside her stood Alex, his hair wet and dishevelled from his efforts with the water pump. The deep lines in his brow told Felicity he was perhaps less intrigued by the new developments and more concerned about them.

Felicity pinched her own eyebrows together to mirror Alex's graveness, but she couldn't stop her mind whirring on.

Ignoring Charles' praise, Edwin looked up at Felicity. "I'll have Horrocks confirm it, but there's no doubt those fireworks were set deliberately. I understand the remnants of a rocket were found in the gutter of the stable roof, although with all that wind, it was likely more down to chance than planning." Edwin looked at Leonard's motionless form. "The ruse worked, nevertheless."

"The ruse?" enquired Felicity, keen to understand Edwin's thinking.

"To draw Leonard outdoors. To take a shot at him. To kill him, I suppose." Edwin rubbed his freckled brow. "By heavens. I suppose that means..."

Edwin didn't have to say it. It was chillingly obvious to everyone. The bullet in Leonard's shoulder had been no accident. That meant the shot that did away with Helen was likely also a deliberate act. There was a murderer on the loose.

Who would want both Helen and her fiancé dead, and why?

"Felicity." Edwin looked up at her, imploringly. "If there's anything you can do..."

"Well, I..." Felicity fingered the beads at the neck of her dress. She remained quite desperate to help, but how? She'd done nothing to prevent or solve Helen's death and had been powerless to stop Leonard from almost being killed.

Alex continued to look grave. Charles puffed his pipe, his alert, curious eyes on Felicity. Their conversation in the gun room threatened to re-enter her thoughts, but she tamped it down. Now was not the time for personal discomfort. She cleared her throat. "The events of this evening will make the papers, you understand."

Edwin's shoulders slumped further. "I had considered it."

Miss Fairchild wept. The housekeeper promptly offered a handkerchief, which Miss Fairchild accepted.

"We'll write things up in the most respectful way possible," offered Felicity.

Alex nodded in agreement. "We certainly shall."

Edwin sighed deeply. Felicity could tell her offer wasn't enough.

"For pity's sake." Charles flung down his pipe. "Who's to say any of us will be alive long enough to read another newspaper?"

Edwin widened his eyes at his friend. "While I appreciate your concern, I'll have you remember we're among the afflicted."

Charles frowned apologetically at the two unconscious men occupying the sofas. "Sorry, old chap. My emotions got the better of me. But it's clear there's a murderer amongst us, isn't it?" His appeal to Edwin went unanswered. He turned to Felicity. "Isn't it?" Charles winced, as though he couldn't quite believe he'd just asked her opinion. The nuances of her relationship with Charles didn't matter, however. Not at that precise moment.

"The shot that did for Helen might have been accidental," said Felicity carefully, still fingering her dress's neckline. "But the bullet in Mr McQueen's shoulder must have been the work of someone wishing to do harm. It, therefore, colours our interpretation of Helen's demise. Indeed, it rather implies there's someone with murderous intentions amongst us."

Edwin nodded grimly. "I doubt the police will arrive before morning. I suppose Charles has a point. Who's to say what will happen in the intervening hours?"

It was clear to Felicity what she must do. "If I can identify that person," she said, "and prevent him or her from doing further harm, then I will do just that."

Alex widened his eyes slightly at Felicity.

It was a bold commitment. Yet it felt right.

Charles exhaled with force. "It's dangerous."

It was. And there was the letter Felicity had received in her coat pocket to consider as well. "Helen was my cousin," said Felicity in answer to Charles. "Edwin is my cousin. If I can help them, then I will."

"And I will assist Lady Felicity however I can," added Alex, although the set of his jaw showed he wasn't entirely at ease with the situation. Then again, neither was Felicity, although she felt better knowing Alex would be at her side.

There came a knock at the drawing room door. The door

opened slowly to reveal Sir Vernon. He was once again wearing his monocle, although it had a rather nasty crack in it.

Charles stiffened and put a hand on the gun at his hip. Felicity wasn't worried. She knew for certain Sir Vernon hadn't pulled the trigger on Leonard.

"I'm frightfully sorry to bother you chaps, but the young lady and I are quite desperate for news about Leonard. Will he live?" Sir Vernon opened the door further to reveal Ariadne, her eyes puffy and pink from crying. Ariadne was also innocent of firing on the businessman.

The net was narrowing.

Faintly, Jambo could be heard howling in despair at being locked away in some distant room, away from his master. Charles scrutinised the two interlopers, his hand hovering by the holster at his waist. "We asked not to be disturbed," he said.

Edwin stood up, a hand raised in a signal for Sir Vernon and Ariadne to keep their distance. "Under no circumstances may you touch Mr McQueen. His condition is extremely delicate, but I can confirm he will survive his wound, if he's given the proper care and attention."

Charles continued to watch Sir Vernon and Ariadne as they gingerly entered the drawing room. Ariadne swallowed hard as she looked from Archibald to Leonard.

"C-can I approach him?" asked Sir Vernon. Edwin nodded. Sir Vernon went to Leonard's side and lowered himself to his knees beside the sofa. He hovered his still-bandaged hand over Leonard, then withdrew it, mindful that he ought not to touch his friend. Leonard groaned weakly but did not open his eyes.

Ariadne kept her distance, her fingers knitted together, her eyes darting between the two unconscious men. Then the tears came.

Felicity stepped forward and put a hand on the girl's shoulder. "Shall we step outside for a moment?" she said gently.

Alex watched closely as Felicity went to the drawing room

door with Ariadne. Felicity gave Alex a look of reassurance before exiting the room.

A cold draught swept along the stone corridor as the lights outside the South Drawing Room flickered. Ariadne sniffed back tears, her face a grimace. "It's my fault. It's all my fault."

"Hush now." Felicity squeezed Ariadne's shoulder. There was no point discussing matters with the girl if she was too upset to gather her thoughts. "I believe we both want to do our best to help your brother, step-brother, and Mr McQueen, do we not?"

Ariadne sniffed and nodded, blinking her periwinkle-blue eyes. "Of course."

"Then we must hold things together. We must be strong. It won't be long till the police get here." Felicity, of course, didn't know if the stablehand had reached the village and had no clue when the ice would thaw. "We should do our best to keep things calm till then."

"I want to help. I've been an absolute menace, I see that now." Ariadne wrung her hands. "Honestly, I want to help."

Felicity smiled sadly. "I know you do. And I know you can be strong." She hesitated before continuing. "Ariadne, there's something I need to ask you. Can you be honest with me? It doesn't matter what your answer is. I just need the truth."

Ariadne nodded earnestly, her pale, frizzy hair bouncing. "Please. Ask me anything."

Felicity withdrew the typewritten note from her coat. "Did you put this in my pocket?"

Ariadne took the paper and read it. Her unwrinkled brow creased suddenly. "No." She shook her head earnestly. "No, I didn't write this. I can prove it, if you like." She handed the note back to Felicity. "My typewriter has a little mark it makes on the tail of the Y, and this one doesn't. There is, however, a mark next to the capital O, which my typewriter does not make."

Felicity was impressed by the girl's attention to detail, although it wasn't the answer she'd hoped for. It would have been much simpler and safer if Ariadne had placed the letter in Felicity's pocket not long after her arrival at Grimstow House. "I believe you," said Felicity gently, hiding her disappointment. "That's all I wanted to know."

"Who did, do you think?" asked Ariadne. Her voice trembled.

"You don't need to worry about that," said Felicity soothingly, although she felt anything but soothed herself.

Ariadne gave a little gasp. "Wait. Archie's innocent, isn't he? He didn't shoot Leonard, so he didn't shoot Helen. That's right, isn't it?" Her eyes sparkled with hope. "He was unconscious on the sofa so can't have gone to the stables."

Felicity wasn't yet ready to make pronouncements. There were people to whom she needed to speak — the first step would be a thorough discussion with Alex — but Ariadne was thinking along the same lines as Felicity. "You need to be strong for your brother, step-brother, and for Mr McQueen," she urged.

The creases returned to Ariadne's brow. "I know that Debenham fellow was angry at Leonard, but he wouldn't have done for Helen, would he?" Ariadne was smart. Perhaps too smart.

"You need to keep yourself safe," urged Felicity. Not wanting to create panic, she wouldn't say it aloud, but without a clear suspect and motive, it was hard to say what might happen next.

Footsteps were approaching along the corridor.

Ariadne wiped at her eyes and nodded. "If Edwin doesn't need my help in the drawing room, I shall return to the attic, as Archie instructed."

"Just what the blazes is going on?" Rex's voice boomed along the corridor as he approached, his fists balled at his sides.

"Go back inside," said Felicity gently to Ariadne, but the girl froze in fear at the drawing room door.

Rex's eyes were wild with anger, and his gaze was fixed on Felicity. "I want answers, and I want them now."

Chapter Twenty-Three

Felicity swallowed as she stepped forward to meet Rex, positioning herself between him and Ariadne. Rex's strong emotional attachment to Helen gave him a motive to harm Leonard, whom he perceived as not having done enough to protect Felicity's cousin, but he wouldn't have harmed Helen. Did that mean Rex couldn't be suspected of either shooting?

In any case, Felicity didn't want Rex exploding into the drawing room. Edwin had been through more than enough.

"Mr Debenham," she said coolly, lifting her chin to denote a confidence she didn't necessarily feel.

Rex stopped close to Felicity. A little too close. "First the fireworks." He jabbed his finger at her as if it were her fault. "Then someone brought that blasted hound back to the house. Practically put it next door to my room." So Rex had taken himself to his room to calm down. If true, Felicity was impressed. "I could hear it barking the whole ruddy—"

Rex broke off as the door to the drawing room opened quietly.

Alex stepped calmly into the corridor. "Lady Felicity," he said with a nod in Felicity's direction. "Mr Debenham." His greeting for Rex was polite enough.

Felicity suppressed a relieved smile. She turned to Ariadne. "Go back inside the drawing room for a moment," she said softly. "I shall join you presently."

"Hang on just a minute." Rex addressed Ariadne, reaching out to catch her arm, but in slipping back into the drawing room, Ariadne evaded his grasp, leaving Felicity and Alex between Rex and the door.

The sportsman looked from Felicity to Alex. He shook from the effort to control himself. "Will one of you just tell me what the deuce is going on?" he hissed.

Alex folded his arms. "Rather a lot," he said.

"Do you know about the fire?" asked Felicity.

Rex frowned. "What fire?"

"Someone set off the fireworks, which caused a fire at the stables," said Felicity. "Mr McQueen was among those who attended to assist with extinguishing the flames. While at the stables, he took a bullet in the shoulder."

"What? Leonard's been shot?" Rex let out an odd little laugh. "Is the blighter dead?"

"No," said Alex firmly. "He's not."

The sportsman ran a hand over his hair. "Lord Archibald woke up then, did he? You know, as soon as I recognised him, I took myself away. I had to. It was that or strangle the beggar with my bare hands." A glimmer of murderous revenge danced in Rex's eyes. Considering his earlier behaviour, his account of his own self-control was hard to trust. Yet Felicity had indeed advised him to contain his emotions, for both Helen's sake and his own.

"Lord Archibald appears not to have woken up," said Felicity. "The precaution was also taken to lock him in the South Drawing Room when everyone went to attend to the fire."

Rex shook his head. "Are you certain?"

"Quite certain," confirmed Felicity.

Rex rubbed his chin, the fire in his eyes weakening. "Upon my soul. Who shot the blighter, then?"

"That's what we're rather keen to find out." Felicity's manner remained serene despite her heart beginning to bang in her chest. Who, indeed?

The lights in the corridor flickered. Alex peered at the sportsman from under lowered eyebrows.

"Don't look at me." Rex's tone was confidently dismissive.

"You have an alibi, do you, Mr Debenham?" asked Felicity.

A smile tickled Rex's mouth. He fixed his eyes on the floor before his shoes. "You know, I thought about doing away with Leonard. Thought about it more than once, actually. In the end, I never felt the need. Helen would have left him, eventually. It was only a matter of time." He shrugged and looked up. "And now she's no longer here, what do I stand to gain? Doing away with Leonard wouldn't bring my Helen back. Although I can't say news of his injury displeases me." Learning of Leonard's misfortune indeed seemed to have tamed Rex's mood.

"We have no reason to disbelieve you, Mr Debenham," said Felicity. "But it would help to know where you were between Lord Archibald being brought back to the house and now."

Rex narrowed his eyes. "It may not seem like it, but I am aware of what a nuisance I can be when I get carried away. I took our earlier discussion in the stables to heart, Lady Felicity, and I went to my room to calm down. I even ignored the fireworks. Found a book to read. The biography of Imperial Tiara. A fantastic race horse. Gripping stuff."

Felicity and Alex exchanged glances.

Rex went on. "But then someone brought that blasted dog along, and well, I couldn't stand all the howling and barking. So I went and found Clem. I owed her an apology, just as you said, Lady Felicity," he added cloyingly.

Felicity raised her eyebrows. Was Rex mocking her?

The sportsman continued. "And would you believe it, I found her on her own. For once that harpy of a sister didn't have her claws in her."

"Where did you find Clemency?" asked Felicity.

Rex let out a deep sigh. He leaned a shoulder against the

stone wall of the corridor. "On the landing near the twins' room. We sat, and we talked. Oh, she got upset. Of course she did. I did my best to explain things. She's a wonderful girl. Rather naïve in some ways, I suppose. When you have feelings for someone…" He looked from Felicity to Alex. "Real feelings. You can't hide it away from the world." Rex looked at Felicity almost tenderly. Had Helen indeed known true love with Rex? It was something everyone hoped to experience.

"If I understand correctly, Mr Debenham," said Felicity, "Miss Clemency Bourgoyne will confirm that you weren't at the stables when Leonard was shot."

"Look." Rex stood up straight and folded his arms. "I already said I didn't do it. I may be many things, but I'm not a liar. Had Clemency asked me outright at any point if there was anything between Helen and I, I would have told her."

"Where's Miss Bourgoyne now?" asked Alex, adding his weight to the effort to keep Rex on track.

"That's just it." The sportsman allowed his hands to clap to his sides. "That blasted sister of hers came storming out of their room. Looked as pale as a ghost, she did. Said they were leaving. Insisted on taking Clem with her."

Felicity widened her eyes at Alex. He looked as alarmed as she felt. The Model T skidding over ice and crumpling against a dry stone wall was the last thing anyone needed. "Did Patience say why they needed to depart so suddenly?" asked Felicity.

Rex's laugh was bitter. "Oh, there's no reasoning with that one. Patience's mind was made up, and she wouldn't say anything further on the matter. She looked rather queer. Much paler than usual, and her hands were shaking, but for once she didn't seem angered by my mere presence. She took her sister, and off they went to collect their belongings. I offered to help, but Patience wouldn't have it. Clem didn't want to go, of course. As long as she lives, she'll never stand up to her sister of hers."

"How long ago did they leave?" pressed Alex.

Rex blew out his cheeks. "Not long before I came upon Lady Felicity and Ariadne. Not long ago at all."

Felicity looked at Alex. "We need to stop them."

Alex nodded, and they set off along the corridor in the direction of the entrance hall.

"Don't waste your time," called Rex. "Patience is practically barmy. Got some funny beliefs, that one. You can't reason with the woman."

Felicity looked back at Rex. "I'd advise you to return to your room, Mr Debenham, and await the police."

Rex held up his hands. "I'm on my best behaviour, your ladyship."

The lights flickered as Felicity and Alex hurried along the cool stone corridor, their footsteps echoing.

"Did Ariadne write the note?" asked Alex, barely turning to look at Felicity.

"No," said Felicity as she hesitated at a junction, unconvinced they were going in the correct direction for the entrance hall.

Alex drew to a stop, his fists on his hips, his expression grim. "I feared as much."

The threatening note remained in the pocket of the brown woollen coat Felicity still had on. She couldn't spare it too much thought. "We've got to stop the twins." Felicity decided which corridor to follow next and promptly set off. "We've got to get to the garage."

Alex kept pace beside her as they hurried along, their footsteps suddenly muffled by carpet underfoot. "I know you want to help your cousin," said Alex, "but there are other ways to go about things. There's no need for you to solve this before the police get here."

Again, this wasn't something Felicity could give space to in her mind at that point in time. "If we take Rex at his word, then

Clemency is an innocent in all this. If those girls go out on the road, there's sure to be an accident."

Alex shook his head, confused. "Are you saying Patience isn't innocent? If it was Rex with a bullet in his shoulder, I'd understand it. But why would Patience shoot Leonard? And do you really think she'd shoot Helen? They were friends, were they not?"

Usually, Felicity would pounce on the opportunity to discuss theories with Alex — and they'd both been witness to what Patience had said to Leonard about his father's hand in the loss of the Bourgoyne fortune — but now wasn't the time. "We just have to stop them."

"Lady Felicity." The butler's voice rang out along the corridor.

Felicity stopped and turned, as did Alex. The Ridgeback's howling was faintly audible. The lights in the corridor dimmed momentarily.

"What is it, Mr Horrocks?" Felicity spoke a little more brusquely than was her habit. The pressure of the situation was getting to her, and she didn't like it.

The greying butler approached, breathing hard. "My apologies, Lady Felicity, for hailing you in such an uncouth manner. There's something I was hoping to discuss with you. To show you, in fact. I was hoping for your advice on the matter. It's just that I'd rather not add any more burden to Doctor Quick unless absolutely necessary."

"Can the matter wait?" asked Felicity.

"It's my duty to take action, your ladyship. If you've not the time to be consulted, then I shall proceed to Doctor Quick and inform him of the matter."

Felicity sighed despairingly. She was torn. She wanted nothing more than to help Edwin, but the twins' predicament was potentially deadly.

A solution stood right before her.

"Will you find the twins?" Felicity asked Alex, although she already felt certain of the answer. With the note in her pocket unresolved, and his duty to Felicity's brother if nothing else, Alex would be loath to leave Felicity's side.

Hesitating for a moment, Alex glanced at the butler. Then he nodded. "I'll stop them." Felicity bit her lip as she watched Alex set off in the direction the butler indicated as the quickest exit towards the garage.

"The twins, your ladyship?" enquired the butler as Alex disappeared down an adjoining corridor. The wind buffeted a nearby window that gave onto the blackness of the freezing night beyond.

Felicity pulled her coat more tightly across herself. "We understand the Bourgoyne sisters are attempting to leave in their motor."

The butler's brow wrinkled. "I hope you excuse my saying this, your ladyship, but after the losses suffered in the war, one would imagine people to have an increased perception of the value of their lives."

Normally, Felicity would have indulged the observation, for the butler made a valid point. Her goal now, however, was to attend to the business from which the butler wanted to save Edwin and to rejoin Alex as quickly as possible.

As Felicity opened her mouth to speak, the memory of Charles' talk of marriage flew back to her and made her stomach tighten. She pushed the thought violently aside. "Please, Mr Horrocks," said Felicity, lifting her chin. "Take me forthwith to whatever it is I must see. There isn't time to dawdle."

Chapter Twenty-Four

On the landing of Grimstow House's first floor, the wind howled at a row of narrow leaded windows, like an angry spirit trying to gain entry. An elegant display of dried flowers in a stylish terracotta vase moved slightly in the cold air the windows couldn't fully exclude. Felicity and Horrocks had ascended several flights of stairs to arrive on the landing, and her pinching shoes were making her feet throb.

"My apologies, your ladyship," said Horrocks, apparently aware of Felicity's discomfort as he indicated the corridor along which they were to proceed. "Normally, we might have used the lift, but in such wind, I'm afraid the electrics cannot be trusted."

Felicity smiled stoically in recognition of the butler's apology. Had she made the right choice? She remained desperate to help her surviving cousin, but what would Alex do if he arrived at the garage to find the Model T already gone? Surely, he wasn't foolish enough to give chase.

Ignoring the pain in her feet, Felicity hurried along the corridor with the butler. Taking action was never the difficult thing. Determining the correct action to take was the challenge.

"Here we are, your ladyship." Horrocks took a large bunch of keys from his pocket, effortlessly found the correct one, and unlocked the door before which they had stopped. He stood aside to allow Felicity to pass into the room.

Electric ceiling lights in shimmering glass settings snapped on to reveal an elegant contemporary bedroom with a nod to medieval styling, much in alignment with the rest of the residence's decoration. Thick, embroidered fabric reminiscent of ancient tapestries draped from a large canopy bed. A chaise longue and a chair before the dressing table were also sumptuously upholstered in shades of gold and blue.

The butler went to a section of the wall hidden under the fall of a set of heavy gold-trimmed curtains that extended across the windows. Sweeping aside the curtain, he revealed a small safe built into the panelling. Using a key to unlock it, Horrocks put the tip of his finger underneath the thick metal door and pulled it open. "I've done my best not to disturb any fingerprints that might be present, your ladyship," said Horrocks as he stepped aside to allow Felicity to look.

Within the safe was a pile of gold and silver chains with settings that clasped precious stones sparkling in a rainbow of colours. It was jewellery, but it was difficult to determine one piece from another. A number of items had been slung in a pile. "I'm afraid I'm not entirely sure what I'm looking at," said Felicity.

The butler cleared his throat. "It's about this safe that I was hoping for your advice ahead of approaching Doctor Quick, your ladyship."

"How might I advise?" asked Felicity, hoping the butler would soon come to his point.

Picking up on the undercurrent of impatience in Felicity's tone, the butler stood up straighter. "My apologies, your ladyship. I've not explained things well. The Earl keeps a portion of the late countess' jewels here in this safe. After the Bourgoyne twins reported the theft of their belongings, we checked this safe's contents. The jewellery had indeed been taken. Yet now… Well, your ladyship." The butler blinked at the safe, as if unsure whether to trust his eyes. "What was stolen appears now to have been returned."

Felicity drew her head back slightly. The situation was baffling. How might the theft and subsequent reappearance of the late countess' jewels have anything to do with Helen's demise and the attempt on Leonard's life?

She glanced around the room. Nothing appeared out of place. "How were you made aware of the jewellery's return?"

"I was passing along this corridor when I noticed the door to the room had been left ajar. I was most concerned, your ladyship, as I was certain I'd locked the room after the discovery of the theft. But then I said to myself, with so much going on, perhaps I'd become forgetful." The butler looked pained, his forehead deeply creased. "Please forgive me for speaking so frankly, your ladyship."

Felicity regretted her curtness with the butler. He was, like everyone, doing his best to handle a distinctly awful situation. "Please, Mr Horrocks. I'm glad you're sharing this with me so that we might spare my cousin the trouble. Do continue."

The butler nodded. "Ahead of relocking the room, I opened the door to check that all was well, especially considering the earlier theft. That's when I saw the curtains were out of place. They're usually lined up precisely with the panelling. A servant here at Grimstow House would never leave the curtains in such a state. We keep everything precisely as the Earl likes it. So I took a closer look, and there it was. The door to the safe was open, and there were the jewels, returned in the same pile we see them now. I haven't touched them. I couldn't quite believe my eyes, your ladyship. I still cannot."

"When did you discover the jewels had been returned?"

"Just before I came to find you, your ladyship."

"Who else has a key to the safe?"

"The Earl keeps a key with him. The only other key is in my possession. Your ladyship, this safe is extremely secure. It takes some level of skill to get into such a contraption, if one can speak of skill in such wrongdoing."

Felicity considered matters for a moment. "Were the jewels stolen from and returned to the safe within the course of the evening?"

"I would say so, your ladyship. This room is checked daily. There was nothing wrong here when I passed by earlier in the afternoon."

Felicity returned to a thoughtful silence. She tapped a gloved finger to her lips as she again looked around the room, more slowly this time. If the butler's testimony could be taken at face value — and Felicity had no reason to believe it could not — then it wasn't only a question of who stole and returned the jewels. Why risk the theft, only to return the stolen items? And what did this have to do with the shootings?

"I hope you understand why I wanted to discuss matters with you first, your ladyship. I would like to avoid further troubling Doctor Quick. He is the most senior family member on site — who is conscious, that is. Not only has Doctor Quick's own sister very sadly passed this evening, but the doctor has two patients to which to attend. None of it's pleasant, your ladyship."

"I wholeheartedly agree," said Felicity. Besides herself and Alex, Horrocks seemed to be the only member of the household who'd given Edwin's suffering a second thought. "My cousin's having an awfully rotten time of it."

Felicity continued to gaze around the room as she considered what the best approach with Edwin would be. Then she noticed something. The blended dark blue tones of the carpet combined with the occasional flickering of the lights made it difficult to spot at first. "Is that mud on the floor, Mr Horrocks?"

The butler's gaze snapped in the direction Felicity was looking. "My apologies, your ladyship. Yes, it is." The muddy scuff mark lay on the route between the door and the safe in the wall. It wouldn't have been brought in by the butler, for whom cleanliness was second nature, and Felicity had been nowhere on muddy ground.

The soles of Rex's shoes had been soiled when he knelt over Helen's body, likely from chasing the still-unidentified woman outside. That would mean the woman likely had dirty shoes as well. Since the incident in the morning room, however, many people had been outside with the opportunity to muddy their feet. In the fire's chaos at the stables, anyone might have stepped onto the rough ground beyond the gravel and cobbles. There was also whoever had set off the fireworks to consider.

A central puzzle remained. Why steal the jewellery and then return it? It simply didn't make sense.

"Forgive me, your ladyship," continued Horrocks. "I'll send a maid to clean it up right away."

"No need to apologise, Mr Horrocks," replied Felicity. "I'm grateful you informed me about the return of the jewels to the safe. You were right to take this approach. I'll share the information with my cousin when the time is right."

"Very good, your ladyship."

"Is there perhaps another secure location for the Earl's precious items? It's clear there's someone among us capable of opening this safe."

"That's an extremely good point, your ladyship. I shall take the proper precautions."

Felicity had a thousand questions in need of answers. "Might a member of staff be able to check if the jewels taken from Helen's necklaces have also been returned?"

The butler's brow creased. "I should imagine it's safe to assume they have been. Wouldn't you say, your ladyship?" Horrocks' resistance to the suggestion was unexpected, yet also understandable. To further disturb Helen where she lay seemed improper. After all, the police were yet to arrive.

Felicity nodded. "Very well," she said. It wasn't as if there weren't other avenues to examine, and it was high time for Felicity to catch up with Alex and the twins, although there remained yet another pressing matter. "May I ask, might you know of any typewriters in the house besides the one used by Lady Ariadne?" If Ariadne hadn't written the note Felicity had found in her pocket, then it was highly possible the note had been the work of whoever was behind the chaos at Grimstow House.

"When the Earl's here, his secretary brings a typewriter along, but besides Lady Ariadne's contraption, there's not a typewriter kept here at Grimstow House, your ladyship. I do, however, believe that one of the Misses Bourgoyne brought one with her for the stay. Miss Patience Bourgoyne mentioned that she's working on a book."

Felicity's stomach tightened. Patience had been scornful towards Felicity from the start of the evening, had she not? Rising above the animosity, Felicity had convinced herself Patience was scornful of everyone, but perhaps that wasn't the case. Perhaps Patience had a specific reason to be upset about Felicity's presence at the disastrous party. If all had gone to plan, Alex was now alone with Patience and her sister.

"I could take you to the Bourgoynes' room, if you'd like, your ladyship? It's at the end of the wing, on this floor. Under the circumstances, it would be acceptable to requisition such a tool for your important newspaper work."

"That's kind of you, Mr Horrocks, but perhaps later," said Felicity evasively, for her dedication to journalism was, of course, not the reason behind her interest in the typewriter. There was also no further time to be lost. "I need to rejoin Mr Cooper as quickly as possible. Would you be kind enough to direct me to the garage?"

"Of course, your ladyship."

Moving swiftly, Felicity went with Horrocks back downstairs. She did her best to tamp down her concerns for Alex's safety, but she couldn't help shifting the puzzle pieces around in her mind. Helen had suspected Patience of sending the anonymous letters, had she not? Perhaps Patience had meant Helen harm. Helen had certainly said an unkind thing or two over dinner, particularly regarding the twins' absence of means. Was theft part of Patience's motive? If so, then the question remained. Why return the jewels? And how would doing away with Leonard resolve any of the Bourgoynes' issues?

"Cici! Heavens. There you are." Charles raced up the staircase towards Felicity and the butler.

Felicity stopped dead. A knot of dread tightened in her stomach. "Charlie, what is it? What's wrong?" Had something happened to Alex?

The butler stood aside as Charles took the stairs two at a time to reach Felicity. He stopped before her, his cheeks red and his hair mussed, his hand gripping the bannister. "I've been racing around, looking everywhere for you. Edwin sent me. Something extraordinary has happened. Quite extraordinary. You must come and see at once. You simply won't believe it."

Chapter Twenty-Five

The choice between Alex and Edwin was agonising but had to be made quickly. Desperately hoping Alex would forgive her, Felicity requested that Horrocks locate Alex and the Bourgoyne twins and do his best to ensure no one was endangered.

"Right away, your ladyship," confirmed the butler, and they set off in different directions, Horrocks towards the garage while Felicity followed Charles, the wind still howling viciously at the corridor windows and the flickering of the lights now so commonplace as to be almost normal.

"It's the most extraordinary thing," continued Charles somewhat excitedly as they hurried towards the South Drawing Room, the awkward scene between them in the gun room seemingly at the back of his mind. Felicity hoped for a quick resolution to whatever wonder lay ahead, so that she might rejoin Alex, as she'd promised she would.

Arriving outside the drawing room door, a voice not yet heard that evening came muffled from the other side. "And that's really everything I can tell you." The voice had a North American twang to it.

Stepping into the room, Felicity was met with a strange,

subdued atmosphere. Most striking was that the two previously unconscious men on the sofas both were now awake. Leonard had barely changed position and seemed rather drowsy, his eyelids low as Sir Vernon loomed protectively over him, his bandaged hand resting on the back of the beige sofa. Opposite, Lord Archibald was sitting upright, his periwinkle-blue eyes shining. Ariadne was perched on the sofa next to him, her gaze locked on her brother and her expression full of tearful wonder. Whatever interest the girl had in her step-sister's fiancé, her love for her sibling outweighed it.

His freckled brow deeply furrowed, Edwin leaned stiffly on his cane, his eyes on Archibald. Miss Fairchild, who stood nearby, looked as though she had seen several ghosts. The housekeeper and the footman stood watchfully at the side of the room and didn't look much happier. Charles resumed his position next to the porcelain clock on the white marble mantelpiece. The wind rattled the windows beyond the thick curtains.

Tick. Tock. Tick. Tock.

Had Felicity's ears played a trick on her? Where was the man with the American accent? "You wanted to see me, cousin?"

Edwin looked grimly at Felicity. "None of us imagined this evening could become any more abnormal, but this is something I felt you had to witness. May I introduce you to the Honourable Anthony Carrington?"

Felicity followed Edwin's gaze, landing on the blue-eyed man sitting upright on his sofa. "How do you do?" he said with a North American lilt.

Felicity's mouth gaped briefly. "You're… You're not Lord Archibald?"

The blue-eyed man laughed a little. "I'm not." He held his ribs before falling into a fit of coughing.

"Go easy, Tony," said Ariadne, putting a hand on the man's back.

As his coughing subsided, the man added. "Although I understand the confusion, your ladyship."

Felicity looked from Ariadne to Edwin, then back to the Honourable Anthony Carrington. "You're Lord Archibald's twin." Felicity was apparently the last person in the room to grasp it. "You look utterly alike," she said, feeling immediately foolish for stating what was obvious.

"I'm just so pleased you're back," said Ariadne, who couldn't take her eyes off her brother. "Archie will be, too."

Sir Vernon shook his head, his cracked monocle still in place. "The likeness is confoundingly uncanny."

The Honourable Anthony Carrington grinned, a hand still at his ribs. "We are indeed that kind of twin." Realising he was the only person in the room to find the situation at all amusing, he straightened his expression. "I gather my brother isn't here right now," he continued with his American twang. "And it seems my arrival, aside from it being rather a disaster personally, has come at a terrible time for the household. My new step-brother Edwin was just informing me that I had a step-sister who I never got to meet."

Edwin nodded stiffly. "Mr Carrington—"

"Please. Call me Tony. We're brothers, aren't we? On top of everything that's happened, let's not start things off by putting up unnecessary walls of politeness between us."

Edwin looked from Tony to Felicity, blinking nervously. Was the appearance of Archibald's twin more than he could bear? "T-Tony was telling us how he'd been in Canada until very recently. He arrived in Devon earlier today."

"We never imagined we'd see you again." A tear escaped Ariadne's eye as she rested her temple on her brother's shoulder. "You went to war and never came back."

Felicity remembered the portraits she'd seen of what she'd assumed to be Archibald at various stages throughout his military career. If she'd looked closely enough, might she have realised the portraits depicted identical brothers?

"I feel rotten about that, Ari," said Tony sheepishly. "Really, I do. That's why I came back. I was thinking about you and Archie the whole time. I absolutely was. I suppose it was piggish of me that I never wrote a letter or anything, but I also wanted so desperately to start completely over again, to be somebody else. I suppose I managed it. Only I could never quite let go of you and Archie."

Ariadne looked up at her brother. "Why did you leave us?"

Tony smiled sadly. "We were born on the same day, but I was unlucky enough to be the second son. I never begrudged Archie his luck in that respect, but I could never quite come to terms with my position in life. Young, selfish, and foolish as I was."

"You've been in Canada, you say?" asked Felicity, her head spinning at the revelations.

Tony nodded. "I used an injury and hospitalisation as a stepping stone for escape. Took myself as far away as possible. I was in a deep hole, that's for sure, but I'm a different person now. I realise the hurt I caused." He turned a sad glance towards Ariadne. "At the time, I was blind to it. Blinded by my selfish pain. I wanted to get as far away as possible."

"What prompted you to return?" asked Felicity.

Tony reached under his thick wool jacket and into an inside pocket of his waistcoat. From there, he withdrew a folded and rather dog-eared scrap of newspaper, which he handed to Felicity. She unfolded it. It was an article about the construction of Grimstow House and its innovative accoutrements, including the hydropower installation. The piece was dated from the year before. It was one of those syndicated types of texts that newspapers around the world use as interest pieces to fill in gaps when news was slow. The publication's name appeared next to the date at the top of the torn page. *The Whitehorse Herald*.

Felicity's heart glowed at the power a newspaper article could have.

Tony accepted the clipping back from Felicity. He nodded towards the grainy reproduction of the photo of Grimstow House. "It just had Archie written all over it. I'm a technical man, myself, you see. And well, it might sound overly sentimental, but it just made me miss him all the more." Tony smiled shamefacedly.

"A technical man?" The statement had piqued Sir Vernon's interest. Even Leonard seemed more awake now, his eyes slightly more open.

"Well," said Tony bashfully. "I suppose I better come clean on that point. I invented a machine to make mining for gold much quicker and more efficient. It caught on a storm and made me rather a load of money."

Leonard's eyes shone with interest.

Sir Vernon spluttered in surprise. "You made a fortune in mining, you say?"

Tony shrugged. "I suppose that's one way of putting it. I'd arrived in the gold fields penniless, you see, but I made something of myself. I suspect it was the boost in self-esteem I needed, as I'm no longer that angry young man I once was." Tony shifted awkwardly, his genial expression becoming serious. "Excuse me for speaking so frankly. I suppose I've rather lost touch with the ways of genteel old England. In any case, I was hoping to share my successes with Ari and Archie. Maybe even Father will be proud. If he can ever forgive me."

Ariadne put a hand on her brother's arm. "Archie and Father would so love to see you, I'm sure of it. Only we don't know where Archie is, do we?" She blinked anxiously at Felicity. Her concern was understandable. The revelation that Tony had been rescued from the frozen hills and not his brother meant Archie's movements could no longer be accounted for.

Edwin looked distinctly worried. The same thought had likely occurred to him. Miss Fairchild continued to look just as frightened as when Felicity had arrived in the South Drawing Room. The housekeeper and the footman watched the proceedings calmly, but while Mrs Rudd's facade was entirely infallible, Mr Wilkinson was a tad wide-eyed.

"There could be a perfectly reasonable explanation for Lord Archibald's absence from the house." Felicity's tone was reassuring, but despite Tony's revelations, she couldn't forget about Alex out in the cold with the Bourgoyne sisters. She sincerely hoped Horrocks was providing support.

Tony sat up straighter, still holding his ribs. "Now, I know I haven't seen him in a few years, but I can vouch for Archie not having a single murderous bone in his entire body."

At the mantelpiece, Charles cleared his throat. "Is it even necessary that we get into particulars? If we stay together, the police will eventually arrive and sort things out." This was mainly addressed to Felicity, although there was a wobble of uncertainty in his voice. "That young stablehand I was riding with will no doubt get through," continued Charles, addressing the room. "He's a most excellent horseman."

"The sooner the better," croaked Leonard, attempting to sit up, Sir Vernon intervening ineffectively with his bandaged hand.

Unnecessary to get into particulars. Charles was perhaps lucky to see matters in such simple terms. Felicity certainly could not. There was so much that needed looking into: the mystery of the returned jewels, the identity of the woman in the feathered headband, the note in Felicity's coat pocket, not to mention Alex's whereabouts.

Edwin sighed heavily, pressing the tip of his cane further into the drawing room carpet. "I'm just sorry you've arrived tonight of all nights, Tony." Use of the short form of his step-brother's name was still awkward for the doctor. "The circumstances, as I hope I've already successfully explained, are absolutely exceptional."

"There's no need to apologise to me," reassured Tony. "I'm the one who must apologise. It was idiotic of me to attempt to arrive here on foot in this weather. It really got the measure of me. I've spent winters in the Yukon, you see, and I suppose that made me over confident. But the weather up here on the moors is clearly not to be underestimated. I'm not only sorry to you, Edwin, but also to your friend here—" he nodded towards Charles "—to whom I owe my life."

"Not at all, old chap," said Charles humbly.

"If there's anything I can do—" Tony attempted to sit up even straighter, but he gasped in pain.

"Tony, please," begged Ariadne, a hand on her brother's shoulder.

"Rest is what you can do," said Edwin firmly. "You've broken ribs and perhaps more. I should be pleased to get you to Exeter for x-rays before determining everything that might be wrong."

Tony chuckled. "I suppose I did take rather a tumble." He straightened his face. He seemed jolly and good natured and glad to be alive, but he was also aware of his surroundings. "I'm only sorry I never got to meet Helen. She sounds like a wonderful woman."

"She was," said Felicity. Tony would no doubt in time learn of the depth of Helen's character, most likely from his little sister, but now wasn't the time. There was so much else that needed looking into. "I'm awfully sorry to change the topic," continued Felicity, "but has anyone seen or heard from the Bourgoyne twins—" the moniker felt inappropriate compared to the alike nature of Archibald and Tony Carrington "—or Mr Cooper?"

"I... I..." Miss Fairchild, who hadn't stopped trembling since Felicity arrived in the drawing room, cast a frightened gaze around the room, her eyes landing on Edwin. "I'm sorry," she blurted and, dashing to the door, left the room.

Edwin frowned, a tremor in his jaw. He looked from the door to the injured men on the sofas. It was too much. All too much.

"Shall I go after Miss Fairchild?" Felicity quickly offered.

"Mrs Rudd will see to it." Edwin turned to the housekeeper. "Mrs Rudd, will you ensure Miss Fairchild is well and return her to us here in the drawing room? It's indeed safest that we remain together."

"Of course, sir," said Mrs Rudd with a diligent nod, and she promptly left to carry out the command. As the only servant now left in the South Drawing Room, the footman swallowed and straightened himself, pressing his spectacles up his nose.

The need to take action weighed heavily on Felicity. Alex had been gone an awfully long time, and there had been no word from the butler. "You're absolutely right, Edwin. Mr Cooper went to fetch the Bourgoyne sisters. I should like to know how he's getting on. Patience can take some convincing, but I believe we should be able to bring everyone back here. As you say, remaining together is the safest option."

Edwin nodded but looked doubtful. Felicity was glad no one but Alex knew about the letter found in her coat pocket.

"What if one of those blasted girls is responsible for this whole ruddy mess?" exclaimed Sir Vernon. "If anyone had a reason to go after Leonard—"

"What my father did..." Leonard went to say something, but a shot of pain cut him off and he groaned.

"Easy, now," said Edwin, urging the businessman to not make any further attempt to sit up.

There was no time for questions, but the relationship between the McQueens and the Bourgoynes was another knot in need of unravelling.

Charles approached from the mantelpiece, fixing Felicity with an earnest look. "I'll go with you."

"No, Charlie," said Felicity firmly but gently, Charles' concern sending a ripple of discomfort through her. "There's no need. I'm quite certain I'll be able to locate Mr Cooper by myself."

"I'd offer my help," added Tony, looking down at his muddy clothing, "but I'm rather incapacitated, I'm afraid."

Ariadne urged her brother to lean back on the sofa. "Tony, you really must rest."

"Cici, there's someone out there doing real harm," insisted Charles. "I simply can't allow you to put yourself in such danger."

Felicity blinked. Not even her over-protective older brother spoke to her in such blunt terms. "I know how to look after myself," said Felicity as a hint of scarlet crept up her neck. Was this how a smitten man cared for his future wife?

"Charles, I'd prefer it if you remained here." Edwin's

intervention came as a relief. "Felicity, Wilkinson will accompany you."

Felicity nodded. As much as she would have preferred to leave the South Drawing Room on her own, the company of the footman was a compromise she could bear for her cousin's peace of mind. The young bespectacled footman lifted his chin in an attempt to appear gallant. "At your service, y-your ladyship." His uneasiness was palpable.

"Thank you, Mr Wilkinson." The puzzle pieces kept rearranging themselves, but it was clear what Felicity needed to do next. "Let us find Mr Cooper."

Chapter Twenty-Six

"Before proceeding to the garage, I should like to re-arm myself, your ladyship."

Felicity had been hurrying towards Grimstow House's main entrance, successfully ignoring the continued pinching of her shoes, when the footman's footsteps ceased in the corridor behind her. She turned to see the footman press his glasses up his nose.

"I should like to make a diversion to the gun room, your ladyship, if you've no objection." There was a tremble to his voice, but he stood firm under flickering lights.

The presence of a loaded weapon had sparked the series of terrible events that had befallen Grimstow House that evening, yet Charles' decision to arm himself had been reassuring. Had he not been on guard in the South Drawing Room, Felicity might not have been able to leave Edwin so easily.

"If you can be certain of handling a weapon capably," said Felicity, unable to hide a large dose of doubt in her voice.

The footman nodded enthusiastically. "I did my military training, your ladyship. The war ended before I reached eighteen, so I was never sent to the front, but the Earl takes us servants pigeon shooting once a year. We all know how to handle a weapon, should the need arise."

"Very well, Mr Wilkinson," said Felicity, somewhat reassured, although not for the local pigeon population. "Lead the way."

Following the footman through stone corridors that took multiple turns on the way to the gun room, Felicity pondered arming herself. In extraordinary circumstances, she'd handled a gun before, but after what had happened to Helen, she wasn't comfortable with the idea. Then it dawned on her.

Felicity stopped. "Mr Wilkinson, would you mind terribly if we regrouped in the entrance hall?"

The footman looked confused. "We're to split up, your ladyship?"

"Only temporarily, while you ready your weapon." *And I ready mine*, thought Felicity.

Having made a concentrated effort to better remember the layout of Grimstow House, Felicity took a route she knew would lead to a set of stairs. En route, she passed the door of the billiard room, from where she heard a gramophone record playing and a combination of sobbing and masculine crooning, which Felicity attributed to Rex. If that was his way of staying out of trouble, then so be it. It was for the best that the emotionally unstable sportsman didn't yet know about Tony's arrival.

Upon reaching a wide, carpeted staircase, Felicity hurried towards the first floor, her coat now feeling rather warm despite the cold draughts whistling through the house. Recalling the butler's description of the location, Felicity made a beeline for the Bourgoynes' room, which lay at the end of the same corridor on which the master suite with the safe was situated.

The lights dimmed for a moment as Felicity examined the two doors at the end of the corridor, one on either side. Between the doors was a recess in which stood a white marble sculpture of a playful nymph. After a quick mental round of heads-or-tails,

Felicity chose the door on the left. She knocked and waited. Twisting the brass handle, she entered the room.

With the room lit only from the corridor, Felicity felt around before her hand landed on the switch. An inverted pendant lamp at the centre of the bedroom ceiling illuminated before she closed the door behind her. The room was richly furnished in the old-meets-new style typical of the house, with two sturdy single beds, a chaise longue, a large wardrobe, and a vanity set all built from warm mahogany.

The space was, however, in a rather extreme state of disarray.

Trunks excessively sized for a few nights away spewed clothes onto the floor. The bedcovers of the twin beds had been pulled back, with more garments slung onto the bedsheets, including two discarded feathered headbands, one in blue and one ruby red. Curtains in sumptuous damask stood partly open, perhaps yanked apart to check on the weather before the sisters again ventured out to the garage, or maybe to see what was happening when the first bangs of the fireworks went off.

Felicity's image was reflected in the glass. Beyond, vaguely picked out in the remaining moonlight, was a steeply terraced lawn at the bottom of which lay the deep darkness of densely planted evergreen trees, their pointed tops rocking in the wind.

Had the room been ransacked? Or was this how Patience and Clemency lived as guests? It wasn't immediately clear. If the latter, then whoever went to steal from their room must have been a talented thief to find anything.

Despite the room's disarray, Felicity located exactly what she needed. In front of the window was a desk, atop which sat a sage-green typewriter, its case set to one side and a sheet of paper on the roll.

If Felicity could get a match between Patience's typewriter and the note found in her pocket, then the culprit would be obvious. Making that confirmation ahead of confronting the Bourgoyne sisters would allow Felicity to tailor her approach, but she had to be fast. She didn't want the footman calling a search party for her.

Careful not to trip on any of the items strewn across the floor, Felicity went to the desk and perched on the chair. Through the windows, one could just about see the garage, the lights glowing through the skylights in the roof. Had Felicity made the right choice in diverting to the sisters' room? It was too late to turn back now. She had to press on.

In addition to the sheet on the roll, upon which had been typed only *Chapter 9*, there were two stacks of paper, one on either side of the machine. One stack was blank, and the other was typed. Felicity scanned the top page. *Chapter 8: An Experience of Ectoplasm at Audley Chambers.* The page's title made Felicity shudder. It was admirable that Patience was writing a book, but the topic of spirits wasn't anything in which Felicity had ever felt the need to dabble. That said, she knew it brought comfort to the enormous number of people bereaved following losses in the Great War.

Not wanting to get too distracted, she ceased reading Patience's work and pulled the typed note out of her pocket. *Keep your nose out. Or you'll be sorry.* As Ariadne had spotted, there was a small mark on the O that made the typed text quite distinctive. Felicity scanned the top page of the typed stack on the desk. The lights flickered dramatically for a moment, but thankfully, Felicity didn't have to read far. On the second line, there it was. *Renowned and respected clairvoyant, Mr Oliver Babbington*— The O had precisely the same mark on it as the note Felicity had found in her pocket.

Unease weighed on Felicity's stomach. Why Patience had wanted Helen and Leonard dead wasn't yet clear, and it was of course possible someone other than Patience had used the typewriter to send Felicity the note, but evidence was stacking up against the dark-haired Bourgoyne sister. Felicity couldn't bear the thought she'd sent Alex to the slaughter.

She went to stand up, determined to reach the garage as

quickly as possible, but the light in the centre of the bedroom's ceiling flickered, then went out.

As the seconds ticked by, despair swept through Felicity, quickly followed by anger. Of all moments, why now to be plunged back into darkness?

She turned in her chair. The moonlight outside was too dim to light the way across the bedroom. Should she go and risk tripping and injuring herself? Or should she wait for the light to come back on? How long would it take? Every second felt like forever.

Eeeek.

A slow creaking penetrated the darkness. Was it the wind?

The creaking stopped. Felicity listened carefully. Her heart jumped into her throat when she heard it: footsteps. Soft, careful. Someone was doing their best not to be detected, but for Felicity, it was clear. She was not alone.

Thump! The noise was accompanied by a cry of pain.

The light at the centre of the ceiling came back on, surging for a moment with brightness before returning to a steady glow that was stronger than before.

There, before Felicity, lay a piece of the puzzle she had so far completely ignored.

Chapter Twenty-Seven

Miss Fairchild was sprawled on the bedroom floor, the hem of her frilly dress caught on the corner of an open trunk, her feet tangled in a bundle of silk scarves. She sobbed where she lay, her face hidden in her hands, her shoulders heaving. Felicity's instinct was to help the woman, but as she rose from her seat before the typewriter, she paused.

Miss Fairchild's distress seemed genuine, and Felicity already had a notion of why she'd been hiding in the wardrobe. Indeed, Felicity's own presence in the Bourgoyne sisters' bedroom wasn't entirely legitimate, and the distraught woman collapsed on the carpet hardly seemed to pose a threat.

Approaching Miss Fairchild, Felicity helped the woman to her feet. She appeared unharmed.

Felicity took a step back. There was a limit to the succour she would offer. "Please, Miss Fairchild. There's no need for such upset."

"Don't comfort me," said Miss Fairchild between sobs as she rubbed her elbow. "I don't deserve it."

Felicity took a shaky inhale. "I believe I know why you're here."

"You do?" Miss Fairchild blinked, surprised for a moment.

She then collapsed into desperate crying, sniffing and bringing the back of her wrist to her forehead, the feathers on her headband quivering.

The urgency to reach Alex and the Bourgoyne sisters remained, but Felicity couldn't rush away. Miss Fairchild had been in front of her nose the whole time. What else had Felicity missed? A more thorough approach had been needed in making sense of the perplexing situation at Grimstow House, yet Felicity had clearly failed to apply it.

Miss Fairchild sniffed. "Edwin said you're very good in these kinds of situations. If he'd told me before time, I wouldn't have done it. Oh, I don't want to cause more pain than I already have. I'm so filled with remorse you can't imagine. Now that you've caught me, I suppose I should tell you everything." She wiped at her eyes with balled fists. "Can I tell you everything?"

Felicity nodded. "Part of it I can already guess."

Miss Fairchild sniffed. "What have you guessed?"

"You're a thief, but you're not a murderer. Do I have that correct?"

Miss Fairchild's shoulders slumped. "How did you know?"

"When the fireworks went off, there was time to either return the jewels to the master suite or to take a shot at Mr McQueen. There wasn't time to do both. And now I've found you here, I presume you're returning whatever it was you stole from the Bourgoyne sisters."

Miss Fairchild's eyes welled with tears as she nodded. "I'll never do it again. I swear. This is the first and last time. The first and the last."

"Did you set off the fireworks?"

"I did, but I didn't mean for the stables to catch alight. I actually care for animals." Miss Fairchild twisted her fingers together. "Oh, I've caused so much damage."

Felicity narrowed her eyes. It was all very well that Miss Fairchild cared for animals, but she had been extremely callous in her behaviour towards the household, not to mention Edwin.

Felicity remembered what the butler had said about the level of expertise required to break into the safe. "You say this is your first time thieving?"

Miss Fairchild shook her head, her lower lip trembling. "It's my first time working alone. I was part of a gang till now. Then I suppose I got greedy, wanting to go it alone and keep the spoils all for myself. So now I've been punished." She wrung her hands as she spoke. "I'm off stealing for good. This is the worst that's ever happened. I didn't want to hurt anyone. I didn't hurt anyone."

Felicity folded her arms over her chest. "You stole gems from a dead woman's body."

"I didn't." Miss Fairchild shook her head adamantly. "I was upstairs while the lights were out. I was... You know." She swallowed. "I needed time to get into that safe, but I've put all the jewellery back now. And I came back here to return the things to the girls." She reached into a pocket in her dress and held out a heavy handful of valuables, including strings of pearls and glittering beads. As with the clothing strewn around the room, it was a ridiculous amount of jewellery for the Bourgoyne sisters to have brought with them for a couple of nights away. "I was putting it back when you came along. Do you see? I'm putting it back." Miss Fairchild trod through the disarray of the room to tuck the jewels under the bedcovers of one of the beds, which was presumably where she'd found them. The room's disarray was apparently the Bourgoyne sisters' doing rather than the thief's.

Felicity remained quiet, watching Miss Fairchild's movements as the light in the centre of the ceiling continued to burn brightly and steadily. It was, of course, possible that Miss Fairchild, in her crisis of conscience, would admit to stealing jewels from unoccupied bedrooms but not to stealing from a dead body. It was equally possible she was telling Felicity the complete truth.

"Did you know you would rob Edwin's family and acquaintances when you met him?" Felicity's tone was stiff. The damage done to Edwin in the course of one evening was beyond imaginable.

Miss Fairchild hesitated, then nodded. "I was looking for a mark when I met him. It was very easy to read what kind of woman he was after and to play a character to fit that role. Of course, I feel awful about it now. As I said, I'll never do it again." The thief paused, knitting her fingers. "Now I've confessed, and the jewels are back, there's no need to inform the police, is there?"

Felicity's stomach squeezed at the thought of Edwin discovering the woman he had set his hopes and dreams upon, in his old-fashioned, awkward way, being revealed as a heartless thief who wanted him only for his connections to wealthy jewel-wearers. Part of Felicity wanted to see Miss Fairchild punished for exactly that. However, further drama, outcry, and publicity wouldn't help Edwin.

"Did you take anything from my room?" asked Felicity. Among her belongings, there was perhaps only a pearl necklace that was of any value to someone like Miss Fairchild.

The thief shook her head. "I'd heard you had to borrow your costume for the ball."

Felicity drew a deep breath. "If you've not stolen from me, then I have no theft to report to the police, but I cannot vouch for what your victims might say or do."

"They won't know it's me unless you tell them." Miss Fairchild sounded both desperate and hopeful. "You're the only one who knows it was me." Felicity saw now that the thief was perhaps younger than she'd made herself appear. She was at once worldly — an experienced criminal — and utterly naïve.

"I shall be honest with you," began Felicity. "The police's view on things matters less to me than my cousin's welfare, and I believe he deserves to know the truth." She lifted her chin. "If you don't tell Edwin about your true identity, then I shall tell him myself."

Miss Fairchild gasped and brought a hand to her throat. "But I put it all back, and I shall never steal again. Never again. You have my word."

"I'm afraid, Miss Fairchild, or whatever your name really is, that your word means little to me. It's my cousin I care about in this situation more than anything else." *And Alex*, added Felicity silently, for it was none of the thief's concern that Felicity wanted to get to the garage as quickly as possible.

Miss Fairchild's chest heaved. "But I… I…" Her eyes darted. Panic was setting in. "I can't go to jail." She rushed for the door, slamming it behind her as she ran into the corridor.

Felicity exhaled with relief. The stand-off in the bedroom was over, but would Miss Fairchild come clean to Edwin? Perhaps not. The picture of what had happened at Grimstow House was growing clearer, however, and Felicity's blood was running colder. Whoever wounded Leonard had taken advantage of a situation not of their own creation, for it was Miss Fairchild who'd set the fireworks and accidentally burned the stable roof.

Had the same quick-thinking brutality been at play when the lights went out for the ill-fated parlour game? Was Alex exposed to an even more dangerous and unpredictable foe than Felicity had realised?

She went to the window and looked outside. Cold gusts of air found their way around the edges of the sash windows. Getting back downstairs and outside would need to be done without a wrong turn. So much time had already been lost. Looking out at the glowing lights of the garage, Felicity tried to instil in herself the direction in which she would need to keep as her North Star despite the many twists and turns of the stairs and corridors en route.

Then she saw something that made her breath catch. It was only the slightest glimpse by lantern light at the base of the pines beyond the sloping lawn, but Felicity knew what it meant.

She flew out of the room.

Chapter Twenty-Eight

Her heart pounding, Felicity dashed downstairs, past the confused-looking footman with a rifle on his shoulder, and along a familiar corridor, passing military portraits of Archibald and Tony, the wall-mounted lights above them glowing brightly. Would she be in time?

A gust of cold air swept along the corridor. A door had opened to the outside. Felicity came to an inelegant halt, her feet sliding a little on the stone floor.

The dignified silver Borzoi entered the building first. Next appeared her master, his large tan leather bag and a glowing lantern all clasped in one hand as he closed the door behind him, its glass panes laced with ice.

"Lord Archibald." Felicity's voice echoed down the corridor.

Archibald had on his heavy great coat and worn leather gloves, his nose and cheeks bright red from the cold. Except for his outmoded moustache, he looked exactly identical to his brother.

His periwinkle-blue eyes widened almost imperceptibly upon noticing Felicity. They remained frozen at a distance from one another. The tall, slender hound looked calmly and inquisitively in Felicity's direction.

"I'm very pleased to have found you." Felicity sounded composed despite being quite out of puff, her heart still going at least three times the normal rate.

There was a pause. Archibald remained still. "Why?" His tone was flat.

Felicity had her own feelings about the matter of Archibald's guilt, but she knew nothing for sure. That he'd done away with Helen and attempted to do the same with Leonard could not be fully ruled out. However, the drama his reappearance would create in the household was guaranteed.

"Have you been out in the grounds all this time, since I last saw you here?"

Archibald nodded firmly. "I have. I went to the hydropower station at the river to fix the electricity, then to the substation at the bottom of the garden. Some of the cabling had come loose in the wind. It's fixed now." The steady brightness of the lights in the corridor bore witness to his account.

Felicity breathed a little more easily. "And you're returning to the house for the first time only now? You've not been to the South Drawing Room, for instance?"

Mina lowered her haunches to the stone floor and lifted her long muzzle towards her master.

"No." Archibald's brow furrowed. "Why do you ask me these things?"

Felicity took a deep breath. "Much has happened. I'm not sure what you already know." Lord Archibald had left the house shortly after the discovery of Helen's body.

"I know my step-sister is dead. The butler informed me. It's why I persevered in taking action on the electricity. Conditions out there aren't easy, but I had to do something."

Footsteps echoed along one of the adjoining corridors. Time was running out. News of Tony's reappearance and the attempt on Leonard's life would have to wait. "Forgive me for speaking bluntly," said Felicity, "but I've reason to believe you may be in danger."

Archibald shook his head. "Why would I be in danger?"

"Certain people here at Grimstow consider you a suspect for the death of your step-sister, Helen."

Mina turned her gaze on Felicity. Archibald looked faintly annoyed. "But I didn't do it."

Felicity continued, speaking quickly. "I believe you. Emotions are, nevertheless, running high. I suggest you return to your room and wait there till the police arrive. Can you get up there without being seen?"

"Certainly. Is my sister up there still?"

"No, but she's in safe hands." Felicity thought of the reliable Charles with the gun on his hip.

The approaching footsteps drew ever closer. "Lady Felicity?" The footman's voice echoed along the corridor. He was unlikely to do Archibald direct harm, but the servant was also unlikely to keep his lordship's reappearance entirely to himself.

"Please, Lord Archibald," urged Felicity.

Archibald wiped a hand over his moustache, then he turned towards the door through which he'd entered, the Borzoi close at his heels. Pushing the door open, the frozen wind whipping inside, Archibald paused. He looked irritated. "The party Helen organised. Did it continue even after she…"

"No," said Felicity firmly. "It certainly did not."

"Then who set the fireworks?"

There had been no time to inform Archibald of the reappearance of his brother. There was certainly no time to explain Miss Fairchild's deception. "It was an accident," said Felicity.

"They went off while I was at the substation, but I couldn't stop my work. I was sorry not to help with the fire at the stables." The corners of his eyes creased. "I saw someone running through the trees."

A chill passed through Felicity. "Who?"

"Lady Felicity?" The footman was very close.

Archibald shook his head. "She was running along the edge of the garden, towards the stables. It wasn't the shortest route."

"A woman?"

"It wasn't Ari. I know that. Someone older. I don't know who."

Wilkinson's footsteps drew closer.

Felicity desperately wanted to hear more. "Please, Lord Archibald. Go. Take care of yourself."

"I will." Archibald extinguished his lantern and disappeared outside, Mina close behind him.

"Lady Felicity." The footman appeared in the corridor. He hurried towards her. "My apologies, your ladyship. I lost you. I'm sorry to inform you that this isn't the way to the garage."

"It's not?" said Felicity innocently, her hand on the door knob as though she were responsible for the lowering of the corridor's temperature. Beyond the glass, there was nothing to see but darkness. "How foolish of me."

Felicity allowed herself to be led briskly back to the entrance hall. It was at last time to find Alex. Would he forgive her for having left him alone for such a long period? He would surely be relieved to know that the matter of the thefts had been resolved, and Archie's reappearance had been delayed till the arrival of more control over the situation in the form of the police. He might be less reassured to learn that Patience's typewriter had been the source of the threatening note placed in Felicity's pocket, and that a feminine figure had been seen in the trees at the edge of the gardens around the time Leonard received the bullet in his shoulder.

"This way, your ladyship," said the footman, opening the front doors to a blast of Arctic air before stepping aside to allow Felicity to exit the house first.

"Thank you, Mr Wilkinson." Felicity pulled her coat tightly over herself and went out into the freezing wind, her heels clicking over the entrance's flagstones, then sinking into the gravel. Compared to the furs she'd borrowed earlier, the wool of her coat was unsuitably thin, and her teeth began immediately to chatter. The brightly burning outdoor lights cast the gravel in warm yellow.

"Please, let us hurry," said Felicity to the footman as he joined her outside, but their progress was immediately halted.

A muscular, dapple-grey horse stood huffing and flicking its ears as its rider dismounted. It was the stablehand who'd gone to telephone the police from the village. "Good boy. Good boy." The young man spoke soothingly to the powerful creature.

"Mr Peabody?" enquired Felicity.

"Your ladyship," he said, practically springing to attention upon noticing her.

"Are the police on their way?" asked Felicity, tugging at her coat's collar, for the wind was vicious.

The stablehand nodded. "Yes, your ladyship. The police gave me a message that I must bring to the household. Plus another message for you in particular, your ladyship."

"For me?" Felicity's head was spinning. Would she ever reach Alex?

"I say. They weren't wrong about you, were they, Peabody?" Rex appeared at the front doors, wincing into the wind, still wearing his dinner jacket with the torn lapel but with no coat. The footman stiffened, his hand going to the strap of the rifle on his shoulder.

Rex approached the horse and took its reins from the stablehand. The young man reluctantly released his grip. "Fine rider you are to make it all the way there and back in these conditions," said Rex. "I congratulate you."

"I… Well, I…" Peabody moved aside as the horse became restless, resisting Rex's attempt to stroke its muscular shoulders. The situation was at an awkward impasse.

Felicity stepped forward. "Mr Peabody, will you go inside and deliver the police's message to Doctor Quick?"

"Right away, your ladyship. What about the message intended for you, your ladyship?"

Rex turned and lifted an eyebrow. "A message especially for Lady Felicity? What could that mean?"

Felicity didn't appreciate Rex's tone, but she would delay her objective no longer. "It shall have to wait, Mr Peabody. I'm on my way to find Mr Cooper, who I believe is at the garage with the Bourgoyne sisters."

"I saw a group heading for the house on my way in, your ladyship," said the stablehand. "A gentleman and two ladies. Might the fellow I saw be the man you're looking for?"

"Oh," said Felicity with surprise and relief. "Well, yes. I suppose so."

As the horse continued to reject the sportsman's affections, Rex looked over his shoulder at Felicity and raised his voice above the wind. "Then we can all go together to listen to Mr Peabody deliver the police's messages, can't we?"

Chapter Twenty-Nine

The scene in the South Drawing Room was much as Felicity had left it. With a hand on his cane, Edwin stood alert, watching over his two patients, while Charles kept an eye on his friend. Still awake, Tony had returned to lying down on the blankets spread over the sofa, Ariadne perched next to him, her sea-green dress still sparkling. Leonard was sitting up straight but was clearly in pain, his face a desperate grimace. Sir Vernon had taken a seat beside him on the sofa, his bandaged hand in his lap. He watched Leonard carefully, as though worried he might stop breathing any moment. The housekeeper stood at the side of the room, her face a mask of impassivity. The clock on the mantelpiece continued to tick as the wind whistled at the windows.

There was, however, no sign of Alex.

As Felicity entered the room with Rex and the stablehand — the footman having been tasked with returning the horse to the stables — all faces turned towards them.

"Felicity. Mr Peabody." Edwin looked hopeful. "Have you news? Are the police on their way? Did you locate Mr Cooper?"

Charles' hand went to the gun on his belt, his eyes on Rex. "Ho. We'll not have any trouble from you."

Rex held up his hands. "Easy, old chap. I'm not here to do anything other than hear what the police had to say. Then I'll be out of your way."

Charles' hand continued to hover near his weapon. "Are you all right, Cici?" he asked cautiously.

Felicity nodded. "Mr Cooper is apparently on his way up to the house," she said, addressing Edwin, "with the Bourgoyne twins, by all accounts." At least, she sincerely hoped the stablehand's report could be relied upon. "And Mr Peabody indeed brings news."

"Excellent. Excellent." Edwin smiled a little, although his eyes bore a haunted look. "Mrs Rudd, might you be able to locate Miss Fairchild? I believe she should hear the news, too." Was the absence of Miss Fairchild conspicuous to the point of alarming Edwin?

"Of course, Doctor Quick." The housekeeper promptly left the room.

Ariadne leaned forward. "Have you perhaps seen Archie?" she enquired quietly of Felicity. Tony blinked up hopefully from his bed on the sofa.

Lord Archibald's was another conspicuous absence.

"All is well," reassured Felicity, although she needed reassurance herself. Even if Alex was on his way back up to the house, was he in the company of a murderer?

"Let's have it then," said Sir Vernon, eyeing the room through his cracked monocle, the effect of the drink he'd consumed earlier in the evening seemingly having worn off and given way to a less sociable attitude.

Leonard said nothing. Without looking up, he leaned wearily with the elbow of his good arm on his knee. His breath seemed laboured.

More eager for Alex's return than the police's messages, Felicity stood patiently beside the sofa occupied by Tony and Ariadne as Edwin approached the young rider, who stood with his cap in his hands, his face still red from exposure to the cold. "You made excellent time to the village and back," said Edwin admiringly.

"The lad helped save my life, too," added Tony.

Edwin nodded in acknowledgement. "Your actions are indeed commendable, Mr Peabody, and I shall see that your deeds are acknowledged accordingly. But please forgive me if I bring us directly to the point, as the situation has developed further in your absence and, unfortunately, for the worst." He glanced at Leonard as the businessman shifted his large frame uncomfortably. "Were you able to make contact with the police?"

"Yes, sir," said the stablehand. "I did."

"What did they say?"

"They said they'd be out as soon as the thaw set in. Tomorrow morning, by their reckoning."

Edwin nodded, his jaw taut. It was as expected. The bullet Leonard had taken in his shoulder had since increased the possibility of Helen's death not being an accident, but the stablehand had left the house before the fire at the stables. He didn't have that information to share with the police. Given the weather, it was difficult to say what difference it might have made to the timing of the police's arrival.

Still, morning felt very far away.

Without looking up, Leonard groaned. Whether the noise he made was prompted by physical suffering or by the estimate on the police's arrival, it wasn't possible to tell.

"It is dangerous out there," confirmed Tony. "Best not to make the mistake I did and underestimate it."

"Did the police say anything else?" pushed Edwin.

"Yes, sir. The police gave the advice that everyone should keep to their rooms."

Edwin tutted. "That's already been tried."

Rex piped up. "I've been in my room." His tone implied it was the behaviour of others that fell short.

Charles remained vigilant of the sportsman's every move. "If only that had been your approach for the entire evening."

Edwin held up a hand to his friend. "Please. No more disagreements. I'm not sure I can—"

A cacophony of voices and clattering in the corridor caught everyone's attention as the door flew open. Patience led Clemency by the hand into the drawing room in a flurry of fur-edged coats and shimmering party frocks. "I absolutely will not take your word for it," said Patience crossly. "I want to see for myself. And if I'm not satisfied, I'm leaving right away, as I told you."

Behind the sisters, in the doorway, stood Alex, his arms full of bags. The volume of belongings the Bourgoynes had brought with them for the ball was staggering.

Felicity's heart leapt at the sight of Alex safe and well, but his usually calm blue eyes burned with a frustration Felicity had never seen before.

"He's right there, Miss Bourgoyne," said Alex through gritted teeth. "Just as I told you he would be."

Charles' eyes darted between Rex and the new arrivals, unsure who he ought to keep the closest watch over.

As Alex set the Bourgoyne sisters' bags down on the drawing room floor, an edge of calm returned to his voice. "I think you'll find he's still alive. At least he appears that way to me."

"Patience, Clemency." Edwin was doing his best to sound welcoming, but his voice wobbled with exhaustion. "I'm glad you've joined us. We've just received word from the police."

Paying Edwin no heed, Patience stopped in the middle of the room, her focus trained fully on Tony. Clemency, her sister's hand still around her wrist, scanned the room nervously. "My darling," she gushed when her eyes landed on Rex, but Patience's grip was firm, and Rex's reaction was cool.

"I say, ladies," said Sir Vernon. "Make an entrance, why don't you?"

"You see?" Alex shook out his hands and managed an ironic

lift of his eyebrows in Felicity's direction. "Lord Archibald's still in the land of the living."

Ariadne peered with confusion at Alex. "You've seen Archie?"

Patience narrowed her eyes at Tony, who lifted his head a little from his sofa bed. "How do you do?" he said in his American twang.

Patience narrowed her eyes. "We've met before, Lord Archibald. Have you moved from that sofa?"

The confusion couldn't be allowed to continue. Felicity stepped forward. "This isn't Lord Archibald. This is Lord Archibald's brother, the Honourable Anthony Carrington."

Alex's face went from relief to distress and confusion. *His brother?* Alex mouthed this at Felicity. He and the Bourgoyne twins had missed the revelation of Tony's awakening.

Felicity gave a little shrug and nodded in reply.

Patience continued to stare fixedly at Tony, struggling to come to terms with what she was hearing. "You are not Lord Archibald?"

"No, ma'am. I'm Tony. I don't believe we've had the pleasure."

"You didn't die in the war?"

Tony looked down at himself. "Not as far as I'm aware."

Ariadne observed Patience, her chin tucked. She was ready to leap to her brother's defence if necessary. Clemency couldn't take her eyes off Rex. Leonard let out another groan.

With a little shake of her head, Patience turned her attention to the injured businessman. "Someone tried to kill you, did they?"

Edwin's shoulders sank further. He looked absolutely drained.

Felicity stepped towards the Bourgoyne sisters. She wasn't sure if further drama could be averted, but she would do her best. "I'm not sure where you've been," said Felicity, addressing mainly Patience, whose grip on her sister's wrist tightened. "But much has happened in your absence." She flashed a glance in Alex's direction. This assessment applied also to him.

"Like what?" Patience spat. "Mr Cooper already told us everything."

Alex folded his arms over his chest. "The Misses Bourgoyne departed the house with only awareness of the fireworks going off. I informed them of Mr McQueen's injury during the fire at the stables. I wasn't aware of the Honourable Mr Carrington's arrival at the house." He nodded respectfully in Tony's direction, then returned his attention to Felicity and Edwin. "You may be interested to know that I found the Bourgoyne sisters stuck halfway down the drive in their Model T. Its wheels were spinning on the thick ice. The butler came to help. He went to fetch the driver to rescue the vehicle, which was left in a rather precarious position." Alex raised his eyebrows at the sisters. "Thankfully, no one was hurt."

Patience wouldn't look at Alex. She swept a lock of brown hair from her forehead. "I had things quite under control."

Sir Vernon stiffened. "You were making an escape?"

Patience fumed. "How dare you."

Edwin grew pale. "Please. Everybody. Do let's keep calm."

Alex addressed Sir Vernon. "Miss Bourgoyne informed me she decided to depart with her sister as she believed she…" Alex pressed his lips together. "Well." It was unlike him to be lost for words.

"Out with it, man," urged Sir Vernon.

Alex sighed with reluctance. "Miss Bourgoyne believed she saw an apparition."

Ariadne looked confused. "You saw a ghost?"

Patience chipped in defensively. "There's been a misunderstanding. I didn't know at the time what I now know. I'm only an enthusiastic amateur on the topic, you understand, and I made a mistake. Now I know who he really is—" she nodded uncomfortably towards Tony "—it changes rather a lot. I can admit that I was rather rash in my assessment."

Alex raised his eyebrows at Felicity as if to say, *Do you now see what I had to deal with?* Felicity empathised, but she was thoroughly distracted by Patience's performance. Did her behaviour fit with doing away with Helen and attempting to do the same to Leonard?

"Where did you see this ghost, then?" The question was Rex's. He sounded extremely sceptical.

Patience glared at Rex for a moment, something akin to hatred for the man burning behind her eyes. "I was in our room when the fireworks went off. That's when I saw someone at the bottom of the garden. It looked like Lord Archibald, but it could not have been because I assumed he was here on his sick bed. So I imagined he must have passed on from his injuries." Patience jutted her chin upwards with defiance. "And that his tormented soul was now wandering the earth."

Sir Vernon laughed heartily. "What a ruddy curious conclusion to draw."

Clemency piped up. "It's not. My sister has a great deal of knowledge in these matters." It was the first show of courage and initiative Felicity had witnessed from Clemency during the evening. "She's writing a book about it, you know."

A fair few eyebrows were raised in Patience's direction. Even Leonard looked up. Felicity remained quiet, her thoughts consumed with making sense of Patience's admissions.

"So you imagined you'd seen an apparition of Lord Archibald," surmised Edwin. "Why did that make you flee?"

Indignance straightened Patience's back. "Have you ever been to a seance? Have you ever had contact with the dead?"

Felicity felt an odd sort of sympathy for Patience. She knew what it was to be questioned and doubted when all you were doing was what you felt was right.

"I find this kind of talk disrespectful of my sister's recent passing." Edwin's tone was sharp.

"Please, Edwin," said Patience, swatting a hand. "You're not the only person who cared for Helen. Clem and I saw more of her these last years than you ever did, despite us all being in London most of the time."

Edwin looked shaken by the accusation, but Patience didn't stop there.

"And you're not the only person ever to have been bereaved," she said. "When you're able to contact the ones you love — and trust me, I shall speak to Helen again at some point — and find reassurance from them, it's incredibly settling. But when I saw that, that… Ghoul stalking around the garden." She shivered. "Well, I know what it was now, thankfully. It wasn't a spirit. It was the man himself. At the time, I got the feeling that nothing good would come of it." Again, the jut of the chin. "So I took Clem, and we left."

"Except you didn't get very far, did you?" needled Edwin. "You might have made ghosts of both your sister and yourself if you hadn't got stuck on the drive. Would you say that was right, Mr Cooper?"

Thrust suddenly into the spotlight, Alex took the measure of Patience, and turned to address Edwin. "When I found the Misses Bourgoyne on the drive, they'd been going at a very careful pace, so nothing was damaged except perhaps a bit of turf at the edge of the drive where they had seen fit to veer from the tarmacadam for better traction. The car and its passengers were intact." It was a clever response, offending no one but also not exactly agreeing with anyone.

Patience threw up her hands. "We're back now, and I know what I saw. I told you, I admit my mistake, but I still wish we'd been able to leave this blasted place. It's not enormously comforting to know that Lord Archibald himself has been stalking around the house and grounds all this time. Goodness only knows what he was up to in the garden. It seems quite obvious to me, as it must do to all of you, that he is responsible for everything that has happened here this evening."

"Whoa, there," said Tony, lifting his head a little.

Ariadne sprang from her seat to confront Patience. "How dare you say such a thing? There's no proof of our brother having done anything wrong. How would he gain from Helen's death? Or Leonard's? Our family is much better off than the Quicks."

Felicity winced. Talk of money was so vulgar, but Ariadne had a point. Charles shot Felicity a glance of concern, but Felicity's taking offence on behalf of the Quick family wouldn't help uncover what was really happening at Grimstow House. Nor would it cool the situation in the South Drawing Room, which risked getting out of hand.

"What about those letters you sent?" responded Patience.

"Yes," echoed Clemency. "What about the letters?"

Sir Vernon nodded vigorously. "Now we're getting somewhere."

Patience continued to address Ariadne. "There's written proof there was ill-feeling from your family towards Helen."

"Enough!" Edwin's voice rang out. The hand gripping his cane shook. "I've heard enough of this. We have instructions from the police. Each of you will go to your room and lock yourselves in. Peabody."

The young stablehand had been doing his best to shrink into the background. "Y-yes, sir?"

"Instruct the household staff to organise an armed patrol. I'm sorry it's come to this, but there's simply no other way. I'll remain here with the patients, but everyone else can clear out. And the doors to your rooms will be locked from the outside."

"But I want to—" began Ariadne.

"Everyone out." Edwin shook with emotion.

"Can I not—" began Sir Vernon.

"Out!"

Leonard groaned and sank against the back of the sofa.

Charles glanced nervously at Felicity before fixing his attention on Edwin. "Do you need me here, old chap?"

"I should be grateful for your support," admitted Edwin, the anger of his tirade already waning.

"Shall I remain here with you, too, cousin?" enquired Felicity gently.

"I think it's safest that you don't," said Edwin. "I shall have Miss Fairchild as my assistant just as soon as Mrs Rudd locates her."

"Very well." Felicity would continue to give Miss Fairchild room to make her confession to Edwin, although Felicity's expectations of Miss Fairchild weren't high. "You may call on me if you need me."

Edwin nodded gratefully. "I know that."

Felicity was partially glad Edwin had released her from the South Drawing Room. She and Alex had so much to discuss. They were surely closer to fathoming out who was behind the shootings, although having heard both Patience's and Lord Archibald's accounts of where they were when Leonard was shot, the waters had been muddied.

As everyone in the room filed out in subdued fashion, with only mumblings like, "But I want to speak to Rex," and "Might as well go fix myself a drink," to be heard, Felicity approached Alex. He was waiting for her by the door, his hands in his pockets, his coat slung over his arm.

"Shall we find somewhere quiet?" suggested Felicity.

"Your ladyship." Before Alex could reply, the stablehand approached Felicity. "I still have a message for you from the police. Would you like to hear it before I go downstairs to deliver Doctor Quick's orders, your ladyship?"

How had Felicity forgotten? She stopped in the doorway. "Of course, Mr Peabody. Please, go ahead."

"It's from Chief Inspector Luscombe, your ladyship. They made certain I would remember his name. They said you'd know who he was, your ladyship."

Felicity raised her eyebrows at Alex as he stepped forward to listen in. Chief Inspector Luscombe and Felicity were indeed acquaintances. While they could never be said to have worked together, exactly, Felicity considered them to have mutual respect for each other's activities. Whatever the instruction, Felicity would no doubt benefit from Alex's support in it.

"Yes, I know Chief Inspector Luscombe," said Felicity. "What would he like me to do?"

Dennis squeezed his hat in his hands, his eyes flicking between Felicity and the drawing room carpet. "He said you're to stay out of things, your ladyship."

Felicity's stomach plummeted. "S-stay out of things?"

Alex's eyes widened. "Are you certain that's what you heard?"

"I didn't speak to Luscombe myself, your ladyship," continued Peabody, "so forgive me if I'm using my own crude language to relay the message. But that was my overall understanding of it. The Chief Inspector had asked for a list of people present at the house. When the constable I was on the line with relayed your name, there was some discussion, and that was the outcome."

Felicity felt the colour drain from her face. What a fool she'd been.

Alex looked at her beseechingly. "I'm sure there's some explanation for this. The full context of what we're facing here won't have reached the police, and I'm sure that the bluntness is, as Mr Peabody says, his."

The attempts at soothing were, however, pointless. Felicity had been reprimanded. She'd been put in her place. How had she dared imagine the police might have special instructions for her? It had been idiotic to imagine she could make any contribution to the investigation.

To make matters worse, the message had been overheard.

"Ha." Patience's reaction was full of spite. "That's told you, hasn't it? A meddler is all you are, and I can vouch for that."

Felicity was so utterly embarrassed. If only the ground would open and swallow her whole.

"Felicity." Alex looked incredibly sad.

"Cici," Charles called out to her, and made his way across the drawing room. "I'd like a word, if you wouldn't mind."

Patience wasn't done yet. "You haven't fixed a thing since you came here. In fact, I'd say you've only made things worse."

She was right. It was all too much.

Felicity fled.

Chapter Thirty

Upon reaching the room where she'd got changed for the party, with the door closed firmly behind her, Felicity's tears came thick and fast. She flopped onto the edge of the bed, her head in her hands, and she wept. She didn't care who heard.

Helen, her own cousin, was dead. She'd done nothing to prevent, solve, or avenge her death. Her surviving cousin Edwin was trying to keep control of a dangerous, chaotic situation at Grimstow House. What had Felicity done to support him? Hadn't she just gone around stirring things up, riling people to the point of outbursts?

Yes, she had uncovered the so-called Miss Fairchild's true nature, but she had clearly been overly naïve in giving the thief the opportunity to come clean with how she'd cheated Edwin. Felicity should have reported Miss Fairchild directly to him. Ripped off the bandage, so to speak. Now, he would hear about it and also learn that Felicity had kept facts from him. And not just about Miss Fairchild.

Lord Archibald was hiding in the attic at Felicity's behest. Who did she think she was, giving commands to people? Keeping secrets and covering things up? She'd also sent Alex off to the Bourgoynes and then, instead of helping him, dashed about playing the detective, which — it was now obvious — she ought never to have done.

She felt deeply ashamed of how she'd handled things. Patience's words had stung so keenly because Patience was right.

The warmth of Felicity's tears soaked her cheeks. She kicked the wretched pinching shoes from her feet and allowed waves of self-pity to overcome her. Felicity was a meddler. The police knew it. Everyone around her could see it. She'd strung Edwin along, indicating that she might have been able to help. She wasn't any kind of detective. She was barely even a journalist anymore. Perhaps the only good thing to come out of the evening had been Charles' talk of marriage. Felicity really ought to put her silly ideas of a career behind her and become someone's wife. Would it truly be that bad? It was what every woman ultimately wanted, wasn't it? It surely couldn't ever feel as bad as the humiliation and failure she felt in that moment, alone in her room, crying in stockinged feet.

She was pathetic. It was pathetic. It had to stop.

Wiping her cheek with her hand, Felicity's eyes landed on the clothes in which she'd arrived at Grimstow House, which had been neatly folded and placed on a chair in the corner of the room. Under the chair sat her blue T-strap shoes. They weren't as eminently comfortable as her Oxfords, but just the familiar sight of them provided solace.

Shimmying out of the frankly now quite ridiculous emerald dress — which took some doing because such clothes weren't designed for ladies without maids — Felicity sighed with relief as she pulled on her comparatively dull cream silk shirt and ink-blue skirt and jacket. Her pearl necklace was thankfully still on the dresser, and her bicorn hat was a welcome addition to her unruly head of auburn curls. After a brief massaging of her feet, Felicity slid back into her T-strap shoes.

It was as she fastened the last buckle that a knock came at the bedroom door.

A lump sprang into Felicity's throat. Her thoughts went

immediately to Alex. She'd abandoned him again, hadn't she? He couldn't see her like this, so hopeless and full of self-pity, when he'd only been dragged into the mess at Grimstow House through his association with her. And despite him just wanting to do his job and report on the incidents for the newspaper in a manner respectful of her family, Felicity had roped Alex into her own futile meddling.

She owed him an apology. Another one. How many times would this have to happen before he went back to London for good? Felicity's brother would be beyond displeased. He valued Alex highly both as a friend and as a reporter. Felicity valued him, too. Perhaps more dearly than she dared admit.

She stood up, straightened her skirt, and wiped her eyes. It was time to rip off her own bandage. She opened the door. Standing in the corridor was Ariadne, the sequins of her dress sparkling under the bright electric lights. She looked pale and nervous. There was no sign of Alex.

"Can I come in?"

Felicity nodded and stepped aside. Absolutely everyone in the household would, by now, know about Felicity being reprimanded by the police. She was officially a meddler and not any kind of sleuth. With that in mind, what could Ariadne want from Felicity?

Ariadne didn't advance far into the room. She clasped her hands tightly, her wispy pale blonde hair floating around her face. "I'm sorry to bother you, but I'm incredibly worried. Tony's worried, too. So I said I'd come and check with you."

Felicity shook her head. "Check what with me?"

"Archie. Patience saw him. Just before we saw what happened to Leonard." Tears threatened in Ariadne's eyes. She sniffed and straightened. "Archie didn't do it, did he? Please tell me he didn't shoot Leonard. Or Helen."

Felicity took a deep breath. She'd drawn conclusions. It was impossible not to. Her mind was apparently built in such a way that Felicity couldn't leave such matters alone, even if all the signs told her to stay away. Answering a question like this aloud was exactly the sort of meddling she shouldn't be doing.

Felicity hesitated. "What's your opinion on the matter?" She spoke gently, for Ariadne was young and unsure, and Felicity still had sympathy for her.

Ariadne looked thoughtful. The wind moaned at the bedroom windows. "Archie can be hard to read. He was always quieter than Tony and myself, but after the war, well, he shut down almost completely. He wouldn't hurt anyone, though. I can't imagine him even wanting to, let alone acting on it."

It was time to confess. Felicity had demanded truthfulness from Miss Fairchild, but she also needed to commit to it herself. It would hopefully start the undoing of the mess Felicity had made with her meddling. "Archie's in the attic," she said. "If you'd like to ask him for clarification, you can do so yourself."

Ariadne's eyes widened with surprise but also relief. "He's here in the house?"

Felicity nodded. "I realise it was wrong of me to tamper with everyone's affairs, but I saw Archibald coming inside, and in light of the revelation of Tony's arrival, I was worried Rex or Sir Vernon or someone else might want to get at him. They seem to consider him a prime suspect. I therefore advised your brother to keep out of the way."

Ariadne's lower lip trembled, then she thrust herself towards Felicity, flinging her arms around her and breaking down into sobs on the lapels of her ink-blue jacket. The gesture surprised Felicity, but she opened her arms and held Ariadne as she cried. Felicity almost slipped back into sobbing herself. So much had happened, and still so much had yet to happen. The police hadn't even arrived, let alone begun their investigation. Could Felicity remain strong? She could at least offer Ariadne a shoulder upon which to cry without sinking again into her own self-pity.

Ariadne drew back, dabbing a knuckle to her eyes, kohl liner smeared under her lashes. "Heavens, I'm so sorry. It's just… Well. You've been an absolute rock through all of this. There were moments when I was deeply unpleasant towards you, and you were completely undeserving, because you've been nothing but nice to me. More than nice, even. And now I'm up here behaving like an absolute child, yet Helen was your cousin. Your own flesh and blood. You knew her better than I did, and somehow you're a pillar of strength while everyone else falls apart. I don't know how you do it, or how I'll ever thank you."

Felicity almost laughed. Where had Ariadne's grandiose impression of her come from? "I'm happy if I've been able to provide you any kind of support, but I'm afraid I got myself too involved in matters to see what ought really to have been done."

Ariadne's face crumpled in confusion for a moment. Her brow shot upwards. "Oh, the police's request, you mean? I'm surprised you've taken it to heart. Isn't that just the way of men, watching out and claiming to care for us when what they really seek is to control us?"

Felicity drew back her chin. She had known Ariadne was a spirited young woman. She hadn't been aware of her interest in female emancipation. "In a criminal investigation, the police have the final say," said Felicity, although she'd practically forgotten that herself at some points. "They have the absolute right to decide who's involved in the process and who isn't."

"But to issue such a command without having seen the work you've done here, when the police couldn't even arrive here themselves," continued Ariadne. "It seems disrespectful of everything you've done for us."

Felicity smiled stiffly. She didn't want to be rude towards Ariadne, but Felicity was quite done with discussing her extremely amateur and unhelpful detection work. "Shall I escort you to the attic?" Felicity offered. Although Grimstow House was more Ariadne's home than Felicity's, it didn't seem right to set the emotional young woman back to wandering the corridors by herself, even with the rest of the house supposedly locked up, which Felicity couldn't quite believe had been achieved. Both Rex and Patience had misgivings about Ariadne. Sir Vernon perhaps also still regarded her with suspicion.

"I would very much appreciate it," said Ariadne, who somehow looked cheered, a healthy pink having returned to her cherubic cheeks.

In the carpeted corridor outside Felicity's room, where wall-mounted lights still burned brightly, all was quiet except the constant whistling of the wind at the windows and the occasional howl or bark from Jambo, who was still locked up somewhere nearby on the first floor. While glad she hadn't left Ariadne to ascend to the attic alone, Felicity wasn't entirely sure what protection she could offer were they to be set upon. There was someone at large who, for some still-unexplained reason, had wanted to harm Helen and Leonard, and perhaps intended to cause further damage.

"Which is the best route to the attic?" enquired Felicity, distracting herself from the potential danger and her mind's inability to leave the unravelling of the mystery alone.

Ariadne put her hands on her hips and looked along the length of the corridor. "Now the electricity's more settled, I believe it's safe to take the lift. This way," she said and disappeared around a corner into a corridor.

Felicity followed, but she didn't get far. Hearing something, she stopped. What was it? Despite being muffled by the carpet and hidden under the moaning of the wind and the Ridgeback's pining for his master, the sound was distinguishable. Footsteps. They were coming along the corridor behind them.

"What is it?" Ariadne had also stopped and turned.

Felicity put a finger to her lips and crept back to the corner. She had no weapon with which to protect Ariadne and herself, but she could put whoever was following them at a disadvantage by removing the element of surprise.

Taking off her bicorn hat, slowly and carefully, Felicity looked around the corner.

Chapter Thirty-One

Alex stopped in the corridor. He tipped his head to one side. "Felicity?"

It must have been confusing to see only the top part of Felicity's face appear around the corner, but she wasn't at all dismayed to see him. Nor was she merely relieved that it wasn't someone to cause trouble.

Felicity smiled as she uprighted herself. "It's Mr Cooper," she called to Ariadne, whose shoulders dropped with relief at the news.

"I'm sorry if I startled you," said Alex as he came together with Felicity and Ariadne at the corridor junction.

"Don't apologise," said Felicity. "I ought to have guessed it was you."

"It's understandable we're all a little jumpy." He gave her a quick, reassuring smile. How was it that Alex never seemed in the least disappointed in her?

"Lady Felicity is escorting me to Archie," said Ariadne, a little too loudly for Felicity's liking. Who knew who else was lurking around the place?

"Shall I accompany you both?" offered Alex.

"Please," said Felicity, already looking forward to the moment she would be alone with him, and the three of them set off in the lift's direction, Ariadne in the lead.

It wasn't long before they arrived at a set of doors in dark, warm cherry with pale-gold oak inlays. Ariadne pressed a brass button mounted on the wall at the side. "Have you ever been in a lift before?" she asked.

It wasn't particularly noisy, but the lift made a rumbling that no doubt could be heard throughout a portion of the house. Felicity had foolishly not considered the noise before agreeing to the method of travel upstairs. The lift also moved rather slowly, but it was too late now. The machine was in motion.

Alex smiled kindly. "In London, there are all kinds of buildings with lifts in them."

"Oh, I know that. I didn't mean in shops and so forth," continued Ariadne as she pulled back the cage door. "I meant in a private house."

Alex stood back as Ariadne then Felicity stepped inside the lift. "No," he admitted. "I don't suppose I have."

He pulled the wooden doors and then the cage door shut. "Top floor?"

"That's right," said Felicity, who hadn't been in a private house with a lift before either. Not a lift that carried people, at least.

As they stepped out onto the top floor landing, the door to Lord Archibald's room opened slowly, and Archibald himself appeared, Mina at his side, a rifle readied in the interlopers' direction. The sight of the weapon sent a chill through Felicity, but her dread was quickly over. Archibald immediately recognised his sister and lowered his weapon.

"Archie!" Ariadne flew to her brother and hugged him around the middle. He didn't hug her back, but he put his hand on her pale hair for a moment. He, too, seemed relieved, having obviously taken Felicity's warning about his safety to heart. The lift was also clearly not the subtlest manner of getting around Grimstow House.

"You didn't do it, did you?" Ariadne looked up at her brother, her eyes gleaming with tears.

"Didn't do what?"

"You didn't kill Helen or shoot Leonard or anything else ghastly like that?"

Archie looked with confusion at Felicity and Alex, then at the rifle, which he kept at a distance from his sister. "I've shot nothing other than pheasants since the war," said Archie, returning his gaze to his sister, who continued to clasp him round the middle.

Ariadne broke down into floods of tears. She knew her brother well enough to trust what he said. It came as a relief.

Felicity put a hand gently on Ariadne's shoulder. "You've an incredible amount to share with your brother," she said, knowing that Archie still had to be informed of Tony's arrival. "But please, stay here together till the police arrive. That's the safest approach."

After a quick but awkward introduction with Alex over Ariadne's weeping head, for Archie and Alex hadn't yet spoken, Felicity and Alex left the siblings with Mina in the attic.

"It's not that I don't trust your judgment," said Alex once they were a little way down the stairs, "but may I ask why you seem so awfully sure of Lord Archibald's innocence?"

Felicity explained to Alex how, in her view, the fixing of the electricity was Archie's alibi. She also shared with Alex what she'd discovered about Miss Fairchild. It was a lot for Alex to take in. They paused on a landing. It was perhaps the same landing upon which they'd had their in-depth discussion about Alex's remaining in Devon while on their first trip to the attic.

The recollection made Felicity anxious. She'd likely done a great deal that evening to damage the feeling of belonging she'd somehow stirred in Alex.

"Heavens," he said, looking rather perturbed by the revelations about Miss Fairchild, the creases in his forehead emphasising the scar there. "Poor Edwin."

"I suppose the only consolation is she's not the murderer,"

Felicity added. "Although that's only my opinion, of course. And my opinion doesn't count for much. The police will have everything sorted out in their own way as soon as they get here."

"Well, I for one am always eager to hear your opinion." Alex wore an expression of perplexedness as he returned to slowly descending the stairs. "Your friend Lord Lorrimer told me he's thinking about marrying you and that he told you as much. I must admit, I've been wondering about your opinion on that."

Felicity felt the colour drain from her face. Why was it such a terribly awkward feeling? Wasn't it what every woman wanted, a good husband? The right kind of marriage? Her movements on the stairs became shaky.

"I don't mean to pry, of course," continued Alex. "You don't have to tell me anything. Although I thought you might appreciate knowing that he's informing just about everyone of his interest in you."

A little zing of anger shot through Felicity. How dare Charles? He said he'd give her time to think.

"I mean, we hardly know one another, Lord Lorrimer and I," continued Alex, "but he wanted to hear from me, as your colleague, how attached you are to your career."

"As a journalist?" asked Felicity, her neglectfulness towards her duties as a reporter adding a dose of shame to the tangled mass of uncomfortable emotions building up inside her.

"Well," began Alex, tugging a little at his shirt collar. "I told him you're the best writer the Western Daily News has — aside from myself, of course — and that your success as a journalist reflects your passion and dedication."

Felicity's insides warmed for a moment, but Alex's words contained a sting in their tail. "You'd be more comfortable if I was focused on reporting. Is that correct?"

Alex stopped on the stairs and sighed. "That's not what I said." He looked a little sad. "You're a fantastic journalist. Among the best there is." Felicity began to protest. Alex cut her off. "But that's not what's most important. I'd rather you were doing what you wanted to do."

Felicity frowned. Over the years, she'd fought for her position at her brother's newspaper. She and Alex hadn't arrived at Grimstow House as reporters, but a huge story was brewing. The scoop of the month, if not the year. "You're right," she said, stopping a little further down the stairs. "I should be reporting."

"Look." Alex put a hand on the bannister, his dark blue eyes earnest. "It was my life's dream to write for the papers. I came from a hard-working family, but I had no connections to newspapermen, yet here I am, working among friends, sharing the news in a way that means something to people. I'm passionate about it. But it's my passion. It's not everyone's. One ought to be able to follow one's passion, regardless of one's background."

Felicity thought for a moment. It was what she admired most about Alex. Not just his skill and experience, but his tenacity and stamina. It was passion that drove him forward. Reporting was Felicity's passion, too, wasn't it? She came from privilege, but to fight for a career as a woman counted for something. She would continue the fight, wouldn't she? There was more than just her career to think about. The partnership Felicity had developed with Alex was founded upon their professional relations.

Suddenly, the thought of Charles' talk of marriage returned to Felicity like an awkward weight slung around her neck. "How did Charles react to what you told him?"

Alex pushed his hands in his pockets. "He didn't seem overjoyed to hear how dedicated you've been to your job, but as far as I'm concerned, that's the truth of it. I hope you don't mind that I told him the way I see things."

"On the contrary. I appreciate it." Felicity's earlier self-pity was almost forgotten. It did wonders to know one had an ally.

Alex smiled. "I thought to myself, this chap's surely not the only fellow interested in marrying my colleague, Felicity. In fact, I know for certain he's not."

Felicity frowned briefly, puzzled by Alex's comment.

He moved the conversation onwards, resuming his progress down the stairs. "While I was gathering the Bourgoynes' bags from their motor, Clemency confirmed Rex's alibi for the time when Leonard was shot."

"She's clearly besotted with the fellow," said Felicity. "Are you convinced?"

Alex shrugged. "It's as convincing an alibi as electricity cables that cannot speak." There was an air of challenge to his voice.

"So that leaves…" Felicity stopped herself.

"Patience?"

They'd come again to a halt, this time on a landing with corridors running off it in several directions.

"She swears she wasn't the lady in the morning room," says Alex. "She told me multiple times, without my asking, how offended she was that you'd dared even suggest it."

As indomitable as Felicity's drive was to untangle everything she and Alex knew about what had happened that evening at Grimstow House, she wouldn't take the bait. "We're to lock ourselves in our rooms till the police arrive, are we not?" She was feeling less sorry for herself and more indignant. "I have orders from the Chief Inspector not to involve myself."

Alex lowered his brow. "Sharing your opinions with me isn't exactly involving yourself, is it?"

Felicity thought for a moment. Technically, it wasn't.

A smile danced on his lips. "And since when have you taken the police or anyone else warning you off very seriously?"

"Now that I take offence to," said Felicity somewhat haughtily. "You make it sound as if I make it my business to defy orders."

"Do you not?"

Felicity huffed. "I make it my business to help where I can. If orders are defied in the course of that, then I've always made the proper apologies. But that's a thing of the past. I've come to realise I've overestimated my usefulness." Felicity folded her arms over her ink-blue jacket. "I'm not sure where your room is, but I'm quite certain mine is—" she turned "—this way."

Felicity stopped, blinking.

Where the corridors split in various directions, there was an alcove. In the alcove, on a pedestal, sat a large antique vase with a gilded rim. Extending from the vase's opening was a collection of large-plumed feathers arranged delicately to form an attractive display.

"I see it now," said Felicity quietly. "I've been completely blind."

Alex joined Felicity in staring at the feathers. He glanced at her. "I recognise that look in your eye."

Felicity's stomach rolled. She turned to Alex. "I've a horrible feeling I know what's going on."

Chapter Thirty-Two

After summarising the breakthrough in her thinking — which was made simpler because Alex was quick on the uptake and grasped what Felicity was saying immediately — Felicity and Alex dashed down the stairs, Felicity moving faster than she had done all evening, thanks in part to her T-strap shoes. The South Drawing Room was quickly located, and Felicity knocked on the door, she and Alex entering without waiting to be summoned.

Both Edwin and Charles looked annoyed at first, then relieved when they saw it was Felicity and Alex who had burst in. Their relief, however, was replaced by expressions of worry, with Edwin's countenance grave. Leonard was sitting up on the sofa, looking pale and annoyed, his head resting on cushions. In the hand of his uninjured arm, he held a cigar, which filled the room with its rich, thick smell. Tony appeared to be asleep, although his eyes fluttered open to watch Felicity and Alex enter the room. Felicity supposed the nature of the drama didn't touch him as much as the other people in the house, especially those who had known Helen.

The butler and the housekeeper stood dutifully to one side of the room, ready to take orders at a moment's notice. Upon

Felicity and Alex's entrance, the two servants had stirred only slightly in the barely perceptible way of long-standing attendants. Miss Fairchild was nowhere to be seen.

"Edwin, might I have a word with you in private?" Felicity and Alex's entrance had perhaps been a little too dramatic, so Felicity spoke gently to downplay it. She'd felt so sure of herself upstairs on the landing. Now, with so many eyes on her, she felt the weight of her deductions more keenly. What if she had things wrong?

No. She couldn't have. There was simply no other way.

"Of course, Felicity." Edwin looked over at Charles. "May I leave my patients in your charge temporarily?"

Charles nodded at his friend. "Certainly." He still had the pistol on his hip, which was reassuring, but when he cast a longing glance in Felicity's direction, she shifted uncomfortably. A marriage proposal amid the savagery of the evening's events was evermore incongruous.

"I'll stay, too," said Alex, joining Charles beside the mantelpiece.

"We shan't be long," said Edwin. "Right, Felicity?"

Felicity swallowed. "That's right."

As Edwin escorted Felicity out into the corridor, his cane tapping on the stone floor, the butler closed the drawing room door behind them.

"What is it you have to tell me?"

"Not here," said Felicity. "I'd rather not be overheard," she added in a whisper.

Edwin's jaw tightened. "Very well," he said, and led her along the corridor. Exhaustion had been replaced by tension and perhaps even anger in Edwin. Felicity hoped she wasn't exacerbating his misery by calling him away like this. Even if she was, it didn't matter. She had a duty to tell him.

"Is everyone in their rooms in accordance with the police's orders?" asked Felicity as Edwin opened a door off the corridor.

Edwin huffed. "What do you think? It's not as if anyone's

shown any willingness to be well-behaved at any point this evening." He flicked on the lights. They'd arrived back in the library where Felicity and Alex had met with Helen and Leonard at the beginning of their ill-fated visit to Grimstow House. This was now a very different situation, and a very different discussion. Remembering that Helen was no longer among them made Felicity shiver.

The wind continued to gust against the windows, which — despite the house being only recently built — could be heard rattling beyond the thick curtains.

As Edwin closed the library door, Felicity said, "I owe you an apology." Before anything else, she needed to clear the air.

Edwin went to the polished oval table and leaned upon it, resting his cane beside him. He folded his arms. "If it's about Miss Fairchild, I already know."

Felicity's hand flew to her chest. "You do?"

"Isn't that why you want to apologise? For not coming immediately to tell me?"

Felicity had other matters in mind for clearing the air, but they could wait. "Do you mean she…"

"Miss Fairchild—" Edwin halted. "I mean, whoever the woman really is, she called me away and confessed. Confessed to everything."

Felicity raised her eyebrows. Miss Fairchild had gone up in her estimation, as much as a liar and a thief could.

Edwin tightened the fold of his arms. "You don't need to apologise, Felicity. You did the right thing. To hear it from her directly… Oh, it was painful all right. She asked for my forgiveness, which I thought was rather premature. I couldn't give it to her. Not yet. Indeed, I don't know if I'll ever come around to that. Not after tonight. Of course, I've been a perfect fool. I've been thoroughly played, and to bring a character like that into a family home. I suppose there's no way of covering up, not with those Bourgoyne women harping on about their jewels. They say they can't find them, even though they've been returned."

Recalling the state of the sisters' room, Felicity suspected she knew why.

Edwin shook his head. "I'll never get over the shame of it."

"It wasn't your fault," said Felicity emphatically. "She had us all fooled."

Edwin looked up. "Everyone except you."

"It was pure luck that I uncovered her misdoings."

"But it all pales compared to the loss of Helen," said Edwin with a heavy sigh, a pained expression on his freckled face.

"Of course it does," said Felicity sadly.

Edwin pushed away from the table, taking up his cane. "But there's no point dwelling. We can't bring her back. I need to get back to my patients." Edwin was being extremely brave. He had no obligation to care for the two men, especially given being so recently bereaved, although it was perhaps a welcome distraction from the sorrow of losing his sister. "Mr McQueen is getting rather restless, which is really the last thing we need. The fellow wants to be reunited with that dog of his, which I will absolutely not allow." Edwin began towards the library door.

"I'm afraid that's not everything I had to share with you," said Felicity.

Edwin paused. "It's not?"

"I'm terribly sorry to bring this up, but did you discuss with Miss Fairchild the matter of Helen's jewels?" It was a deeply unpleasant topic.

Edwin grimaced. "She mentioned it. The woman insists she didn't take them, yet they're gone."

"May I ask who provided the evidence about the gems from Helen's necklace being missing?" pressed Felicity, making a point. She knew the answer.

"Why, the butler confirmed it. You were there yourself when he told us, were you not?"

"You haven't since confirmed it yourself?" Felicity asked, yet she might have guessed the answer. She was circling around the issue rather than going straight to it. She had to be careful. Edwin had been through so much, and she'd already witnessed his rage brought on by the hurt.

"I've not been back in that room, if that's what you're asking." Edwin's brow drew low. "Look, Felicity. You've been an enormous help and a great comfort to me, but if you'd kindly just get to the point and spare me further misery."

Felicity nodded. Coming to the point was the least she could do for her cousin. If this was meddling, and the police's special order for her was being defied, then so be it. She would rather live with the consequences of having been wrong and defiant in her behaviour than having been right and not bold enough.

"We've invested a lot of trust in the servants here at Grimstow House," said Felicity. "We've depended on them thoroughly. I believe that's why we've not examined them deeply. How well do we know them?"

"How well does anyone know a domestic?" Edwin blinked and shook his head. "Felicity, please. Speak plainly."

"The butler, Horrocks, has vouched for everyone below stairs, and we have taken him at his word."

"Are you saying we cannot trust Horrocks? Are you implying that young Mr Peabody is not to be relied upon in terms of his account of reaching the village and contacting the police? Or any of the men who helped prevent the stables burning to the ground?"

Felicity nodded with understanding. The relationship between master and servant was both intimate and impersonal, and — in order to be maintained — rarely examined. It was a delicate subject. "What I mean to say is—"

Edwin cut her off. She'd pushed his patience too far. "I can't see how, on top of all the drama and rivalries swirling around the guests, there would be some layer of intrigue that would drag the servants down into it. They're all extremely dedicated to the Earl, as I'm sure you realise."

Felicity hesitated. Colour rose in Edwin's cheeks. He pushed the tip of his cane into the library carpet, his grip on it vice-like.

"Or do you see it differently, Felicity? And remember, we are far beyond playing parlour games now."

Within Edwin's agitation was the same vexation Felicity herself had felt when she'd realised what she'd overlooked. Her first reaction had been to chastise herself, because Felicity's tendency was to direct her frustration inwardly. Kind though he normally was, Edwin, like many men, directed his frustration outwards. Knowing her cousin, knowing everything he'd been through and what he would have to face even after this awful night was over, Felicity could look beyond Edwin's irritated manner.

She spoke gently. "Exactly what the intrigue might be isn't something I've yet—"

A rumble like furniture being moved in an adjoining room startled them both.

"What the deuce was that?" said Edwin.

They paused and listened. There was the howl of the wind at the windows. Then raised voices.

Felicity's heart pounded.

Crack!

She looked at Edwin, her mouth gaping, the blood draining from her face. It was obvious to both of them what the second sound had been. A gun had gone off in the room next door.

Chapter Thirty-Three

As Felicity and Edwin reached the South Drawing Room, their footsteps clattering along the hallway, the door flew open. Breathing heavily, Leonard stood with the hand of his good arm pressed against the door jamb. He was as white as a sheet except for his cheeks, which glowed pink with irritation, and his dark eyes, which blazed with anger.

Behind Leonard stood Charles, his face full of regret, the pistol in his hand. Beyond Charles was Alex, his eyes wide with warning. Tony was awake and watching, although still lying back on the sofa. The butler stood at the side of the room. He looked frightened. One of his cheeks was rather red. On the carpet in the middle of the room lay a small pile of white plaster that had collapsed from a hole in the ceiling.

"It wasn't my intention to f-fire," stammered Charles. "It really wasn't. He came at me. I—"

"Out of my way." Leonard lurched forward, pushing Edwin to one side.

"Where are you going, man?" Edwin tried to catch Leonard's arm, but he slipped past. "You're in no fit state to be standing up, let alone walking around."

"I'm no one's prisoner," said Leonard as he stumbled and

smacked into a side table in the corridor. The impact had such force it made Felicity wince.

"Horrocks," said Edwin forcefully. "Do something."

"I-I tried, sir. Mr McQueen has been rather insistent about his need to leave Grimstow House." The butler touched his cheek.

"I'm going to get my dog," said Leonard as he careened along the corridor. "And I'm going to leave."

"You're not thinking straight," said Edwin, approaching Leonard briskly. "You don't have the strength to handle your dog, and the weather outside is deadly." Edwin put a hand to Leonard's good arm, but he violently shrugged Edwin off.

"Don't touch me," said the businessman. He groaned in pain and rested his weight against the wall.

Alex approached Felicity, raking a hand through his hair, his brow knitted with concern. "We tried to stop him, but as you can see, he won't be reasoned with."

"I'm certain you did your best." Felicity sympathised with Alex's exasperation — how many people thought they would find success venturing into the freezing night? — but she had to think quickly. Leonard had already been shot once. By leaving the safety of the drawing room, he was exposing himself. Danger could lurk anywhere in the house.

"Mr McQueen, you are delirious," said Edwin, dropping his hand hopelessly to his side.

"I want my dog back."

"Please, Mr McQueen," said Felicity, stepping forward. "We'll bring your dog to you."

Leonard turned, a glimmer of interest in his eyes.

"If you'll just stay in the drawing room, where we can—"

The lights went out. The drawing room and the corridor were plunged into darkness.

"—look after you." A horrible sinking feeling hit Felicity in the stomach. It was as if a switch had been knocked. There'd been no flickering. The darkness was absolute. She put a hand out to feel for the wall, to help gather her bearings.

"Just what is going on?"

"Don't go anywhere."

Felicity stayed still, but with the disembodied voices and the sound of people moving around in the dark, it was difficult to orientate herself.

"The lights will be back on soon." The voice was Edwin's.

Someone brushed past her, exiting the drawing room. But who? She knew instinctively it wasn't Alex.

There was a thud as someone stumbled into a piece of furniture in the drawing room and an oath or two was uttered.

"What's going on?" A woman's voice echoed along the corridor. It sounded like Patience.

Felicity remained on the spot. There was so little to see. Then the curtains in the drawing room opened. The light from the moon didn't flood in like it had done in the billiard room, but it was enough to make out who was who.

Alex had opened the curtains. Tony remained on the sofa, though he was attempting to sit up. Charles was still frozen to the spot, his gun still in his hand. Edwin had remained in the corridor, close to where Felicity was standing.

The light barely reached the corridor, but it seemed Leonard and the butler were gone.

"This is completely unacceptable." Patience's voice drifted through the dimness of the corridor. Sobbing accompanied her words, presumably Clemency's. "We see you, Felicity. We're coming to you."

Felicity had to think fast. "Mr McQueen is in grave danger," she said to Edwin. "We have to get to him."

"Lady Felicity's right." Alex joined Felicity in the corridor. Sweeping back his jacket and putting his hands on his hips, he revealed that he, too, had a pistol attached to his belt. How long had it been there? "Someone put the lights out on purpose this time."

"Aren't we all in danger?" asked Edwin, sounding more scared than he had all evening.

Leading Clemency by the hand, Patience appeared in the pale pool of moonlight spreading from the drawing room door, their party dresses shimmering. "And just what are we supposed to do now?" Patience had the air of a disgruntled customer, addressing Edwin and Felicity as if it were their responsibility to assist.

But there was a more pressing concern than Patience's discontent.

"Mr McQueen intended to fetch his dog, did he not?" asked Felicity. "Do we know in which room Jambo was locked up?"

Horrocks came trotting down the corridor, a lantern swinging in his hand. He spoke breathlessly, addressing Edwin. "I did my best to follow Mr McQueen, sir, but I lost him. He went to the entrance hall and then outside."

"Outside?" Felicity frowned at Alex.

"And he wasn't alone, your ladyship."

"Who was he with?" pressed Alex.

Horrocks shook his head. "I couldn't tell, sir."

"A man? A woman?" asked Felicity.

"A woman, your ladyship."

Felicity had an inkling she knew who.

"Mr McQueen is badly injured," muttered Edwin. "And I don't suppose he collected a coat before going outside. Where the deuce do you suppose he's going?"

Felicity's mind whirred. They could go to the garage to see if Leonard and whoever he was with were attempting to leave with a motor, but if he wasn't there, it would be valuable time lost. Finding anyone outside in the dark expanse of Grimstow House's grounds was like finding a needle in a haystack.

"I'd like to help, if I can." Tony was trying to sit up.

Edwin went to him. "Please, Tony, you mustn't exert yourself." His patient's suggestion was valiant but indeed ridiculous.

"Just what is going on?" whined Patience. "Horrocks, turn the lights back on this instant. I demand it."

"I already tried that, ma'am, but the main panel has been sabotaged."

Felicity turned to the butler. "Mr Horrocks, can you take us to Mr McQueen's Ridgeback?"

The butler looked at Alex and Felicity. "Y-yes, your ladyship. But Mr McQueen didn't go for his dog. He went outside."

"I realise that," said Felicity rather curtly. "Can you take us?"

"Of course, your ladyship."

Felicity looked at Alex. He nodded his approval. It was clear to both of them what needed to be done.

Felicity turned to Patience. "You and your sister should wait here in the drawing room." Seeing little need to spend extra time on the formalities of politeness, she ushered the girls into the room as one might round up a pair of geese. "Charles will look after you."

Still frozen by the mantelpiece, Charles perked up a little. "I will?" He cleared his throat. "I will."

"But what are we to do here?" said Patience as Felicity deposited the sisters on the sofa Leonard had vacated.

"Sit and wait," said Felicity. "And don't leave this room."

Clemency nodded obediently at Felicity as she took a seat. She was more accustomed to accepting authority than her sister.

"The lights will come back on at any moment, won't they?" asked Patience, lowering herself awkwardly next to Clemency.

No, thought Felicity. *They will not.* But there was no point in sharing her opinion and worrying people all the more.

"I shall ensure your safety, Miss Bourgoyne," said Charles, his confidence in his abilities returning. He gave Felicity a firm nod as if to say, *Leave them to me.* Felicity was grateful.

Edwin rose from beside Tony and addressed Felicity. "I don't know exactly what it is you plan to do, but I wish you good luck."

Felicity couldn't be sure what lay ahead, but inaction wasn't an option. One murder had already happened under her nose. She wouldn't allow a second.

"I shall do my best," she said as she joined Alex and Horrocks at the drawing room door. Time was ticking. Felicity wouldn't say it aloud, but she was secretly glad Alex had armed himself. It made relying on the butler easier.

"Lead the way, Mr Horrocks," said Felicity. "Take us to Jambo."

Chapter Thirty-Four

Racing along passages and up staircases, Horrocks leading the way with his lantern, Felicity and Alex stopped briefly at the butler's pantry to fetch a supply of confit de canard — the first vaguely appropriate edible they could lay their hands on — and then by the cloakroom, where they gathered coats and a length of rope usually used for fastening valises to luggage racks.

As Felicity pulled on the furs she'd borrowed earlier, which were immediately located by the butler, she wondered if they weren't already too late, but she quickly silenced that voice. They had to try. And they had to be prepared.

"Please, let's hurry," she said as they climbed the stairs to the first floor, the butler in the lead.

"Going as fast as I can, your ladyship."

Horrocks led them directly to a door on the other side of which Jambo could be heard scratching and barking. Alex winced. He wasn't a dog person, and this wasn't helping. Even Felicity, who would never be without a canine companion, wasn't quite sure she could carry things off. She'd little experience of large, powerful dogs like the Ridgeback.

"You may return to the drawing room now, Horrocks," said Felicity. "I'm sure Edwin will be thankful for the extra support."

"Y-your ladyship. If I may, I'd like to be of further assistance to you in seeing this through. I feel I've let everyone down, and I should like to make up for it."

"How have you let everyone down?" she asked.

The butler shook his head. "It's just a feeling I have, your ladyship."

Felicity looked at Alex. He gave a little shrug. "Very well, Horrocks," said Felicity, for she knew how it felt to want to redeem oneself, "but please stand back."

Felicity opened a fragrant tin of confit de canard and approached the door, speaking soothingly towards the Ridgeback. Jambo howled in response, his tone switching from aggression to distress. Opening the door just a crack, Felicity held the tin near the door to allow the dog to sniff its contents. Jambo quietened, whimpering, and sniffed the food eagerly. He licked his jowls, then barked. He was interested.

Opening the door just a little further, this time with Alex's help so that Felicity could control the tin of duck confit with both hands, Felicity gave Jambo a piece of meat. "You're hungry, aren't you, boy?" she said soothingly as the Ridgeback wolfed down the offering. Thankfully, Felicity had brought a second tin along.

Very slowly, and while still eating, Jambo allowed Felicity to pet his velvety head. "What a good boy you are." The Ridgeback continued to eat as she gently reached for his thick leather collar and strung the rope through it, tying a very firm knot and taking the length in her hands.

When the second tin was empty — thankfully, there was a third and even a fourth — Jambo looked up at Felicity rather docilely, his flopped ears perked in hope of even more delicious duck.

With the door to Jambo's room now fully open, Felicity encouraged the large dog to join them in the corridor, where she urged him to sit. "Good boy. Good Jambo." Felicity stroked the Ridgeback's head, his velvety fur shining in the light of the lantern.

The butler looked unsure of Felicity's methodology. Alex looked vaguely amused.

"We need to find your master," she said softly to the Ridgeback, putting the confit to one side. "Can you take us to him?"

Jambo sniffed the air thoughtfully, barked, then set off.

"Good boy," said Felicity as she allowed herself to be led by the Ridgeback, Alex and the butler close behind her. As they went back downstairs, the dog kept looking over his shoulder at Felicity, clearly hoping for more food, but once in the entrance hall, Jambo's nose went to the ground. He whimpered and pawed at the big front doors. He had his master's scent.

"Good boy," urged Felicity, as the butler opened the doors and the cold, hard wind whipped around her ankles. "Find him. Find Mr McQueen for us."

Once outside, Felicity had to hold the rope rather tightly as Jambo's paws scrambled in the gravel, the dog eager to follow the scent.

"Do you believe he knows where Mr McQueen is, your ladyship?" enquired the butler, raising his voice above the wind.

"We have to hope so," said Felicity as Jambo tugged hard on the makeshift lead. He was taking them in the opposite direction of the garage, over the grass and down a steep slope. "Good boy, Jambo," urged Felicity as they headed into the woods at the side of the house, where the trees blocked out the moonlight. Only a vague pool of light from the butler's lantern allowed them to see where they were treading.

The forest floor dipped steeply, and this allowed Jambo to speed up. Felicity struggled to keep her balance, her T-strap shoes with their little heel not being well suited to navigating an uneven floor. The dog lurched forward. "Easy, boy." As Felicity stumbled, Alex was at her elbow, helping steady her, his calm gaze meeting hers, then they were off again in a flash, Jambo whimpering with longing and excitement, Felicity praising him and doing her best not to slow him down as she clung to the rope attached to his collar.

Pushing branches aside, the forest floor steepened further. The sound of rushing water mingled with the hiss of the wind through the trees. "We're approaching the river," said the butler. Jambo whined as they continued to surge forward and downwards. A dim light appeared up ahead.

"What's that?" asked Alex.

"I believe we're approaching the turbine house, sir. It's part of the hydroelectric system that powers the estate."

The wind picked up, carrying with it snatches of voices that Jambo had no doubt heard long before any human ears.

"—your hands off me!"

"You'll do as I—"

Jambo barked and strained on his improvised lead. It appeared he'd done his job in leading them to his master, but the dog couldn't be prevented from barking. There was no chance of taking anyone by surprise.

Felicity pressed onwards.

The trees thinned as the rush of water grew louder. "Easy, boy." She did her best to slow Jambo, her feet slipping as the Ridgeback yanked her forward. Alex took the gun from the holster on his belt as they slowly approached the dim pool of light thrown from a lantern that had fallen on its side at the foot of a rough stone building. Two figures were lit gloomily in its light. It wasn't yet possible to see what was going on. The pair appeared to be huddled beside a low wall, beyond which, down a sheer drop of several feet, the waters of the River Teign splashed and roared, the blackness of the flow highlighted by glittering slivers of moonlight.

Jambo whined and pulled hard on the rope. Felicity had to use all her body weight to stop the powerful hound rushing towards the two shadowy figures. Alex stepped forward and put a hand on the rope attached to the dog's collar, adding his strength to the battle to keep Jambo under control. "Easy, boy," he said.

"Mr McQueen?" Felicity called, raising her voice above the rush of the river, the whistling of the wind, and the Ridgeback's barking.

"Get this madwoman off me," came Leonard's response.

The butler stepped forward. "Don't come any closer!" came a woman's voice through the shadows.

"Mrs Rudd?" called the butler, raising his lantern and squinting through the darkness. "Is that you?"

"It's the blasted housekeeper, all right," shouted Leonard. "And she's got a gun jabbed in my side. I just wish she'd tell me why!"

Jambo snarled and yanked on the rope, reacting to his master's voice. While it was clear the Ridgeback had a good heart and cared immensely for his master, there was no telling the damage of which he was capable when caught up in his emotions.

"And I'll use it," cried Mrs Rudd. "I'm not afraid to. We're at the end of things now. So stay back!" From the tremble in her voice, the housekeeper was as much frightened as she was defiant. As the trees moved in the gusting wind, a thin cast of moonlight pitched across her outline. Mrs Rudd's dimly lit form resembled that of just about every other woman in the household. The addition of a borrowed feather tucked into her hair would have confused matters even more.

"Mrs Rudd, please." The butler sounded quite desperate. "Don't do anything you'll regret. There's no need for this."

While Alex was armed, so was Mrs Rudd. There was also the distance and the darkness to consider when taking a shot, while the housekeeper had the barrel of her weapon trained directly on her victim. How to get out of this stalemate?

"It's too late for that, Mr Horrocks," came the housekeeper's reply. "But don't worry about me. You all stand to benefit from my sacrifice. I promise you."

With her hands still tight on Jambo's lead, Felicity flicked quickly through the options available.

"Your sacrifice?" spat Leonard. "What are you talking about, woman? You killed Helen, shot me in the shoulder, and now you want me to throw myself in the river? You're the one sacrificing us, you lunatic!"

It sounded as though Mrs Rudd had planned for Leonard's death to look like suicide. That plan had now obviously failed. Whatever her motives, Mrs Rudd was desperate.

"Mr McQueen," said Felicity, still working with Alex to keep Jambo under control. "Please remain calm. Mrs Rudd has her reasons. She's not a lunatic. Are you, Mrs Rudd?"

"Has her reasons? Pah!" If Leonard had known his life depended on his keeping his mouth shut, would he have been able to control himself?

"That is correct, is it not, Mrs Rudd?" continued Felicity firmly but calmly. "Your thoughts are perfectly rational, are they not?"

The river continued to thunder below. "Yes, your ladyship," replied Mrs Rudd after a pause.

The housekeeper's use of the polite form of address threw Felicity slightly. She quickly decided it was an advantage. "Then would you do me the honour of speaking to me before any further action is taken?"

There was another pause as gusts of freezing wind whipped through the trees. The butler stood very stiffly and closed his eyes, as though willing for something to happen.

"There's nothing to discuss, your ladyship," came the housekeeper's answer.

"What do you mean, nothing to discuss?" barked Leonard. "How about we discuss the— Ow!"

Felicity couldn't see exactly what was happening. She guessed Mrs Rudd was controlling Leonard by putting pressure on his injured shoulder. It was a stark contrast to the care she'd shown in dressing Felicity for the ball, caring for Sir Vernon's injured hand, and all the assistance Mrs Rudd would have provided during her many years in service. What had driven her to this?

"Mr McQueen." For his own safety, Felicity had no choice but to use a remonstrating tone with Leonard. "If you would be kind enough to allow Mrs Rudd and I to have a civilised discussion without constant interruption, it would be most appreciated."

Leonard groaned. "I've had quite enough of this, I can tell you."

"Please, Mrs Rudd." The butler sounded deeply upset. "This isn't how things ought to be. We've a duty to the Earl."

"I know that, Mr Horrocks," replied the housekeeper with determination. "I know it only too well. That's why I'm here. I'm here for his lordship. I'm here for all of us. Don't you see?"

"I've got him," whispered Alex to Felicity, bracing a two-handed grip on the rope attached to Jambo's collar.

"Thank you," said Felicity, allowing the rope to slip from her fingers. "Mr Horrocks? May I borrow your lantern?" There were tears in the butler's eyes as he handed the light to Felicity. Holding the lantern aloft, she stepped forward. "I shan't come any further without your permission, Mrs Rudd, but I should like to speak to you, if I could." There was no guarantee it would work, but Felicity had to try. "May I approach?"

Chapter Thirty-Five

The rushing of the river below grew louder as Felicity carefully approached Mrs Rudd and Leonard. Holding the lantern out before her, Felicity's knuckles stung from the biting cold, for in her haste to leave the main house, she hadn't taken gloves with her.

"I'm coming closer, Mrs Rudd. I do hope we can discuss things sensibly." Drawing nearer to the kidnapper and her hostage, Felicity's lantern cast light on how serious the situation really was.

Wearing his dinner jacket and no coat, Leonard was pushed against the low wall, beyond which was a steep drop into the churning waters of a weir that, via the nearby turbine house, powered the Grimstow estate. Behind Leonard, Mrs Rudd stood very close in her black housekeeper's dress. She had a hand on the businessman's injured shoulder. With her other hand, she pressed a pistol into Leonard's back.

Felicity didn't know how to resolve the predicament, or even if there was a resolution to be had. She just knew she had to keep Mrs Rudd talking.

"It's quite the situation we find ourselves in here, isn't it, Mrs Rudd?" Felicity struck an almost friendly, commiserating tone, attempting to identify with the housekeeper. Now that they were closer to one another and didn't have to raise their voices as much, Felicity could control her tone much better.

In the light from Felicity's lantern, Mrs Rudd's expression changed from sombre determination to a tearful grimace. She hadn't a hand free to wipe away the tear that rolled down her cheek. "I suppose you could say that, your ladyship."

Leonard narrowed his eyes at Felicity. *I hope you bally well know what you're doing*, his look seemed to say. He had at least understood the need to bite his tongue.

"How did we get here, would you say, Mrs Rudd?" asked Felicity coaxingly, for the precise nature of the housekeeper's motive remained opaque.

Mrs Rudd wept for a moment, then gritted her teeth, fastening her grip on the gun. "Oh, I've made mistakes, your ladyship. I'll be the first to admit it. I tried to warn you off with a note, only that didn't work. I didn't want anyone else getting hurt, you see, but it seems I overestimated my capabilities in several areas." She sniffed. "In any case, I'm here to see things through." She looked down at her captive. "And see things through I shall."

There were so many options for what to say next. Which was the right one? There was so much riding on Felicity's every word. "What mistakes have you made, Mrs Rudd?"

Again, the housekeeper sobbed. Her emotions threatened to overwhelm her. Straightening, she bit her lower lip and pulled on Leonard's injured shoulder, making the man groan in pain. Jambo barked ferociously. Mrs Rudd's fearful eyes widened at the commotion.

Felicity continued. "I understand you to be an extremely dedicated and capable servant to Earl Carrington. In fact, I've witnessed your skills myself since my arrival at Grimstow. You've maintained your poise and dependability, despite everything the evening has thrown at us." Felicity continued to imply empathy with the housekeeper.

Mrs Rudd sniffed. "That's kind of you to say, your ladyship."

The rushing of the water was fierce and the cold bit hard into Felicity's knuckles where she gripped the lantern. She pulled the fur coat more tightly around herself. "We all make mistakes, Mrs Rudd," continued Felicity. "Which of yours were you alluding to just now?"

Another tear rolled down Mrs Rudd's cheek. "Miss Helen, your ladyship," she said with a gasp of pain. "She wasn't meant to get hurt, your ladyship. She fought with me. I didn't expect it. The gun went off, but that wasn't the intention. I meant for this one to receive the bullet."

"Ow!" Leonard's body arced in pain. Jambo snarled viciously.

"Easy now." Alex was doing his best to control the dog.

"Mrs Rudd, please!" The butler couldn't prevent himself from crying out, no doubt shocked by Mrs Rudd's complete lack of respect for Leonard's welfare.

"It was a clever plan," said Felicity through gritted teeth, for there was nothing admirable about what Mrs Rudd had done, but she had to keep the housekeeper's focus on talking. "Even the best of plans go wrong."

"They certainly do, your ladyship." Mrs Rudd's eyes sparkled in the lantern light. "When I heard about the thefts, I simply informed Mr Horrocks that someone had stolen from Miss Helen as well. I thought I might get away with things that way. It seemed cruel to deprive the Earl of a faithful servant as well as a step-daughter." Mrs Rudd laughed bitterly. "There's no chance of that now, of course."

Felicity shivered. The housekeeper's logic was twisted. She had been happy to allow someone else to take the blame for Helen's death, maybe even to hang for it, yet it was clear Mrs Rudd wasn't entirely heartless. She cared deeply for Earl Carrington. Too deeply.

Felicity swallowed. Despite the pressure of the situation, she couldn't rush the discussion. "The fireworks going off was another opportunity of which you took advantage, was it not?"

Mrs Rudd hung her head. "Yes, but I made another

mistake, your ladyship. I used a rifle hunting rabbits with my pa as a girl, and then there was the annual pigeon shoot with his lordship. The Earl is so good to us servants, your ladyship. You can't imagine. And I'd always been a good aim, but I didn't consider I'd have only one clean shot. I didn't miss by much." The housekeeper gave Leonard a hateful glance. "But there were too many people about for a second attempt." She laughed bitterly. "And now look at me. Caught like an animal in a trap."

"Easy, boy. Whoa, there." Alex was trying to calm Jambo, but he must have lost his footing as he skidded forward, the snarling Ridgeback bounding closer.

"Stay back, I tell you!" Mrs Rudd stiffened and jerked the hand with the pistol at Leonard's back.

Felicity's breath caught in her throat. Alex quickly regained control of the dog. The businessman groaned. "We're not coming any closer, Mrs Rudd," said Felicity gently. "I promise."

The butler remained frozen where he stood, watching the housekeeper with wide, frightened eyes. *Keep her talking*, repeated Felicity to herself. Buying time was all she could do. Perhaps by digging deeper, there was even a slim chance she could talk the housekeeper into letting her hostage free.

Leonard muttered something under his breath.

"Mrs Rudd," continued Felicity, "from everything you've told me, it seems you've had an awful run of bad luck."

The housekeeper's chest heaved. "I have, your ladyship. I really have."

"And yet you've pushed ahead with your goal. You've done your absolute best to achieve your target. You've been extremely dedicated."

Mrs Rudd sobbed. "I have. Indeed, I have."

"What was that goal, Mrs Rudd?"

Mrs Rudd looked down at Leonard. Her face twisted into hate. "To stop him."

Leonard turned to look at his captor. Then he looked at

Felicity. He was doing his best to keep quiet, his mouth pursed under his thin moustache, his eyes ablaze with fear and anger.

"To stop Mr McQueen from doing what, Mrs Rudd?"

"Ruining the Earl."

Felicity exhaled slowly. It had been clear the servants at Grimstow House were extremely dedicated to their master. She hadn't guessed that in the housekeeper's case the attachment was fanatical.

"Forgive my ignorance, Mrs Rudd. I'd not met Mr McQueen before this evening. Could you tell me more about the threat he poses to your master?"

Mrs Rudd's jaw tensed.

"You're hurting me, blast it," muttered Leonard. Felicity silently prayed he would hold his tongue.

"This one's ruined many a good family," said Mrs Rudd. "I couldn't sit back and let it happen to ours."

Her use of 'ours' wasn't uncommon among dedicated servants, but Mrs Rudd had taken her dedication to an unfathomable level.

"That sounds indeed like something one would want to go to great lengths to avoid," said Felicity, adding as much sympathy as she could to her voice. "How has he ruined other families?"

"By stealing their money."

Leonard couldn't control himself. "I'm not a thief," he growled. "I'm a man of business, for heaven's sake!"

Mrs Rudd responded to Leonard with fervour. "I might be just a servant in your eyes, but I'm not stupid. None of us are. We all see what it is you really do. You're a cheat. You take old families for a ride, dazzling them with investment opportunities and then leaving them with nothing."

"That's not me," growled Leonard. "I swore I'd never be like my father," he added quietly.

"Mrs Rudd, Mr McQueen," Felicity said in a futile attempt to bring the attention back to herself.

"Look at the Bourgoynes," continued Mrs Rudd, trembling

with anger. "Rinsed them dry. Their father made one investment in mines or machinery or whatever it was you sold them, and it was gone. All of their money, gone."

"I told you, it wasn't me. It was—" Again Leonard arced in pain and cried out.

Jambo leapt forward, barking. "Steady, boy." Alex was doing his utmost to keep the Ridgeback under control, but the lead had slipped, and he held it now with only one hand.

Leonard breathed deeply, his nostrils flared. "That wasn't me, you barmy woman. Why won't you listen? My father oversaw the Bourgoynes' investments. I never touched their blasted money."

"What does it matter?" said Mrs Rudd. "You're all the same. And we've come too far now to turn back. There weren't meant to be witnesses, but it doesn't matter. There's no chance of it looking like an accident, but at least it'll all be over."

Felicity couldn't restrain herself from stepping forward. "That's not true, Mrs Rudd. That's simply not true. It's not too late to turn back. It never is."

Mrs Rudd sobbed. "Forgive me, your ladyship, but I know what's at stake here. I'll hang for Miss Helen's death. I know I will. So I might as well make it count." The housekeeper turned her full attention on Leonard, the pistol clicking as she readied it.

"No!" cried Felicity.

Crack!

The sound of the gun going off split through the night. For a moment, there was only the rush of the river, the wind in the trees, and the freezing, biting cold.

Chapter Thirty-Six

The sunrise blazed red in a sherbet orange sky over the pine forests surrounding Grimstow House. Ice was melting and sliding from the tree branches at the edge of the garden and from the corners of the leaded panes of the library. The sleek radiators beneath the windows provided a welcome, comfortable heat.

Felicity was back in the chair she'd first occupied upon her arrival at Grimstow House. Snippets of everything that had happened in the preceding hours replayed in her mind. Looking with Helen at Ariadne's letters. Her cousin on the floor of the morning room. The fire at the stables and the shot from the trees. Everything that had transpired at the turbine house. All of it seemed like a terrible dream she was glad to have woken up from, not that she'd had a wink of sleep.

"Lady Felicity?"

Across the oval table from Felicity sat Chief Inspector Luscombe of the Devon County Constabulary. He had the tips of his long fingers pressed together. As well as making the wooden panelling glow, the electric light on the ceiling cast a glint on the policeman's balding head and threw deep shadows into the lines on his face, the expression upon which was down-turned and grave.

Despite the treacherous weather on the moors, and contrary to the impression the young stablehand had been given by whichever constable had answered his telephone call, Chief Inspector Luscombe and his men had set out from Exeter as soon as news reached them of the situation at Grimstow House. The run from Exeter to Cheriton St Mary had been without incident, the lower-lying roads being unaffected by the freezing temperatures that had afflicted the moors. But from the village onwards, the hilly roads had been coated in ice, which slowed the police's progress considerably.

At a certain point, they abandoned their vehicles and made the rest of the journey up to the house on foot, which they made in good time, having been aware of the conditions and well prepared. When the chief inspector and his men arrived at Grimstow House, however, the drama had already reached its conclusion.

Felicity adjusted her position on her seat. "Forgive me, Chief Inspector. My attention wandered for a moment."

The policeman tapped his fingertips together and considered Felicity carefully with wary, intelligent eyes. She'd already given him her full account of the events, but it was as though they were reaching the nub of their conversation only now. There was certainly some reason Chief Inspector Luscombe had wanted to interview Felicity alone, while for the other interviews there were always two policemen present.

"I appreciate you must be tired," said the chief inspector, "and I'm mindful you must be left in peace to grieve, given the untimely passing of your cousin. Naturally, we appreciate your willingness to make yourself available to assist our enquiries."

Felicity smiled somewhat stiffly. Why wouldn't she assist the police? Had she, as Alex intimated, given everyone the impression she considered herself above the law?

"However," continued Chief Inspector Luscombe, "you'll forgive me for asking why you disobeyed the order I sent specifically for you."

Felicity lifted her eyebrows. There it was. The nub of it. The chief inspector had got Felicity on her own to give her a telling off.

The policeman went on. "Have you not been close to death and danger quite enough to make a point of wanting to avoid it?"

An uncharacteristically blunt response along the lines of *Do you think I came here hoping all this would happen?* nearly escaped Felicity's lips, but she caught it in time.

"Chief Inspector," she said. "If you were to find yourself faced with an opportunity to redress the balance between mercy and cruelty in the favour of mercy, would you pass up that opportunity?" A sting of regret flashed through Felicity that she hadn't had the same opportunity with Helen, but she held her chin high.

The lines around the policeman's already down-turned mouth grew deeper. "Does a woman, particularly a woman of your standing, not have a duty to protect herself?"

Felicity couldn't prevent her reaction from escaping her mouth. "I'm in one piece, am I not, Chief Inspector? There's not even a scratch on me," she added, glossing over the blisters the shoes she'd borrowed for the party had given her.

The policeman sighed deeply. "I appreciate that, your ladyship. What I'm saying is that there are ways of helping matters without becoming so involved."

Felicity bit her tongue hard. She wondered, had the chief inspector been in precisely her position, what he would have done when the lights went out and they realised Leonard was missing? Would he have done nothing? Waited for someone else to take action?

Were Felicity a young lord instead of a young lady, would she still be chastised? Or would she be lauded for her bravery?

"What's next for Mrs Rudd?" she asked, changing the subject pointedly.

"She'll survive her wound," said the detective, speaking of the bullet that caught her in the leg and prevented her from pulling the trigger on Leonard. "But despite her being stopped from committing murder outright, and despite her being a beloved servant of the household, the tragedy of Miss Helen's death cannot be ignored. Rudd's admitted culpability, and although it was in a sense accidental — a death was planned, though not your cousin's — I don't see it as the type of crime upon which a jury would be lenient."

Felicity nodded, deep in thought. If the outcome was to be the same, then would it not have been better to put Mrs Rudd out of her misery by the turbine house? And spare the family her appearance in court? But Felicity hadn't pulled the trigger. She didn't deal in death. She was interested in the restoration of balance and the order of things. "Is there truth to Mrs Rudd's claims about the criminal dealings of the McQueens?"

The chief inspector narrowed his eyes. "Leonard McQueen's father had a certain reputation, I suppose you could call it, but no charges were ever brought against him. Crimes of that nature are much harder to police, you understand. It's easier to catch the ragamuffin dashing out the baker's shop with a loaf of bread under his dirty arm than the suited businessman behind the investment that — perhaps deliberately — made no returns."

Felicity nodded. It was a regrettable but truthful observation.

"But Leonard McQueen himself has no claims of wrongdoing against him, to our knowledge." Chief Inspector Luscombe sighed. "Not yet, at least."

"Let's hope it stays that way," said Felicity.

"Speaking of thieves, my men are out looking for that Miss Fairchild character. Unfortunately, she's got rather a head start on us, and I'm not sure we've much on her that will stick. By all accounts, everything she took she returned."

Felicity had no wish to protect Miss Fairchild, who'd disappeared into the freezing night, perhaps directly after her confession to Edwin. Felicity's desire to limit the burden on Edwin, however, remained strong. "She swore to me that the incidents of last night put her off thieving for life," she said.

The policeman's face lit up with an unexpected smile. "If I had tuppence for every time I'd heard such a claim. She may go off it for a while, all right, but she'll be back to it soon enough. The way of the criminal is a hard thing to give up. If it weren't, I'd be out of a job. And to have fooled your cousin as she did, the woman's clearly got some talent at it, whoever she is."

"Edwin feels quite terrible about the whole matter. On top of everything else that's happened."

"Oh, I can imagine. That's why I came up here as soon as I could, your ladyship. People of standing need a level of protection the other classes perhaps don't."

"I'm certain my cousin appreciates your efforts," said Felicity, doing her best to sound gracious. While she appreciated the detective's efforts on behalf of her family, it was her belief that everyone, regardless of status, should have the same level of protection from the authorities. "How's Mr McQueen's condition?" Felicity moved the conversation onwards yet again. She remembered how, in the past, the chief inspector had been less willing to give her attention and time. For all his chastising of her behaviour, he humoured her questions admirably.

"He's in a stable state." The police had an operator dispatched urgently to the local exchange, so the telephone at Grimstow House was now in perfect working order, allowing reports to be received from the hospital in Exeter to which Leonard had been taken. "Wasn't easy getting him down to our vehicles, especially with that dog of his. He insisted he wouldn't be separated from it, but I'm afraid there was no question of the hound escorting him to the Royal Devon and Exeter."

Felicity considered Jambo an odd sort of hero of the evening. Were it not for his tracking abilities and deep attachment to his master, there would have been little chance of locating Leonard in time to prevent the worst. If it weren't for the Ridgeback, Mrs Rudd might have thrown Leonard over the wall into the freezing, churning waters of the Teign and reported a suicide, perhaps bundling a confession regarding Helen into her invented testimony. It was understandable Leonard felt more attached to Jambo than ever.

"Mr McQueen will probably not have the same use of his arm again," continued Chief Inspector Luscombe. "It'll take some rehabilitation. Mr Anthony Carrington, on the other hand —" the policeman shook his head "—has discharged himself already. A bit unwise, if I may say so, but he can't be held at the hospital against his will. Some of my boys are bringing him back here as we speak. It was that or he insisted he'd set out on foot again, and well, we know how that ended last time."

Felicity smiled a little as she reflected on Tony's tenacity. To have adapted so well to the Canadian gold fields, one must have that kind of resilient and energetic character, she supposed. "He's quite something, isn't he?"

The chief inspector sighed. "We checked, and he's fully legitimate. There's proof of his passage from Montreal to Liverpool, and from there down to Exeter. Not to mention crossing the breadth of Canada beforehand. It was quite the journey. I suppose we shouldn't be surprised he won't stand for being separated from his family for much longer. The Earl and his wife are on their way down from London, having returned from the continent this morning. Of course, it's mixed blessings for them. A daughter lost, and a son regained."

They sat in silence for a moment. Felicity would be present for her aunt's arrival at Grimstow House and for her grief. Felicity's grandmother, Lady Henrietta, was also travelling to Grimstow to offer her support. To organise a funeral for one so young was particularly painful.

Chief Inspector Luscombe knitted his long fingers together. "I don't mean to sound discourteous, your ladyship, but I noticed you don't have your notebook with you. I can't imagine your brother's paper won't be covering this?"

"Oh, it will," said Felicity confidently, having already spoken to Jasper on the telephone. "The write-up is in the very capable hands of my colleague, Mr Alex Cooper." As long as Alex was covering the story for the newspaper, Felicity's brother was happy for her to dedicate her resources to supporting her cousin and aunt.

"Of course, your ladyship. A man of many talents is your Mr Cooper."

Felicity couldn't help but glow on behalf of her friend at the compliment. Alex had fired the shot that had prevented Mrs Rudd from ending Leonard's life. That he had taken such careful aim and still hung onto the Ridgeback was nothing short of miraculous, but of course he refused to accept any praise, putting the resolution down to Felicity's calm discussions with Mrs Rudd, which gave Alex time to manoeuvre subtly into position and take aim. Felicity insisted they both deserved credit.

"While Mr Cooper concentrates on the reporting," explained Felicity, "I'm entirely at the disposal of my cousin and aunt for the coming period. You seem under the impression, Chief Inspector, that I seek death and danger for the sake of it, but if there is a peaceful pathway for doing good, then I will take it."

The detective smiled grimly. "I'm only mildly surprised to hear that."

There was a knock at the library door. Ariadne entered without waiting to be called in. "Am I interrupting?"

"Not at all, your ladyship." Although the policeman's frown said, *Yes, you are.*

"Cousin," said Ariadne, approaching Felicity. She'd changed out of her party frock into a coral dropped-waist dress, her pale wispy hair tamed with a set of silver clasps. "I can call you that now, can I not?"

Felicity smiled. "You can."

Ariadne held out a hand, inviting Felicity to take it, her periwinkle-blue eyes sparkling. "Cousin, please, you must come with me. You simply must. There's something I have to show you."

Felicity looked at Chief Inspector Luscombe. He nodded his approval, and Felicity stood up. Her legs were heavy with fatigue, and she wasn't particularly in the mood for more revelations, but Ariadne could indeed be considered a sort of family member, and if she needed Felicity's support, then Felicity would give it to her.

She smiled at Ariadne, doing her best to hide her weariness. "Please, cousin. Lead the way."

Chapter Thirty-Seven

Ariadne moved swiftly as she led Felicity by the hand through a warren of corridors, the warm glow of the morning light making Grimstow House's stonework appear almost honey-coloured. Felicity had lost her bearings by the time they arrived at a door that Ariadne pushed open without knocking.

The curtains of the South Drawing Room were wide open, offering a sweeping view across Grimstow's steep gardens and forests. Bathed in golden light, the grounds expanded into the rolling Devon countryside, the Teign snaking and glistening through the valley below. The room's peaceful splendour was a contrast to the chaos that had erupted there the night before. The carpet had been swept perfectly clean, but the damage to the plaster ceiling remained.

Tony, his hand resting on a walking stick he'd presumably collected at the Royal Devon and Exeter, sat on one of the two beige sofas, a smile on his clean-shaven face as he spoke to his mirror image, Archie, who also wore the hint of a smile underneath his outmoded moustache. The brothers still had on their somewhat shabby outdoorsy clothes in dull tweeds and corduroys. All traces of mud had at least been removed. Mina, who was seated beside her master, twisted her elegant muzzle in Felicity's direction as she entered the room.

"Cousin." Tony's eyes lit up when he saw Felicity. The siblings had clearly had a discussion about Felicity's status as a relative. He quickly dropped his smile, however. "I never knew my step-sister, but Ari and Archie have told me about Helen. I'm extremely sorry I didn't get to know her. We offer our condolences for your loss."

Ariadne's eyes went to the floor. Archie rested a hand on Mina's head. Felicity wondered what exactly they had shared with their brother about Helen, but Tony's regret seemed genuine. "Helen will be sorely missed," said Felicity.

"It is absolutely no way of making up for your loss," continued Tony, "but we want to give you something. From Archie, Ari, and myself. We feel you've been instrumental in bringing things to a… Well, it wasn't a satisfying conclusion by any means, but we believe you had a hand in ensuring it wasn't worse."

"Oh," said Felicity. "There's no need to give me anything."

"Don't be like that," urged Ariadne good-naturedly.

"Please," said Tony, his smile returning.

"Please," echoed Archie. He held out a hand towards a side table upon which stood a shining wooden container about the size of a hat box. Atop it was a large silken bow in a shade of champagne not unlike Grimstow House's stone in the morning light.

Felicity hesitated. Considering everything that had happened, it was an incongruous moment to be accepting a present.

"We insist," said Tony.

Felicity reminded herself that she was a guest in the Carringtons' home. "Very well." She moved towards the box. Carefully, she lifted the lid and peeked inside. "My goodness." She set the lid down on the table. "Is it…?"

Tony nodded. "It's fully electric. And much quieter. You can use it late into the night and disturb no one."

The keys on the machine inside the box made it instantly recognisable as a typewriter, but the blocky dark grey device was otherwise unfamiliar. It wasn't clear where the paper went in, although Felicity would no doubt fathom it out for herself.

"Archie simply can't resist acquiring the latest gadgets," said Ariadne. "We thought this one would find a better home with you."

"How extraordinarily kind." Felicity turned to the Carringtons, a hand lifted to her chest, but her gratitude was tinged with guilt. In accepting assignments as a sleuth, she'd strayed from her love of journalism. Was the guilt she felt towards herself for scuppering her own dreams? Was it towards her brother, for dashing the chances he'd given her on the Western Daily News? Or was it perhaps towards Alex, who was working alone on the story about the events at Grimstow House?

"You deserve it and more," continued Ariadne. "We shall also arrange something to thank Mr Cooper for his bravery."

Felicity smiled. "He certainly deserves the recognition."

Mina stiffened. Her ears pricked in the door's direction.

"What is it, girl?" asked Archie of his canine companion.

A series of feisty barks rose from the corridor. Then came a knock.

"Come in," called Tony.

The unlikely pairing of Sir Vernon and Jambo entered the drawing room. Sir Vernon still wore his cracked monocle and tailcoat, which, by the look of its creases, may have been slept in. The Ridgeback was on a beautifully tooled leather lead, which Sir Vernon had wrapped several times around his unbandaged hand.

"Apologies for the interruption," said Sir Vernon.

"You're not interrupting anything," said Tony.

"I shan't take much of your time. Got to get this old beast out to the hospital." Sir Vernon glanced down at Leonard's dog, who sat uneasily beside Sir Vernon's spats.

Jambo looked at Mina with confusion and eagerness. He barked a little without opening his mouth fully, his jowls puffing out. The Borzoi returned the Ridgeback's attention with a wary glance. She was right to be cautious. Jambo was extremely loyal, but he needed a firm hand to keep his impulses in check. Felicity hoped Sir Vernon had a tight grip on the lead.

"We've had to make friends, Jambo and I," continued Sir Vernon, looking at his new companion out of the corner of his eye. "For Leonard's sake. The blighter swears blind he'll never get better if he doesn't have his dog with him. I'm sure the doctors and nurses will insist otherwise."

"How is Mr McQueen?" asked Ariadne, her eyebrows pinched together.

"Not doing too badly, by all accounts. Not doing too badly at all. Shall I pass him a message from you?"

Ariadne glanced at her brothers. "Just that we all wish him a speedy recovery," she said to Sir Vernon. "From the Carringtons. Thank you." Felicity hoped for the girl's sake that any amorous interest in the businessman had well and truly passed. Ariadne had so little in common with Leonard, and it couldn't be certain that Ariadne's wealth wouldn't colour Leonard's view of her.

"Anyway," said Sir Vernon. "Just wanted to say thank you to you, Lady Felicity. I would shake your hand but, well." He looked down at his hands, one bandaged and the other squeezing the Ridgeback's lead. "If it weren't for you, Leonard might not have even made it to the hospital."

"If I was able to help, then I'm glad to have made a difference," said Felicity. "Although I'm certainly not the only person whose efforts need acknowledging."

Sir Vernon frowned, his broken monocle glinting in the morning sunshine. "Ah, yes. That journalist chap. Of course, of course. But it was you who tracked Leonard down, your ladyship. Had you not done so, I dread to think what might have happened. Thankfully, Leonard reassured me on the telephone from the hospital that the investment in the Central American gem mines will go ahead as planned."

Felicity raised her eyebrows, unable to hide her surprise. Even if there was nothing untoward about the investment — and Felicity sincerely hoped there wasn't — was it not rather soon to be discussing these matters? Especially as it was precisely this deal that had apparently inspired Mrs Rudd to take action.

Ariadne was also surprised. "Has Mr McQueen spoken to Father?"

Sir Vernon nodded. "He telephoned him from the hospital. They're united in grief, naturally, but business is business."

Felicity looked at the Carringtons. Tony shrugged. "People handle bereavement in different ways, I suppose. I've seen it myself. A mine collapses. Friends and even family are lost, yet the survivors aren't deterred. They keep digging for the gold."

The idea sent a chill through Felicity. Thankfully, Lady Henrietta was on her way to Grimstow House. With the Earl being so hard-nosed about the investment deal, Felicity's aunt would likely need the extra support.

The butler appeared behind Sir Vernon. He knocked softly on the drawing room door, which still stood open. "Sir Vernon. The driver's ready for you."

"Splendid." He addressed Jambo. "Let's get you to your master, eh?" Sir Vernon saluted the room with his bandaged hand. "Farewell," he said and turned, keeping Jambo at heel on a short lead. "That journalist chap's not still hanging around, is he?" Sir Vernon asked this of the butler in low tones. "He gave me a tougher time than the police did."

Felicity smiled to herself. Alex was exacting when it came to questioning his interviewees, and as the only journalist on the scene, with a huge scoop for the paper all to himself, he was in his element.

Sir Vernon and Jambo having departed, the butler was closing the drawing room door when Ariadne interrupted him. "Horrocks, your bravery also needs acknowledging," she said.

After Alex shot Mrs Rudd in the leg, giving Leonard the opportunity to escape, the butler had dashed forward and removed the gun from Mrs Rudd's grip. Horrocks had then insisted on being the one to help Mrs Rudd up to the house, where he and the footman kept her under guard until the police arrived.

"That's not at all necessary, my lady," replied the butler with deep humility.

"But Horrocks, you were there when it all came to a head," continued Ariadne. "I don't know that I could keep my calm and do my job the next morning if I'd been through everything you had."

The butler shot an almost imperceptible glance at Felicity. The police having taken Mrs Rudd into custody, Horrocks had confided in Felicity about the guilt he felt at not doing a better job of investigating his fellow servants after Helen's passing. Felicity insisted that if Horrocks was at all to blame for what had happened, then Felicity should also bear responsibility, as she might have investigated the staff herself but had not done so.

In the end, they agreed no one was to blame for Mrs Rudd's actions except the housekeeper herself, with some blame to be apportioned to Miss Fairchild for adding further deception and confusion to events.

"I'm certain Mr Horrocks gains enough satisfaction from fulfilling his daily duties in the service of the Carrington family," said Felicity.

The butler nodded his thanks to Felicity. "Might there be anything else?"

"Our cousin perhaps would like her new typewriter taken to her motor." Tony used his walking stick to press himself up to standing. "Although we hope she's not leaving us soon." Three sets of hopeful periwinkle-blue eyes turned towards Felicity. Mina let out a faint whine.

"I shall indeed stay a while," confirmed Felicity, "to assist Edwin and my aunt as soon as she's back. If you've no objection to my remaining a guest in your home, of course?"

In an uncharacteristic display of emotion, Archie's eyebrows shot upwards. "You're very welcome here."

Ariadne clasped her hands together. "Oh, I'm thrilled. It's absolutely wonderful you're staying."

Felicity may have lost Helen, but her trip to Grimstow House had somehow resulted in her having more relatives than she began with. She would mend her ways and make a better effort to stay in touch with them, starting of course with Edwin, whom she hadn't seen since before her interview with Chief Inspector Luscombe.

Taking leave of her step-cousins, Felicity went with the butler into the corridor. "Do you know where I might find Edwin, Mr Horrocks?"

The butler closed the door to the South Drawing Room. "In the billiard room, your ladyship. Doctor Quick is being interviewed by Mr Cooper."

It was incredibly reassuring that Alex was not only doing what he loved best but also making an excellent job of setting the narrative straight before any of the scandal rags swooped in on the story. "Would you be kind enough to show me the way to the billiard room, please, Mr Horrocks?"

"Ah, yes, your ladyship. It's ah… It's just along the corridor." The butler sounded oddly unsure. His gaze went over Felicity's shoulder.

She turned.

Charles was approaching, his footsteps marking a steady, determined beat that echoed along the corridor. His face was awfully serious.

Chapter Thirty-Eight

"Charlie," said Felicity as brightly as possible as the butler withdrew.

"Cici." Charles stopped before her. He'd changed from his dinner jacket into a dark green wool suit with a fine mustard check, and he looked vibrant and dashing with his shining brown hair and smooth skin, but there was an edge of tension in his jaw.

Felicity maintained a polite smile, although she sincerely hoped Charles didn't require another private conversation in a cubby hole somewhere. "Thank you again so very much for taking on the Bourgoyne sisters last night. I was immensely grateful for the way you allowed me to hand them over to you."

"Not at all, not at all," said Charles distractedly. He straightened, his hands on his hips, his eyebrows drawn low. "Listen, Cici. About what we discussed in the gun room."

So the whole awkward affair hadn't been miraculously forgotten. And though she herself had tried, Felicity hadn't been able to forget either. The matter had to be faced. "Yes," she said in a tone somewhere between shy and just plain reluctant. "What about it?"

Charles ran a hand over the waves of his hair. "I don't suppose you've thought about it any further, have you?"

"Charlie." Felicity was taken aback by his directness. She had told herself she would round off her duties at Grimstow House and get back to Bradley Court before giving Charles' proposal any serious consideration, but was that simply delaying the inevitable? "You said you wouldn't rush me."

"Of course, I do apologise," he said quickly, holding up his hands. "With everything that's happened, it was silly of me to imagine you'd had the time to think things through. It's just…" He laughed nervously, then met Felicity's gaze. "I've given thought to very little else but what we spoke about."

Felicity sighed. It was time to rip off the bandage. "Charlie," she said gently. "Do you really believe we're a match?"

Charles blinked. "We've known each other practically forever, have we not?"

A door opened further along the corridor. Edwin exited the billiard room first. He was followed by Alex, tucking his notebook back inside his jacket pocket. The two men were still deep in discussion with one another, but Alex caught Felicity's eye and gave her a smile so subtle it was barely there, yet it warmed her from the inside.

Charles nodded. He stroked his jaw. "I believe I see what you're saying. Gosh. I've made a ruddy fool of myself, haven't I?" His cheeks coloured. "I didn't even stop to consider whether your interest lay elsewhere."

"Oh, Charlie, you're not any kind of fool," said Felicity, relieved that they were now on the same page but eager to soften the blow. "You'll make a good woman very happy one day, but please don't rush into things. Do yourself the decency of finding a good match."

"You're a good woman, Cici. I hope you know that." There was a sadness to Charles' smile. "My ideas about women's capabilities have been considerably expanded in just one evening, and that's thanks mainly to you. I imagine that will stand me in good stead in these modern times."

"I imagine it will."

"Friends?" asked Charles.

Felicity nodded. "Friends." They shook hands. While Felicity regretted Charles' discomfort, she didn't regret that their betrothal was no longer on the table. Yet he was a good, honourable man, and a suitable husband. She didn't feel it in the moment, but would Felicity live to regret her decision?

Charles' brow creased. "Say, there is one other thing I would like to ask of you."

"As a friend?"

"Yes, absolutely." Charles glanced up the corridor where Alex was still speaking with Edwin. "You'll take good care of your cousin, won't you? I'm afraid I've got to dash back up to London. Duty calls at the Foreign Office."

"Of course," said Felicity, as Edwin and Alex approached. "I've taken temporary leave of my work at the newspaper for precisely that reason. I'm here for Edwin."

Charles looked relieved. "You're one in a million, Cici," he said in low tones. "I really hope you know that." As Edwin drew close, Charles slapped his friend on his shoulder. "Eddie, old chap. I'm afraid I'm off. I'll be back to Devon just as soon as I can."

"There's no rush, Charles," said Edwin, who was dressed in a comfortable-looking brown suit and had much more colour in his freckled cheeks than the night before. "We have everything under control, don't we, Felicity?"

Felicity nodded, content that her cousin knew he could rely on her. "That's exactly right."

Charles wished everyone farewell. "You're a lucky man," he said to Alex as he shook his hand. The comment made Alex frown, the pale grey wool of his suit highlighting his dark blue eyes as he gave Felicity a confused glance, but there was no room for further investigation. Charles departed right away, the heels of his shining brogues tapping along the corridor.

"Did you interview Charles already?" enquired Felicity.

"I did." Alex smiled. "He was extremely impressed by your bravery. Everyone is."

Edwin nodded his agreement.

Felicity swept away the compliment. "Did you speak to Mr Debenham or the Bourgoyne sisters?" Just because she wasn't, on this occasion, contributing to the article, it didn't mean she wasn't interested in it. "I haven't seen them."

"I located Mr Debenham at the stables," said Alex.

Edwin frowned. "Does the stable master tolerate his presence?"

Alex nodded. "Mr Debenham has calmed himself and apologised for his earlier behaviour. He says he finds solace tending to the horses." Alex lifted an ironic eyebrow. "He also claims the night's events have changed him for good."

Felicity shook her head. Rex wasn't someone Felicity would trust with any animal she cared about, but the stable master certainly knew how to handle things should anyone get out of line.

"And the Bourgoyne sisters?" In light of Archie and Tony's alikeness and Patience and Clemency's dissimilarity, it didn't seem appropriate to refer to the Bourgoynes as twins anymore.

"I'm afraid I haven't been able to find them," said Alex.

"They left shortly after the police's arrival," said Edwin. "As soon as they knew they could make it through in their motor. 'Returning to civilisation' is how I believe they termed it."

Alex smiled, amused. "Might you know where I can find the chief inspector?" he asked Felicity.

"I was with him in the library not an awfully long time ago," said Felicity.

"He's been wanting to speak to me, but I needed to carry out my own investigation first. I now have all my questions lined up for him." Tapping the breast of his jacket, where his notebook lay in the inside pocket, Alex set off along the corridor.

Smiling, Edwin shook his head as he watched Alex leave. "A frighteningly efficient interviewer, isn't he?"

"Poor Chief Inspector Luscombe," said Felicity, although she hardly pitied the policeman. She and Edwin were now alone. "Mr Cooper didn't give you too difficult a time, did he?"

"Oh, no. He's fast with the questions, but he was extremely easy to talk to. Gave me ample room to tell my side of things and to, you know, remember Helen. I realise it's a blessing we get the chance to set the narrative straight before the scandal rags get hold of things."

Felicity was relieved her cousin was satisfied with Alex's approach. She stifled a yawn. Leaning on his walking cane, Edwin looked as tired as Felicity felt.

"And it's a blessing you'll be staying with us for the time being," added Edwin. He smiled wistfully at Felicity.

"Oh, Edwin." She suddenly felt extremely sad. "I'm so very sorry."

Edwin frowned. "Sorry for what?"

"That I couldn't save Helen."

"No, Felicity. You mustn't think like that. If it weren't for you, I'm sure the whole night would have been much, much worse. And it's simply too kind of you to stay on to help us like this." Edwin looked a little embarrassed. "After what Miss Fairchild did to me, I might have lost my faith in women entirely if it weren't for you."

"Hush," said Felicity. "Miss Fairchild was the exception. Whoever she is, and wherever she is now, you were extremely unlucky to have met her."

"You've a knack not only for resolving situations but also for saying the right thing at the right time." Edwin smiled kindly. "I know you've got your work to keep you busy, but whoever you eventually choose to marry will be an extremely lucky man."

Felicity smiled back at her cousin. "I'm quite certain you'll make some lucky woman an excellent husband long before I'm anyone's wife."

Chapter Thirty-Nine

TWO WEEKS LATER

When Felicity left Grimstow House earlier that morning, guiding her two-seater Alvis down the steep tarmacadamed drive — which was thankfully free of ice — she noticed clumps of dark green shoots spouting from the grass lining the roadway. Now, as Felicity crossed Exeter's cathedral green in the chilly February sunshine, dressed in a suit of dark grey French serge, a black velour coat, charcoal one-strap shoes, and a simple storm-grey beret, Pip trotting at her side, she saw the same dark green leaves rising from the grass with the white flower heads of snowdrops dancing delicately on the breeze above them.

Such were the variations in climate across the county of Devon. No doubt the snowdrops were in bloom in Lower Diddleton, too, but it wasn't yet time to return home.

At Grimstow House, Felicity had supported her cousin Edwin and her aunt through the police's investigation, the inquest, and the build-up of the court case, which hadn't yet started. Although Mrs Rudd was keen to plead guilty to save the family from further unease, there were still procedural steps to follow, and that took time. Naturally, there had been keen interest from the press, including an encampment of journalists at the gates of Grimstow House, many having travelled down from London for the spectacle. Felicity weeded out the most gossip-mongering publications and sanctioned some reporters for interviews with the family, which Edwin gave with Felicity at his side, both of them shielding Helen's mother from exposure to the press. Losing her only daughter had been a tremendous blow.

Thankfully, Felicity's grandmother was on hand to provide comfort to the bereaved mother, Lady Henrietta's often overbearing presence somehow a salve in a context of complete despair. There were also the arrangements for Helen's funeral, which was to take place in London the following week, that had to be seen to. Edwin had been loath to leave Grimstow House, but with Felicity accompanying him, he'd made a couple of trips up to the capital to discuss plans for the ceremony.

In providing her support to Edwin, Felicity felt useful and appreciated. Her time at Grimstow House also allowed her to get to know the Carringtons better. Tony would stay in England for the time being — he had some ideas to work on with Archie for improving the reliability of the house's electricity supply in bad weather — and Ariadne's entry into a Swiss finishing school had been delayed. She'd expressed to her father her desire to attend university, although she wasn't yet sure what she wanted to study. Earl Carrington, while upset about Helen's death and moved by his wife's grief, could lose himself in his business affairs and matters pertaining to his various estates. As Leonard predicted, the Earl remained committed to the investment opportunity in the Central American gem mines.

But Felicity wasn't in Exeter on behalf of Edwin, her aunt, or poor Helen. She was there on personal business.

Her brother Jasper, editor-in-chief of the Southwest's most-read newspaper and Felicity's boss, had summoned her for a meeting. He'd not specified the topic exactly. He'd only said that he wished to discuss what Felicity 'really wanted'. That he'd called her into the headquarters of the Western Daily News, however, was a signifier of what was on his mind. They might have met at home, at Bradley Court, but it was clear Jasper wanted a frank and business-like conversation about Felicity's role at their family's paper, which was understandable.

Felicity's attention on her career as a journalist had wandered, even before the events at Grimstow House. Jasper had a business to run, of course, and Felicity had been a reporter upon which he depended, and although it had never once been her express intention to involve herself in a criminal investigation, Felicity had repeatedly veered in that direction.

While the meeting with her brother was not a discussion to which she was looking forward, Felicity was ready for it.

As she neared Exeter's bustling high street, with its colourful shop awnings, bicycles, and omnibuses, the scent of coffee being roasted mingling with the smell of exhaust fumes, Felicity lifted Pip under her arm. The Yorkie had hidden under a chair in the South Drawing Room when Felicity announced her intention to bring him to Exeter. Upon his arrival at Grimstow House in the company of Lady Henrietta — all traces of sausage grease and mud removed from his blue-and-tan fur — Pip had formed an immediate bond with Mina. The sight of the tall elegant hound and the tiny terrier scampering about like lunatics in gleeful play made everyone laugh. They even slept curled in the same basket.

Being carried to the Alvis against his will seemed to have been forgotten as the smells, sounds, and sights of the city transfixed the Yorkie, his shining eyes, twitching nose, and pricked ears taking everything in.

As the bells of St Stephen's Church rang the hour, Felicity quickened her pace. Arriving late wasn't how she wanted the meeting with Jasper to begin. Emerging from the alley beside the church and onto the high street, Felicity almost collided with a pedestrian moving in the opposite direction.

"I'm awfully sorry," she said, barely looking up, so keen was she to hurry onwards.

"Lady Felicity. As I live and breathe. How splendid to see you." Rex Debenham wore a wide grin, an extremely well-tailored tan-coloured coat, and an oversized cap in a garish hounds tooth, which he lifted briefly from his head.

"Felicity, how darling you look dressed in mourning." Clemency Bourgoyne clung to Rex's arm. She wore a splendid set of white furs, her lips were painted brilliant red, and her honey-gold hair was styled into perfect waves under a luxuriant turban-style hat.

"Mr Debenham, Miss Bourgoyne," said Felicity with smiling politeness. "What a surprise to see you. You both look awfully well." Felicity hadn't seen Rex or Clemency since the night of the ill-fated ball, but she'd read about them in the papers. Alex had, naturally, done excellent work following up on everyone, and Felicity always read every article Alex wrote.

Leonard had returned to London and was recovering well from the injury to his shoulder, his beloved Jambo ever-present at his side as any photograph published of him attested. While Mrs Rudd was certainly regarded as the wrong-doer in the situation and as someone quite unbalanced, debate about what constituted a sound investment arose in the press. The attention, however, seemed to have done Leonard's business no harm. People clamoured to place their money with him.

Accordingly, a new investment opportunity had rather hastily been established, with input from both the Earl and Sir Vernon, who, it seemed, would remain close to Leonard through thick and thin. A stud farm was to be established in Helen's memory, honouring both Helen's and the Earl's love of horses and the interests of everyone involved in generating income. From an article Alex had published just the day before, Felicity understood Rex had been chosen to be involved in the stud's running.

It was queer how such terrible events could cement relationships, although Felicity had read nothing about Rex and Clemency patching up their bond.

"Congratulations on your appointment at the stud," continued Felicity.

Rex waved a dismissive hand. "Oh, I'm just an advisor. Nothing more."

A well-paid one, thought Felicity, judging by Rex and Clemency's clothing.

Rex's grin returned. "You're our heroine of the moment, Lady Felicity. Have you found another life to save or mystery to solve since our paths last crossed?"

Under the editorial guidance of Jasper, Alex's coverage of Felicity's involvement in events at Grimstow House had been deliberately sober to spare Felicity from a type of attention she had no interest in receiving. Unfortunately, nothing could be done to prevent less salubrious publications running headlines such as *Lady Sleuth Saves Businessman* and *Peer's Daughter Foils Murder Plot*, which put Felicity rather too much in the limelight for her liking. It was, in any case, Alex who fired the shot that incapacitated Mrs Rudd and ended the stand-off.

Felicity smiled at Rex as though amused by a pleasant joke. She moved the conversation onwards. "What brings you back to Devon?" She was particularly interested in what Clemency might say, seeing as she and her sister had branded Felicity's home county 'uncivilised'.

Rex tugged at the peak of his cap. "Looking for the right patch of land for the stud. Devon might be right for it, but certainly not the moors. Not after what we experienced of the weather up at Grimstow."

"Rex said we could do some shopping in Exeter while we're here," said Clemency with a giggle. "Although it's all rather quaint. The shops are small, the fashions old. It's nothing like Bond Street."

Had she not been on her way to a meeting with her brother, Felicity might have launched a defence of Exeter's boutiques. "How is your sister?" she enquired of Clemency, maintaining her polite smile and lifting a grey-gloved hand to shield the winter sun from her eyes.

While Clemency kept a low profile, Patience was speaking to

any journalist willing to give her the time of day. Besides providing an unstable account of the events at Grimstow House that changed between interviews, Patience claimed to be using mediums to attempt contact with Helen. The attempts so far had, by Patience's own admission, come to nothing, but for Felicity and the rest of the Quicks, it was still extremely bad taste.

While Miss Fairchild had returned everything she stole before disappearing without a trace, Patience also insisted on raking up the matter of the 'thefts' and how Edwin had been tricked, which Felicity thoroughly resented. Alex had given plenty of column inches to Edwin's achievements in the medical field and his valiant treatment of Leonard and Tony's injuries. Even if it was only the less salubrious papers that gave her significant attention, Patience's indiscretions still hurt Edwin.

At the core of her thirst for publicity was undoubtedly Patience's book on spiritualism, which she never failed to mention in any of her interviews. Just thinking about it made Felicity angry.

"I admit," said Clemency tightly, "I've not spoken to my sister in a while."

"Patience does not approve of our engagement," said Rex.

Clemency whipped off her glove and showed Felicity a ring with a large, sparkling sapphire at its centre.

"My heartfelt congratulations," said Felicity good-naturedly. It was clear Clemency had got what she wanted, but with Rex, it was harder to tell.

"And how's the darling Lord Charles?" purred Clemency.

Felicity scratched Pip under the chin. Had she been mistaken to imagine all talk of Charles' interest in her had died at Grimstow House? "I believe he's well, although I haven't spoken to him since that night."

Clemency frowned. "Oh. I thought..." She trailed off.

Felicity picked up on the opportunity. "Please do excuse me for being frightfully rude, but I've an appointment with my brother at the newspaper offices."

Rex raised his eyebrows. "Certainly. I trust we'll be able to call on you for coverage of the stud farm when it opens?"

"Of course," said Felicity with a confident nod, although based on the outcome of the meeting with Jasper, her position at the newspaper was far from certain.

After a round of goodbyes and with Pip hugged tightly to her side, Felicity crossed the busy high street, passed the Lyon's tea rooms on the corner, and found the familiar door to the headquarters of the Western Daily News, the name of the title etched in gold on the glass.

Felicity checked her reflection in the glass. Upon arriving in Exeter, she'd felt fortified and ready to face whatever her brother threw at her. Now, as she examined her likeness in the door's reflection, Felicity considered how her jaw looked bigger than she remembered, and there was a mark on her forehead she'd not noticed before.

Beyond the glass, someone was smiling at her.

The door opened.

Felicity's heart skipped. "Alex."

"Hello, Felicity." He looked as handsome as ever in a brown overcoat over a pale grey suit, a grey homburg hat tucked under his arm. His dark blond hair was swept into a side parting, his blue eyes shone with elevated interest.

"I haven't seen you since…" Felicity's voice trailed off as Alex stepped onto the pavement beside her, shoppers and tradespeople hurrying by. Pip extended his neck and sniffed the air, keen to get Alex's scent.

Alex's smile fell. "Since the morning after your cousin's passing. I hear the funeral's next week?"

Felicity nodded. Although she never felt far removed from Alex, reading his articles every day as she did, he might have the impression of having been rather abandoned by her. "You know, I can't emphasise enough how grateful I am — how grateful everyone is for what you did. For what you're doing."

Alex's smile returned as he pulled on his hat. "I'm simply doing my job. You know that."

"But to take that shot the way you did." Felicity could feel herself becoming flustered, almost tongue-tied.

Alex's frown was quick and dismissive. "We went to Grimstow House as partners, don't you remember? With Lady Henrietta's blessing. I had to do my bit."

Felicity smiled, embarrassed. It was touching that Alex had taken their sleuthing assignment so seriously. She opened her mouth to speak, but the words didn't come out.

"Do you have another job for us?" asked Alex.

Perhaps he was just joking about taking their sleuthing together seriously. Felicity couldn't tell.

Gently squeezing Pip to prevent the Yorkie's little wet nose touching Alex's woollen lapel, Felicity cleared her throat, her voice at last unstuck. "I'm here to speak to Jasper about my work for the paper."

Alex beamed. "So we'll be writing together again."

Felicity frowned. "Oh, I don't think you need my help." She knew he didn't. Alex's coverage of the affair at Grimstow sold papers across the country, with regional and national titles paying handsome sums to syndicate the articles Alex wrote for the News.

Alex narrowed his eyes. "You've a knack for being in the right place at the right time. Or the wrong place at the wrong time, depending on how you look at it."

Felicity bit her lip. "And how do you look at it?"

They stood to the side for a moment as a woman pushing a large pram passed by. Alex smiled. "I believe we had this discussion already. Do you not remember?"

Felicity remembered. She thought often of how Alex had said Felicity was part of why he felt at home in Devon. She wanted to hear him say it again. A familiar flush crawled up her neck.

"I'm terribly sorry, but I really must dash. My appointment with Jasper..." Felicity pushed open the door to the newspapers' offices, Pip scrambling a little under her arm.

Alex nodded and stepped aside, his smile gone. "I shan't stand in your way."

Whether sleuthing or reporting, Alex had never stood in Felicity's way. Felicity wouldn't stand in the way of his successful journalistic career, either. She stepped inside the building. Felicity's and Alex's paths couldn't go on being so tangled, could they? It was just as Jasper had said. What did she really want?

Dash it, she thought.

Felicity turned. Her stomach tightened. "Might you have time for tea and a bun later?" A stiff breeze ruffled Pip's ears. Felicity clutched at the neck of her coat.

Alex held onto the brim of his hat. His smile returned. "I thought you'd never ask."

Claim your free Lady Felicity Quick ebook!

Sign up for my email newsletter and you'll get **Murder at Afternoon Tea** absolutely free.

This exclusive story isn't available anywhere else.

As a newsletter subscriber, you'll also receive writing updates, special offers, and peeks behind the scenes…

Use this link to sign up and claim your copy today:
https://BookHip.com/XMGPNZC

Read the next in the series...

Murder on the Coast

A Lady Felicity Quick 1920s Cozy Mystery
Book 5

Devon's coastline has crystal blue waters, stunning views from the cliffs, and ... is that a corpse on the beach?

England, 1922. Determined to focus on her role as a journalist, Lady Felicity Quick travels to Ottermouth, a picturesque fishing village and haven for artists, to report on the opening of a new art exhibition.

But when a lifeless body washes onto the foreshore, the coastal community's peace is shattered. Accusations fly as fishermen, painters and even the authorities turn on one another. And when an important friend is implicated, Felicity strays from her duties for the newspaper...

Trusting her sleuthing instincts and reunited with a faithful ally, Felicity attempts to unpick the deadly case and deliver justice for the residents of Ottermouth. Will she solve the perilous puzzle in time, or will Felicity's daring efforts result in her own watery end?

Join Felicity on her quest for truth in this captivating 1920s British mystery, filled with suspense, humour and unforgettable characters! Perfect for fans of Agatha Christie, Verity Bright, Helena Dixon and Magda Alexander.

Read Murder on the Coast today!
mybook.to/Coast

The Lady Felicity Quick Mystery Series

Murder at Afternoon Tea

(Novella | Exclusive for Newsletter Subscribers)

Murder on the Village Green

(Book 1 | Available Now)

Murder at a Country House

(Book 2 | Available Now)

Murder at the Tea Rooms

(Book 3 | Available Now)

Murder at the Ball

(Book 4 | Available Now)

Murder on the Coast

(Book 5 | Available Now)

Murder at a Boarding School

(Book 6 | Available Now)

Murder at a Flower Show

(Book 7 | Coming Soon)

About the Author

Rosie Hunt is a British author of cozy mysteries both puzzling and historical. Her books include the Lady Felicity Quick mystery series set in the green and pleasant countryside of southwest England in the 1920s.

A history addict and former journalist, Rosie grew up immersed in the worlds of Poirot and Miss Marple. This early exposure to baffling murder mysteries rather coloured her outlook on life, and it was only a matter of time before she began writing her own.

Rosie loves clotted cream, knitting, and Golden Age crime fiction, and she'll never miss an opportunity to visit a National Trust property. She lives with her husband and their four-pawed overlord on a river in Northern Europe.

Join Rosie's mailing list:
bookhip.com/XMGPNZC

Follow Rosie on Facebook:
facebook.com/RosieHuntAuthor

Made in United States
North Haven, CT
21 September 2024

57653632R00178